D1757609

Books should be returned or renewed by the last date above. Renew by phone **03000 41 31 31** or online *www.kent.gov.uk/libs*

Libraries Registration & Archives

C334009343

First Published by

THE GARANSAY PRESS, 2013.

1

The Glenrannoch Hotel, on the Scottish Island of Garansay, stood imposingly above the pretty port town of Kilross. It was constructed in the late nineteenth century from the reddish brown sandstone that was quarried on the island itself. The Hotel attracted some of Garansay's most prestigious visitors.

The 'Glenrannoch' was refurbished a couple of years ago, when a luxurious pool and gym complex were added to the original building in a tastefully designed extension. It now advertised itself as a 'Spa Hotel' and catered for 'high end' weddings and corporate events. On this bitterly cold Saturday afternoon, in the non-descript week between Christmas and New Year, the formal dining room was being hastily prepared for the Hindu wedding of the Malhotras from Glasgow.

Krish Malhotra was closely supervising the transformation of this late Victorian setting. The scene being created was now more reminiscent of a Hindu temple in the midst of a religious festival in downtown Delhi. Krish worked for a Middle Eastern bank, based in their Glasgow office. His fiancé, Akuti Gupta, was a legal executive for another financial institution in the city. He was fast approaching his forties, well established and comfortably off. His wedding to Akuti promised to be an outward expression of their joint economic success, as well as a celebration, in the presence of family and friends, of a lifelong commitment to one another.

The dining room was almost unrecognisable. The walls, tables and floors were covered by colourful strings of lights, ribbons and flower petals. Most impressive of all, was the tableau that had been created in the centre of the hall. Underneath a four-postered canopy of red and gold, two throne-like chairs were placed in front of a decorative grate. During the ceremony, a fire would be lit. The bride and groom would then take seven steps before the sacred flames, declaring the vows intended to bind their union.

When Krish was finally satisfied the details of the scene were exactly as he had envisaged, he invited his guests to make their way from the Ardroch Lounge Bar and take their seats for the ceremony. By Indian standards, this was not a large wedding. Krish and Akuti had only invited their closest family, friends and work colleagues.

As neither bride nor groom were in the first flush of youth the couple decided to keep the numbers down so they could have a 'blow out' three week honeymoon in the Seychelles. Krish and Akuti were reasonably well off, but had to work long hours for their money. Quality time together is what they craved most.

The hospitality team at the Glenrannoch Hotel had successfully hosted many weddings, but this was their first Hindu service. The manager, Gordon Ingle, was surprised by the informality of the proceedings. The costumes and decorations were far more elaborate than he was used to, certainly, but Gordon was taken aback by the ceremony itself. The guests did not adhere to the customary hush whilst the priest spoke his sacred words, or even during the wedding vows themselves for that matter. The guests simply continued their lively chat and laughter throughout. Although initially alarmed, Gordon came to realise this was a sign the event was going well.

At a table in a far corner of the room, underneath one of the tall, arched windows that looked out over the extensive wooded grounds, Krish's boss, Richard Fleming, was trying to catch Gordon Ingle's eye. The Flemings had only been living in Scotland for the past six months, having spent the previous sixteen years in Dubai. After much deliberation, Richard finally decided the time was right to return to the UK. He brought his wife and two children back with him. Krish Malhotra did not know Richard Fleming and his family very well. However, he thought it prudent to invite them to the wedding. He made the judgement that it would not be wise to risk offending his line manager, a man whom Krish felt he did not yet have the measure of.

When the harassed Events Manager finally made it over to the Fleming's table, Richard bellowed over the background noise, 'we've hired a private helicopter. It's coming to pick us up in an hour or so to take us back over to Tarbert. It will be setting down at the pad near the Harbour. Can you inform me as soon as the pilot has landed?'

'Certainly Sir,' Gordon Ingle replied, not unused to this type of request.

Many of the Glenrannoch's clientele reached Garansay by chartered helicopter, although in recent years, it had become a rarer occurrence. The recession had put the financial squeeze on a number of the businessmen and women who regularly visited the Hotel. Gordon had noted that their Middle-Eastern guests still appeared to possess unlimited funds.

Just at that moment, the bride swished past the Fleming's table and scooped up Isla Fleming and her daughter, leading them onto the square of plush carpet tiles that denoted the temporary dance floor. The volume of the music was then cranked up. Conversation became virtually impossible over the steady, repetitive beat of the bhangra tunes being supplied by a tiny laptop wired to two huge speakers.

Isla Fleming was a very trim woman. Although naturally fair skinned, she had been deeply tanned by nearly two decades spent in the hot Arabian sun. Her daughter, Lucy, still possessed the natural paleness of her Celtic ancestors. Clinging tightly to her mother, she seemed to be enjoying the good-natured attempts being made by Akuti's sisters to teach them the basics of Indian dancing. Lucy's creamy skin and simple, ivory dress differed sharply from the heavily bejewelled and intricate outfits worn by the bride and her family.

Richard and his son, Cameron, gazed upon the antics of the ladies with solemn expressions.

7

Richard was drinking steadily from his glass of Saint Emilion whilst glancing every few minutes at his flashy wrist watch. His son simply looked bored. Cameron was nearly twenty years old and knew no one else in the room other than his own parents and younger sister. Blond-haired and tanned like his mother, Cameron was a handsome young man who had taken full advantage of the privileged upbringing he enjoyed in Dubai. His father's decision to move back to Scotland had been most unwelcome to him. He had spent the last few months considering whether or not he would return to his life in the Middle East without his family.

As far as Cameron Fleming was concerned, the jury still remained out on that decision. He was intending to spend a year travelling the world before making a final choice about where he might settle down and study. His father craned his neck around in order to peer irritably out of the window behind them, where the sky was rapidly darkening.

'I wonder if Tom has landed yet. He should be here by now,' Richard muttered. 'Looks like it's clouding over. I hope we get back to the mainland this evening. I've got plenty of work to be getting on with.'

Cameron didn't reply but instead scanned the room to see if the bar was open yet. He fancied a beer and had never managed to develop a taste for red wine. The girls swooped back to the table. Garlanded and giggling they collapsed theatrically into their seats, exhausted by the energetic dancing lesson. Richard gazed upon his wife with disapproval.

'We need to be heading off soon, so finish up your drinks,' he advised ominously. 'If we wait for the weather to close in we'll never get out of this place.'

Just then, Gordon Ingle's tall and wiry figure began to approach their table, manoeuvring itself unsurely through the revellers. When Richard spotted the manager advancing towards them he immediately sprang to his feet.

'That's it,' he declared, without waiting to hear what Gordon had to say. 'The chopper must have arrived. Get your things together and we'll say our goodbyes. Where the hell has Cameron got to?'

Isla and Lucy reluctantly reached down for their handbags. As the Flemings weaved their way past the complicated pattern of tables dotted across the packed dining room, they finally spotted Cameron at the busy bar, handing a crisp Scottish note to one of the hotel's serving staff. Richard's son happened to be standing next to Krish Malhotra. The family was able to thank their host profusely for his hospitality. Meanwhile, Cameron quickly downed his bottle of lager, keenly aware of his father's eagerness to leave.

As the Fleming clan collected their exquisitely tailored coats from the Hotel's lobby cloakroom, Isla tentatively suggested to her husband that they be allowed some time to change out of their formal clothes before getting into the helicopter. Richard gave his wife a look of pure disdain but he reluctantly agreed. The receptionist patiently directed them towards a ground floor bedroom, which Isla had earlier asked the hotel if she could set aside for this very purpose. Inside the room was a small case filled with what constituted 'casual' clothing to the Flemings.

9

Richard became increasingly agitated at the time it took his wife and daughter to get changed and carefully fold and pack their dresses. When they were finally ready to leave, he was short tempered and red in the face.

'Let's just get going shall we?' Richard hissed through gritted teeth, 'I hate flying at night.'

No one replied in sympathy to this observation. As the Fleming family rushed down the marble steps leading out onto the hotel's flood lit gravel drive, they could still just about hear the merry hum of the celebrations, now in full swing, fading away behind them.

2

The strengthening wind was rattling the old, wooden framed window in the kitchen of Lower Kilduggan Farm. Michael Nichols pulled across one of the sturdy oak chairs so he could reach up to close the flimsy catch that in theory, secured the smallest pane of glass at the top. Michael was a silver-haired, elegant man in his late fifties. Lower Kilduggan Farm was his family home. He inherited the place, along with his brother and sister, when their mother died a couple of years ago.

Michael was a partner in a successful architectural firm in Glasgow, where he owned a beautifully renovated Victorian flat in the West-End of the city. He had found himself spending increasing amounts of time in recent months on the Isle of Garansay. The farmhouse, and the three acres of land which surrounded it, were in desperate need of update and repair at the time Michael's mother passed away. When Michael started to use Lower Kilduggan as a weekend retreat about a year ago, he couldn't resist the temptation to consider plans for its refurbishment. For the past six months, Michael had been spending a few days of each week at his Glasgow flat and the rest of the time here on Garansay, working from the farmhouse and gradually restoring the old building to its former glory.

The farm was situated up a steep gravel track on the western side of the island. It faced the Kilbrannan Sound and the Mull of Kintyre, which was the thin strip of mainland just visible on the other side of the channel. On this cold evening, in the week between Christmas and New Year, Michael could barely see to the far end of the farm's courtyard from the kitchen window, let alone to the hills and sea in the far distance. It was now very dark and there was a mixture of sleet, hailstones and rain falling simultaneously outside. This must be what the Met Office means by the term 'wintry showers', Michael thought wryly to himself.   Michael Nichols had just lit the wood burning stove which he recently had installed into an inglenook at the far side of the old kitchen. The lively flames that it was producing, along with the Christmas decorations hung gaily around the ground floor of the house, were giving the place a cheerful atmosphere. Michael spent Christmas here with his daughter, Sarah, and her fiancé, Ross. He might not have made the effort to celebrate the festive season otherwise. Since Michael's wife died over a decade ago, he had found this time of year particularly difficult to get through alone.

The room was only just beginning to experience the warmth radiating from the smouldering logs and kindling when Michael heard a sharp knock at the front door. He was certainly not expecting any visitors tonight and the urgency of the continuous assault on the old wooden panels which followed made Michael immediately fearful.

'Hold on - I'm coming!' He called out, making his way quickly down the wide hall.

A rush of freezing cold air greeted him as he opened the door. Standing on the step, in full waterproofs, was his nearest neighbour, Colin Walmsley. The man owned the farm that bordered Lower Kilduggan along its north-eastern boundary. 'I'm sorry to bother you so late, Michael,' Colin said with his characteristic politeness. 'There's been an accident. The lifeboat's been called out. We need all the help we can get. Can you come?'

'Of course. I'll be five minutes.' Michael grabbed his waterproof trousers and jacket, swiftly pulling on his wellington boots. The two men ran out of the house and jumped into Colin's 4X4 which was parked diagonally across the farm's courtyard. When Michael was a younger man, he had been a volunteer on the inshore lifeboat, although it had been decades since he'd attended an emergency call-out. He was secretly hoping he would be asked to stay at the lifeboat station and man the radio. On the drive over to the Kilduggan Point, where the new vessel was housed, Colin filled Michael in on what he already knew.

'A helicopter took off from Kilross Harbour about an hour ago. Conditions at take-off were acceptable; the pilot logged in with the private hire company in Prestwick at eight forty five pm. But no one's heard from him since. It was due to land at the helipad in Tarbert at nine thirty. The coastguard at RAF Kinloss picked up an automatic mayday signal at three minutes past nine.'

'What is the significance of an 'automatic'

mayday and why do they think the helicopter might be in the Sound?' Michael enquired.

'By nine pm the chopper should have cleared the west coast of Garansay and would have been following a bearing north-west along the Kilbrannan Sound. The automatic mayday is triggered when the helicopter crash lands. It will release its signal whether the pilot has pressed the button or not. There were four other people on board and it appears as if none of them were wearing buoyancy gear.'

Michael sat in silence as Colin expertly negotiated the narrow and winding lanes that led from Lower Kilduggan Farm to the lifeboat launching point. The station lay at the end of a small rocky headland which pointed the way to some of the deepest and most treacherous waters in the Kilbrannan Sound. It was now that Michael began to fully contemplate the magnitude of what he was going to have to do. Colin had been going to sea on this lifeboat since he was a teenager, but Michael had very little recent experience on the water, especially since moving to Glasgow. It was his younger brother, Allan, who was the adventurous one.

'Do you want me to go out in the boat too?' Michael shouted, above the noise of driving wind and rain, as they climbed out of the jeep.

'I'm sorry Mike, but we're really shorthanded. We need you on board. Don't worry, the adrenaline will kick in as soon as we set off. Just listen to instructions and do as you're told. It will all come back to you.'

The two men joined the rest of the volunteer crew down by the jetty. Tasks were handed out by a man of about Michael's age, who seemed to be the one in charge. When the six men were in their correct positions on the boat, the signal was given to launch.

As the vessel was propelled down the steep jetty, it felt to Michael like the log flume ride he had taken Sarah on once at Disneyland in Florida, the only difference being, this time around there was genuine danger involved. He tried to keep his head up and a tight grip on the thick rope threaded around the inside of the boat. As soon as they plunged into the surging water, the skipper, whose name was Rab, switched on the huge search light fixed high up on the bow. They began the job of scanning the waves for signs of the helicopter's flashing emergency beacon and, hopefully, life. Visibility beyond the searchlight's beam was very limited. As the vessel powered out into the middle of the Sound, further away from the headland, it seemed to Michael as if they had been given an impossible task. The fierce southerly wind became ever stronger as they moved out of the protection of the Garansay hills and into open water. Luckily, it was too dark for Michael to see the horizon, which he knew must be rising and falling at extreme angles as the lifeboat was tossed about by the towering waves. Just as nausea and exhaustion were threatening to get the better of him, Michael heard the skipper calling out an instruction over and over again. As the lifeboat suddenly lurched to the left, abruptly changing its course, he worked out that Rab was urgently shouting: 'Come About, Come About!' although the words were practically swallowed up by the thunderous noise of surf and spray.

There was now a sudden burst of activity on

15

board the vessel. Unsure of what to do, Michael took hold of one of the smaller torches, which were attached to the gunwales of the boat. He pointed it towards the area of sea which Rab appeared to be focussing his attention on. There, amongst the purple darkness, was a dimly visible flash of orange light. It seemed to take forever for them to reach the source of this eerie flickering. When they finally did, Michael let out a gasp. The scene set out before them was totally surreal.

The helicopter was floating, seemingly in one piece, on top of the water. Scattered around it lay numerous fragments of buoyant debris, including several padded squares of material. As they approached the chopper, on low engines, Michael could see the front glass double panel had disappeared and that the right hand side of the cabin had completely broken away from the rest of the structure. The heavy pieces must have sunk to the uttermost depths of the Kilbrannan Sound. The tail boom was still in place. The rotor blades hung limp, but intact. They were entirely at the mercy of the pitiless wind which was steadily twirling them around, in a sad parody of their proper function.

'No sign of survivors yet. Remember - 'Air Accident' will want the Black Box!' Rab shouted back to them as they visually combed the detritus of the doomed helicopter.

Then, a man positioned at the bow of the boat started shouting excitedly to the rest of the crew, madly waving his flashlight. 'There's someone in the water! There's someone in the water!' he cried.

The lifeboatmen leapt into action. This was the scenario for which the volunteers spent countless hours in preparation. The procedure was performed seamlessly. Michael was given no task, so he gripped the side of the boat and watched, as the rescue vessel slowly moved up alongside the body, which was lying across one of the helicopter's landing skids. The unconscious form was gently hauled into the boat by the bowman and promptly wrapped in sheets of heat conserving material by the remaining crew.

At this point, Michael was finally provided with a function. Rab barked at him, 'look after the boy and keep him warm until we get back.'

Causing it to pitch in a terrifying manner, the skipper turned the lifeboat around. With its engines on full throttle, the ship motored straight ahead, driving into the remorseless winds, speeding alarmingly along a direct route back to Kilduggan Point.

3

Michael did exactly what he was told and tried to keep the young man they pulled out of the Kilbrannan Sound as comfortable as possible during the choppy voyage back to Garansay. The survivor seemed to be breathing evenly but had not yet regained consciousness. When they arrived on dry land, he was swiftly transferred onto a stretcher and lifted into the medical room of the lifeboat station.

'Stay with him and wait until the ambulance arrives,' Rab commanded, before dashing back out into the dark night.

'Where's he off to?' Michael asked his neighbour, nonplussed.

'They're going to re-launch. The crew need to find out if there are any other survivors out there,' Colin explained. Michael shuddered, incredibly relieved to be left playing nursemaid to the young man on the stretcher in front of them.

'Shouldn't we get him to Glasgow as quickly as possible?'

'The Rescue Helicopter can't fly in this weather. The medical centre in Kilross will have to look after him for the night. Look, Mike, can you go with him in the ambulance? Only I've got some contractors who need my supervision arriving at the farm first thing in the morning.'

'Of course. My building designs can wait.'

Whilst the two men shared this friendly exchange, the boy in the stretcher started to wriggle around uncomfortably, letting out a low moan. Michael quickly moved across and placed his hand on the boy's forehead, noticing then that he had a nasty gash above his left eye.

'Can you hear me?' he asked in a gentle and soothing tone, 'you're okay now. We are going to take care of you.'

The boy rolled over onto his side and drifted back into unconsciousness, although somehow, he seemed more settled than he was before.

'Do we know who he is?' Michael whispered. 'Was there a passenger list?'

Colin said, 'just a second,' and disappeared off into the main office of the lifeboat station. He returned a couple of minutes later with a scrap of paper, on which Rab had scrawled down a message sent from the control centre at Kinloss.

'Unless the pilot was unusually young looking, this must be Cameron Fleming. He is nineteen years old and lives with his parents and sister in Tarbert. When he does wake up you're going to have to be very gentle with him. If the guys don't find any other survivors out there in the Sound, then this lad has just lost his whole family.'

'Bloody hell,' Michael muttered, as the last of the adrenaline finally left his system and he began to realise the full implications of this horrible accident. He set about busying himself by cleaning up the cut on Cameron's forehead and finding a suitable dressing to place over it. Michael was just wondering whether or not he had dealt with the injury correctly when he and Colin

19

heard the ambulance pull up outside. As soon as they set off for the cottage hospital in Kilross, the medics started giving Cameron the once over, closely monitoring his vital signs.

'He seems amazingly well, considering,' said one of the medics, 'although you can never tell what's going on inside - he could have an impact trauma that's making him bleed somewhere. The docs will have to keep a very close eye on him.'

'What about his head?' Michael pointed out, as if the highly trained paramedic might not have noticed the giant plaster that had been hastily stuck across the boy's temple.

'It's stopped bleeding, but they'll probably do a scan when he gets over to the mainland. The fact he's not fully conscious yet is a bit of a worry, I must admit.'

They spent the rest of the journey filling out the seemingly endless forms which accompanied this type of call out. Michael was compelled to inform the medic that he couldn't be of much help since he didn't even know the boy. But the men did their best to tick the appropriate boxes before the ambulance arrived at the small but modern hospital building.

It was nearly midnight as they entered the quiet lobby. The hospital staff showed Michael straight into the relatives' room, handing him a scratchy blanket and urging him to get some rest. The doctor on duty told him Cameron was quite stable for the time being and they would let him know immediately if there was any change. The doctor explained that Cameron would be flown to the Western Infirmary in Glasgow as soon as the weather had settled enough for the helicopter to reach them.

By the following morning, Cameron's condition

remained good. The doctors at Kilross were happy for him to stay on Garansay for a few days longer. Michael went in to see the boy. He wanted to reassure himself that it was okay for him to return to Lower Kilduggan, for a few hours at least. When Michael entered the small but pleasant room, he ventured cautiously towards Cameron's bedside. The boy was still sleeping, but his face had some colour in it. For the first time, Michael was able to fully examine his appearance.

Cameron was fair-haired, but his skin had been deeply tanned by the sun. Although he was connected up to wires and tubes and his head now properly bandaged, Michael could still observe that he was a very handsome young man. A fortunate physical trait, Michael thought to himself. One which would either be enhanced or impaired, depending upon what the boy's personality turned out to be like.

As if in answer to the query, Cameron began to move his face towards the light filtering in through the thin hospital curtains. Slowly and tentatively, he opened his eyes. Michael stepped back a little, so as not to intimidate the boy. But he saw immediately that he need not have been so cautious. The steely blue eyes now resting steadily upon him were exuding both self-assurance and determination.

'What happened?' the young man demanded, in a pleasant accent which was undeniably Scots, but with a hint of other, unidentifiable influences.

Michael moved in closer again. 'I'm afraid there was an accident - Cameron, is it?' the boy nodded his head. For the first time since wakening, those piercing eyes displayed a flash of fear.

Colin Walmsley had called Michael in the early hours of the morning, to inform him the lifeboatmen found no other survivors in the water or within the wreckage. Now it had simply become a salvage exercise. Michael found he was faced with a difficult choice. He must decide just how much to reveal to this poor boy.

'You were in a helicopter; travelling back from a wedding at the Glenrannoch. Do you remember that?'

The boy nodded again, this time adding, 'yes, the weather suddenly turned. It was OK when we set off, but after just a few minutes, once we got beyond the hills, we seemed to be in the eye of a storm.'

'Well, we don't know exactly what happened yet. But we were very lucky to come across you in the water.'

'Were there - did you - find anyone else?' Cameron faltered over the words.

Michael took a deep breath and gently laid his hand over Cameron's. 'They did everything they possibly could. I know what it was like, because I was out on the lifeboat with them for a while. The conditions were terrible. They searched for hours but they couldn't find any trace of your mum, dad or sister. I'm so deeply sorry.'

Cameron looked away and lay very still, staring blankly at the stark, whitewashed wall for several minutes. When he turned back again his face was contorted with anguish.

'Then how did I survive? I'm no better at swimming than they are, in fact, Mum used to swim every day...' his voice trailed off and he started to sob, great heaving shudders that threatened to dislodge the tubes which were delicately taped to his chest. Michael said nothing but took the boy in his arms. He held him tight until Cameron had finally exhausted himself and was lying limp and spent against Michael's shoulder. But the silent tears were still falling, uncontrolled, down his handsome young face.

4

Michael Nichols had always found the days leading up to the New Year bleak and slightly depressing, even before Miriam died. The Christmas decorations suddenly seemed sad and redundant. Although a Scot, Michael had never found himself drawn into the spirit of Hogmanay. This year, however, he had more important things on his mind. After the high winds and rain of the past few days, the weather on Garansay had settled down. The sun was blazing across the Kilbrannan Sound. It was still freezing outside, but the bright clear skies made the cold seem more bearable.

As Michael looked out across the water from the kitchen of Lower Kilduggan Farm he wondered at the calm stillness of the scene. On a tranquil morning such as this, who could comprehend the countless lives that had been lost in those murky depths? He shivered at the thought, in spite of the warmth radiating from the wood burners which were lit both in this room and in the large sitting room that lay beyond the hallway.

The renovations to the ground floor of the farmhouse were halfway towards completion. The kitchen had new units and a large, modern, range-style cooker. Michael had also had the downstairs bathroom refitted. But the sitting room that ran from the front to the rear of the house still remained much as it was. Michael was contemplating the possibility of creating French doors that would lead from the sitting room out onto the lawned garden at the back of the property. He knew he would have to speak to his sister and brother, Imogen and Allan, before making any final decision about this.

Michael had packed a suitcase for a return visit to his flat in Glasgow. He had not planned to go back to the mainland before New Year's Eve. But Cameron Fleming was flown over to the Western Infirmary yesterday and as he was leaving, the boy had implored Michael to drop in and visit him as soon as possible. Michael had given the lad his old smartphone, so they could keep in contact once they both got back to the city. Sarah and Ross had just bought him the most recent version for Christmas. Michael thought that giving away his current one would force him to get to grips with the newer technology.

Michael's second storey tenement flat was only about a mile away from the hospital. He decided he would be better able to keep an eye on the boy from there. Cameron seemed to be recovering very well physically. There were still some tests that needed to be done, but it appeared he had been extremely fortunate to have escaped more serious injury.

Psychologically, Michael was not quite so sure the boy was coping. Cameron was still very tearful and seemed full of guilt and remorse that he escaped the crash relatively unscathed while the rest of his family wasn't so lucky. The boy had been replaying the last few minutes of the flight over and over in his mind. It was frustrating him that he could not recall what happened after the helicopter hit the water.

Michael suspected that Cameron desperately wanted to believe he did something to help his father, mother and sister after the crash. The accident itself had become national news. There had been reporters all over the island for the previous forty eight hours. The staff at Kilross cottage hospital had done an excellent job of protecting Cameron from the worst of the whirlwind of media attention.

Michael had been a little concerned at the thought of Cameron having to get back into another helicopter to return to the mainland. He even offered to take the boy over himself on the ferry. But the determination that Michael had initially observed in Cameron Fleming, as soon as he had opened those piercing blue eyes, seemed to have kicked in and the boy insisted that he would travel in the tiny aircraft. Michael sensed then that this was a young man who liked to take on his fears and have mastery over them.

All of the men who had gone out in the Kilduggan lifeboat on that awful night had been interviewed by both the local and the national press. Photographs were taken and one journalist in particular made a big thing about the role Michael had played. She seemed to think that by staying overnight at the hospital he had somehow gone 'beyond the call of duty'. Michael stressed to her, in very strong terms, that the real heroes in all this were the regular lifeboatmen, who went back out into those stormy seas to search over and over again for further survivors.

Colin Walmsley told Michael that the debris

from the helicopter was recovered by the Air Accident Investigation people and sent to the mainland for testing. They had not been able to find the 'Black Box', which was the recording device that would provide the investigators with valuable data about the last crucial moments before the crash. But he said it might still get washed up somewhere. They hadn't entirely given up hope of recovering it. The same went for the bodies. Colin pointed out that the chances of ever finding them were not good. The Kilbrannan Sound joined the Firth of Clyde, the North Channel and then the Atlantic Ocean itself to the south. The pilot and the rest of Cameron's family could have ended up anywhere.

Michael had a good look around before gathering up his case. He took a moment to reflect upon how just a couple of years ago he would not have dreamt of spending so much time back here on Garansay. The island had never really felt like home to him.

He had helped his father to run the farm and knew the business inside and out before he left to study for his degree in Aberdeen. But Michael's father, Angus, had been a tough task master. He was always made to feel as if he had to 'sing for his supper.' This meant he had never been totally comfortable here. Last year, however, his brother and sister found out some things about their family that had forced him to reconsider his relationship with this place. He realised that great sacrifices had been made in order to allow him to spend his childhood on this beautiful island. Lower Kilduggan seemed different to him now.

Michael believed that only one place you lived in during the course of your life ever truly felt like home. For Michael, this special place was the house he had shared with Miriam and Sarah in Bearsden, in the north-western suburbs of Glasgow. He and his new wife moved into that house, just an ordinary looking three-bedroomed new-build, after they got married in 1983. Sarah had been born just a couple of years later. That was the place Michael would always consider his home. On those rare occasions when he recalled his dreams, in the semiconscious haze of early morning, they all seemed to be set in that neat little house, positioned in the middle of its wrap-around garden. He vividly conjured up Sarah's pretty little gabled bedroom in his mind's eye. The one they had built above the garage when his daughter had grown bigger and wanted more space of her own.

Michael shook off these thoughts, which would only make him maudlin if he allowed them to. Instead, he promptly took his leave of Lower Kilduggan Farm, thoroughly determined to fill his mind with plans for the future.

*

The Western Infirmary in Glasgow was next to the sprawling campus of the University and just across Kelvingrove Park from Michael's flat. He received a text from Cameron Fleming the previous night, asking him to come over and visit today. Cameron said the Strathclyde Police would be interviewing him and he could do with some moral support.

It would be perfectly natural if Michael felt

imposed upon by this request, but he did not. As the dust began to settle in the aftermath of the crash, it became increasingly clear that Cameron had very few family and friends in the UK who he could call upon at this difficult time. The Fleming family solicitors, a large corporate firm based in the financial centre of the city, had been doing their best to trace Cameron's relatives, not least so they could fulfil the bequests made by Richard and Isla Fleming in their will.

Isla's mother was still alive and living in Dunkeld. She was quite elderly and unable to come and visit her grandson whilst he was still in hospital. So Michael was perfectly happy to act *in loco parentis*, for the time being, at least.

When Michael was directed to Cameron's room, he was cheered to see the young man propped up in bed, reading a motoring magazine, surrounded by dozens of vases bursting with flowers, presumably sent by well-meaning members of the public.

'How are you doing?' Michael asked quietly, hovering in the doorway.

Cameron lifted his pale blue eyes from the glossy pages and responded immediately, 'Michael! Please come in and sit down. I'm fine, thanks, but a bit tired still.'

'Totally understandable,' the man replied as he seated himself in the soft visitor's chair at Cameron's bedside.

The young boy shifted himself forward a little, as if he were about to impart a great confidence. 'I'm a little nervous about this interview with the Police Inspector, although he promises it's purely

29

routine. I don't want to get upset when I have to talk about Mum and Dad. I desperately want to do it properly, so we can find out exactly what happened - you know?'

Michael placed his hand on Cameron's arm. 'The Inspector will understand that. He will take it very slowly and be patient, I'm sure. He'll want to find out the truth just as much as you do.'

Cameron lay back again and looked happier. Michael suddenly wished that his brother-in-law were there. Hugh was a Professor of Psychology at a University in the south of England, but before he entered academia he had practised for a few years. Hugh was the most sensitive and perceptive person Michael knew. He felt as if he would know exactly what to do in this situation. Not only that, but Hugh might also begin to help Cameron come to terms with his devastating loss.

This train of thought was interrupted when a burly looking man in a brown suit appeared at the door of Cameron's room. Even without the uniformed WPC standing next to him, this chap would still be immediately identifiable as a police officer. The man broke into a wide smile, revealing crooked and tobacco stained teeth which, rather than being grotesque, actually made his face strangely appealing.

'Hello Cameron,' he began, taking a small and respectful step into the private room. 'My name is Detective Inspector Zanco. This is WPC Barrie, who is here to take a few notes for me, if that's okay with you?'

Cameron nodded.

The two police officers entered the room and brusquely pulled up a couple of seats, preparing themselves for the interview.

'My name is Michael Nichols. I'm not a relative.

In fact, I was one of the volunteer lifeboatmen who pulled Cameron out of the water. The lad here wanted someone to be with him whilst he was questioned and I agreed. If it's acceptable, I would like to be permitted to stay.'

'Of course,' said DI Zanco. 'We'll need to take some details from you afterwards and I would ask that you don't interrupt or prompt Cameron in any way during the interview.' The detective made a start. 'Cameron, I know this is going to be very difficult for you, but I want you to do your best to tell us everything you can remember about last Saturday. If you need to stop at any time for a break, just say the word.'

Cameron Fleming described the day his parents and sister were killed in as much detail as he could recall. He explained how the cottage in Tarbert had been their holiday home in Scotland for the past four or five years, but up until recently, it hadn't had much use. They had been living in the old fishing port since they came back to the UK six months ago. It was only supposed to be a temporary residence as his father had been looking for a house for them to buy. It was taking so long because his dad was really quite particular about the type of place he wanted. Their previous house in Dubai had been very large, with a swimming pool and a huge garden.

'It must have been difficult to leave Dubai,' DI Zanco put in lightly, 'and return to Britain just in time for an infamous Scottish winter!'

'Yes, I found it pretty tough at first. I wasn't sure if I wanted to come back at all. But I'd enjoyed Christmas and was just starting to get used to it when -' Cameron broke off mid-sentence and blinked his eyes ferociously. 'Anyway, we had to leave the wedding party early because Dad doesn't like flying at night. He had a really bad experience once in a small plane, years ago. We were running later than planned. It was actually pretty dark by the time we took off. Dad wasn't in a very good mood.'

'Did your father get on well with the pilot, Thomas Watson?' Zanco asked.

'Oh yes, Dad's used Tom loads of times before, so he trusted him. But Dad was nervous, so he was snappy with me and Lucy. Then he was really quiet during the flight.' Cameron said.

'I know it's upsetting, but could you explain to us, in as much detail as you possibly can, what happened on board the helicopter.'

Michael placed his hand next to Cameron's arm in a gesture of silent support.

The boy took a very deep breath. 'OK. It was nearly dark when we got into the helicopter at the landing pad in Kilross. The pilot made sure we were all strapped in, then he spoke to Dad for a bit. Dad was asking if the weather was going to be a problem. Tom was telling him that he'd checked the forecast and there was no reason to delay or cancel the flight. After that, Dad got into the back with us. Tom spoke on his radio for a few minutes before we took off.

I remember looking out of the window and watching the flashing Christmas decorations strung along the main road. They followed the shoreline and I recall thinking how pretty they were. The illuminations disappeared as we flew out of the village and into the hills. The chopper glided through a deep valley where there were tall mountains on either side of us. It was getting darker, but we had our lights on and everything. No one was saying very much. I think Lucy might even have been dropping off to sleep. The steep sides of the valley suddenly fell away and we were flying over what must have been the opposite side of the island. I could see the streetlamps of a little village twinkling beneath us. This was when the ride started to get a bit bumpy. I glanced at Dad. I could tell he wasn't happy. After that, we crossed the coastline and found ourselves over open water. This was when the helicopter really began to vibrate. We appeared to be bearing the full force of the wind. Tom looked to be working hard just to keep us steady.' Cameron paused here.

'Would you like to take a break?' Zanco asked, leaning forward with concern.

'No, I want to get it over with. It was then that we seemed to be at the centre of a storm cloud. It suddenly went very dark and we couldn't see anything out of the windows at all. This was when Dad started to panic. That's what he really hated about flying at night - not being able to see anything outside. It made him feel claustrophobic. Dad shouted ahead to Tom. He was telling him to try and land as quickly as possible. Dad was saying that maybe we could make it across to Campbeltown. Tom didn't respond. He was too busy trying to fly the chopper, I expect. Because we were really shaking badly by that time and had to hold onto our seats. Mum and Lucy were absolutely quiet, Mum had her eyes tight shut and they were holding hands. We were juddering so violently that at one point I thought the helicopter might break into pieces in mid-air. But that wasn't what happened. We suddenly pitched forward and it felt like we were dropping. The sensation didn't last long and then there was nothing. I don't recall anything after that.' Cameron fell back against the pillows.

'Thank you very much, Cameron. You are being extremely helpful,' Zanco said kindly. 'So, what is the next thing you *do* remember?' he pressed. Trying his luck a little, Michael thought.

But Cameron raised his upper body again and a faint smile flickered across his tanned features. 'I remember Michael,' he stated blandly, turning towards his temporary guardian.

Then the young man tightly clasped the hand that had been resting, gently and reassuringly next to his own, on the plain starched sheets of his hospital bed.

5

The Cumberland Arms Public House, situated halfway along the aptly named Rotten Row, was a Glasgow haunt that the city's respectable tourists would do well to avoid. Situated south of the Clyde and in the heart of that sector of the city which was once notorious for its filth, poverty and crime, 'The Cumberland' had clung stubbornly to its down market pedigree, despite the surrounding area having been totally revived and regenerated in the meantime. Sitting, semi-slumped at a table in the far corner of 'The Cumberland's' lounge bar, was Pat O'Connell, his strange posture being on account of his age rather than the effects of the pint of 'shilling ale that his right hand was gripping.

Pat's peace was shattered by the arrival of one of the pub's regulars, a good generation younger than the solitary man in the corner, who made his unsteady way across the filthy stone floor. This wiry fella had a scrunched up copy of the 'Herald' held out in front of him in an accusatory manner. He proceeded to shove the paper directly under the nose of the timeworn drinker.

'Take a look at this yin, Pat,' he slurred, tapping the front page with a grubby finger; 'tha's somethin' that's rarer than hen's teeth - it's tha' tale aboot tha' lad they pulled oot o' tha' whirlybird th'other nicht. Surviv'd tha' 'Soond' in a storm like tha' yin. I jus' canna believe it, man.'

Seeming to require no response to this observation, the drunkard zigzagged his way back towards to the public bar, without giving Pat so much as a backward glance. But if he had, he would have seen that the old man had slowly propped himself up and was now staring, open-mouthed at the photograph that accompanied the front page article.

'Well I'll be damned,' he muttered quietly to himself.

With a surprising amount of strength, he shoved the full pint glass out of his way and began the painfully slow process of manoeuvring himself free of the snug and then of 'The Cumberland' itself. When he finally stepped out into the moderately fresher air of the street, the hunched figure determinedly shuffled its way the short distance along Rotten Row to the tiny set of ground floor rooms that Patrick O'Connell liked to call home.

Part Two

6

Imogen's nerves were a little frayed by the time Hugh guided their heavily loaded estate car onto the mezzanine level of the Garansay ferry. The drive had been a relatively uneventful one but they did have to take a detour into central Manchester to pick up Ewan from his student digs, which added an extra hour to the journey. As a result, the Crofts had been lucky to reach Gourock Harbour in time for the last boat of the day. The youngsters were tired and frazzled, but were also excited and looking forward to a scotch pie and beans in the cafeteria, the promise of which had been sustaining them for the last hour or so.

The trend in recent years towards short and very wet summers seemed to have been broken. Like the previous year, July had been extremely hot and dry. The spell of good weather helped Imogen to persuade Hugh and the boys to accept her older brother's invitation to spend a few weeks of the summer holidays with him at Lower Kilduggan Farm. Bridie was enthusiastic about the idea right from the start. Ewan and Ian were more sceptical.

Ewan was under no obligation to holiday with

his family at all. He was twenty years old now and in his second year at university. But the eldest of the Croft's children was also completely skint and a plan he had with some of his pals to backpack around Europe had fallen through. So their eldest son unenthusiastically asked if he could come along with them to Garansay. Ian was sixteen years old and going through that 'difficult age'. The worst of his behaviour only amounted to being quiet and sullen, with a tendency towards spending his spare time listening to music or playing online games. Ian still loved his sailing and that was how Imogen lured him into this trip. She assured her middle child he could go out on the water every day if the weather permitted.

Whilst the youngsters tucked into their 'high tea' in the ferry's busy cafeteria, Hugh and Imogen had bagged the window seats and were gazing out at the calm waters as they slowly sipped their coffees. Hugh was reluctant to accept Michael's invitation to join him on Garansay, not because he didn't love the beauty of the island, but because he was worried about the emotions that it might stir up in his wife. Last year, they discovered some unpleasant facts about Imogen's family. It had tainted the good memories she had of the farm she grew up in. Hugh was concerned that coming back here again would upset her.

Imogen laid a hand on his and said, 'I can't wait to see what Michael has done with the place. He tells me it is a total transformation. He's really very excited about us coming, you know.'

'I know, darling,' Hugh replied. 'I'm looking forward to it too and it's probably good therapy for you to return to Lower Kilduggan Farm under happier circumstances.' He gave a tight smile.

'Exactly, I'm just really pleased that Michael is

spending so much time back on Garansay, he was never very enthusiastic about being there before.'

'It's amazing what the onset of old age will do to you,' Hugh gave her a wink and this time his face broke into a proper grin. Imogen gave him a gentle kick under the table, but felt relieved her husband finally seemed to be warming to the idea of the trip.

'So who is this kid that might be joining us at the farm?' asked Ewan, who had polished off his pie and beans and was about to wash it down with a large glass of cola.

Ian and Bridie also looked up from their plates, intrigued by the thought of a potential holiday companion close to their own age.

'Well, he is called Cameron and is nineteen, only a year younger than you, Ewan. According to Uncle Michael, he is very sporty and loves to sail so you should get on like a house on fire. But guys, just be aware that he has had a very tough time. His parents and sister were killed in an accident earlier this year, so he is still a very fragile boy. You will all have to be extremely sensitive, okay?' Her offspring dutifully nodded their heads, returning immediately to their refreshments, smart phones and MP3 players.

'I'm sure they will,' Hugh said. 'One of Ian's classmates lost his father last term. His tutor told me the class handled it really well.'

'Oh yes, the kids will be fine. I'm just concerned Michael is taking on too much by spending all of this time with the boy. I know it's uncharitable, but it isn't really his responsibility to look after the lad in this way.' She peered down at her empty cup, feeling ashamed of airing these worries.

'Don't feel guilty. I completely agree with you. Michael found out some earthshattering news about his childhood just last year. Now he has befriended a damaged young man who has lost his own parents, just as Michael effectively 'lost' his, when you told him what you had uncovered about the family.' Hugh gazed out of the cabin window, just as the hills of Garansay began to come into view along the horizon.

'But Cameron does seem to be a fairly independent person. His parents had a lot of money and although it is being held in trust for him until he reaches twenty one, the trustees are still making sure that he is well looked after,' Imogen stressed, trying to add some balance to the discussion.

'Yes, and he has taken a flat in Glasgow hasn't he? I would be more concerned if he were spending all of his time with Michael. Once the boy starts to get back on his feet, finds a girlfriend and what have you, Michael will probably see less and less of him.'

'Speaking of girlfriends,' Imogen said, in a change of tack, directing this line of conversation towards her eldest son. 'When is Chloe coming over - has she decided on a day yet?'

Ewan thought about this, his thin but handsome face furrowing in an attempt to recall a phone conversation or an e-mail exchange he had lodged in his mind somewhere. 'She's definitely coming, but she's got two weeks of work experience first. I'll just give her a text to check on the date.'

'Put in the message that we will come and meet her off the ferry. She just needs to let us know when she's going to arrive.'

'Okay Mum, okay,' Ewan replied, letting out a heavy sigh, as if the demands made upon him by this simple request were really quite unreasonable.

Imogen had seen the photos Michael sent them of the work he was having done at Lower Kilduggan Farm but they had not prepared her for how different the place now looked. As Michael led them on a grand tour of the farmhouse she was truly impressed at how well he had used the space. The old kitchen now had a cosy inglenook area with a wood burning stove and a small armchair placed by the fire. The units themselves were solid wood and for the first time in decades the room looked light and airy. But in particular, she liked what Michael had done with the sitting room, which now had large patio doors opening out onto an outdoor seating area. The back garden itself, which had not been properly tended for years, now possessed a good number of flowering shrubs. Michael had planted a small apple tree in the centre of the lawn which he said should be bearing fruit by next year.

Imogen felt a lovely warm glow inside at what her brother had achieved here. This was not the same farm anymore and yet they had not completely given up on the piece of land their Stewart forebears had worked so hard to make their own. She walked over and gave Michael a hug, as the youngsters scampered off to stake a claim on the rooms they wanted.

'What was that for?' Michael said with a smile.

'I'm just so glad you've decided to come back to Garansay and make it your home,' she gushed, feeling happy tears prickling at her eyes.

'I've still got my flat in Glasgow you know.' Michael gently corrected.

'I know, I know, I just feel that this is how it was supposed to be. Oh, just ignore me, Michael. I'd better go and help Hugh unload the car.'

Later, when they were settled in, with the boys sharing the back bedroom and Bridie taking the old box-room which was once Imogen's, they sat around the kitchen table with a pot of tea, eager to catch up on family news. After about ten minutes of chatting, the kids were keen to go and investigate the hillside. As they pulled on their trainers and headed out of the kitchen door Imogen told them to make sure they were back in time for dinner.

'It's wonderful to be able to give them that freedom,' she said, when the room was quiet again and the adults had a chance to talk in peace.

'We have some lovely countryside around us in Cooper's Creek,' Hugh continued, 'but the traffic on even the smaller country roads is frightening. It makes us very nervous about letting them wander too far on their own. Now we're just not used to it.'

Michael shook his head sadly. 'It's a terrible shame when you think of how independent we were as children, Imogen.'

'Yes, but I'm not convinced we always used our freedom wisely,' his sister replied, almost absentmindedly. When she realised she might be straying onto a dangerous topic, Imogen quickly changed the direction of the conversation. 'So, Cameron must like coming here, especially if he enjoys sailing.'

'Oh yes, he seems to. You will both like him. He is an intelligent young lad and although he has some dark moments, he seems to be coping pretty well.' Michael became quite animated at the mention of Cameron. 'Actually Hugh, I was wondering if you might spend a little time with the boy when he is here. I know it's an imposition, but he is still very troubled by the fact he was rescued while the rest of his family was not.'

'Survivor guilt,' Hugh supplied. 'I'll do my best, but to have any real impact Cameron would need to be seeing a counsellor on a regular basis. It could take months or even years to deal with his grief.'

'Thank you, and he does have his own counsellor. The trustees of his father's estate arranged it for him. But I just really wanted the benefit of your opinion. I completely trust your judgement.'

'Well, I appreciate the vote of confidence, Mike. But if I am going to be effective you'll have to fill me in on the boy's background a little bit. I only know what I read in an article in a Sunday supplement a couple of months ago.'

'Sure.' Michael refilled their tea-cups. 'Cameron lost his mother, father and younger sister in the crash. His sister, Lucy, was fifteen years old. They had only just moved back to Scotland after spending the last sixteen years in Dubai.'

'So his sister was born out there and Cameron was just a toddler when they left the UK?' Imogen asked.

'That's right. Lucy had just spent a term at a girls' boarding school in Perthshire at the time of the accident, so she'd made a couple of friends here. But Cameron had completed his A Levels at the British school he attended in Dubai and was on a gap year. He hadn't yet had the chance to make any real connections in the UK before he lost his family.' Michael paused to sip his tea.

'Are there any relatives still living in Scotland who can help him out?' Hugh enquired, hoping not to sound as if he was keen to off-load the boy onto them.

'There are some aunts and uncles, but Cameron's father sounds as if he could be quite a difficult man. These relations had, at various times over the years, fallen out with the Flemings. Cameron's grandmother is still alive and she lives in Dunkeld. In fact, I took him to visit her myself. She is a nice lady but is pretty frail and can't travel at all. Cameron tries to get up to see her whenever he can. She is extremely upset about losing her daughter and granddaughter. She is very emotionally fragile.'

'Even if Cameron's relatives had fallen out with his father, it's no reason to abandon the boy. Not when he's been left all on his own,' Imogen added indignantly.

'But he's not actually a boy, Imogen.' Hugh interjected. 'Cameron is nineteen and he has left the education system. It would be different if he'd been five years old but he's not. Only because we have a son of that age do we know what a tricky time it can be for them and that they are anything but grown-up yet. In the eyes of the law, he's an adult and therefore no one's responsibility.'

'Hugh is right,' Michael agreed. 'If Cameron's father hadn't been wealthy and left trustees in charge, then he would have been completely alone.'

'Ah, but he would still have had you,' Imogen said and leant in to give Michael a peck on the cheek before standing up to clear away the cups and saucers.

'There's another thing I wanted to talk to you about,' Michael suddenly said. There was something about his tone that made Hugh shoot his wife a warning glance, which she totally ignored.

'What is it?'

Michael went over to the wooden dresser that sat behind the door. He opened one of the drawers and brought out a piece of paper. He unfolded it and left it lying on the table top in full view. Imogen padded back over from the sink to have a closer look.

'I received this in the post back in January. It's probably a mistake of some sort, but I thought it was the kind of thing that you two are quite good at puzzling out,' Michael explained, trying to adopt a light tone.

Hugh and Imogen both looked down at the sheet of paper. It was surprisingly crisp and white when compared to the writing on it, which was just a blotched and spidery scrawl. It took them a little while to work out that it said, quite simply:

I did what you asked.
Now I want to be paid.

7

Michael had gone over to Kilross to meet Cameron off the morning boat. The children wanted to get out onto the water as soon as they could, so the Crofts drove up to Port na Mara, the fishing village on the northern coast of Garansay. There was a natural harbour there and the ruins of a Norman Castle stood imposingly on a tiny spit of land stretching out into the bay. There was a sailing club by the pier, where beginners could happily take to the calm and protected waters of the cove, or more experienced sea-farers could make this headland the starting point for a trip to Kintyre or even up to Loch Fyne.

Hugh had taken the boys out in an eighteen foot yacht the family had rented for the day. Bridie and Imogen decided to visit the craft shops and Castle instead. Imogen felt it was good for them to have some 'girlie' time every so often. Bridie had really grown up since they were last on Garansay as a family. The girl was tall girl for her age and although she possessed her mother's dark brown eyes, her hair was a much lighter shade and could turn a honey blond colour in the sun. Bridie loved to make jewellery and to paint. She was pottering happily around the little village shop, which stocked local crafts as well as doubling up as a small art gallery.

Imogen was glad that Hugh had taken the boys

out because it gave her time to think. Hugh was grumpy the previous night about Michael having shown them the letter. 'We're supposed to be on holiday for heaven's sake!' were his exact words as they unpacked their suitcases in the old guestroom which possessed the best view over to Carradale on Kintyre. But later on, when the three of them had downed a couple of glasses of single-malt out in the garden after dinner, Hugh had begun to soften a little, as his natural curiosity got the better of him. He surprised Imogen by saying, 'Could it have been sent by one of the contractors you used here at the farm? The note, I mean.'

'I did think of that,' Michael replied. 'But I've mainly used the Monroes and any of the work they weren't able to carry out Danny subcontracted himself. I have found Danny Monroe's billing process to be a little more sophisticated than an anonymous scrawl sent in the post.'

Hugh chuckled and added, 'I just thought you might have used a self-employed tradesman at some point - to re-paint the old windows, or something of that sort.'

'Yes,' Imogen had put in, with a wry smile, 'someone who's an expert at intricate paintwork but has atrocious pen control.'

Michael laughed and Hugh gave her a gentle shove.

'Okay, if that's not where the note came from then what are we thinking? What did it say on the envelope? Was it addressed to you?'

'Yes,' said Michael. 'It was sent to me

personally, here at the farm.'

'You've been in the papers a lot over the last few months Michael, especially back in January, just after the crash. It isn't difficult to find out someone's address online if you've got their name and you know the general area where they live,' Imogen suggested.

'It must have been some kind of crackpot then,' Hugh stated with obvious relief.

'That's the conclusion I came to as well,' Michael had said, and the conversation about the letter ended there.

In the cold light of day, Imogen was thinking about it again. Bridie had chosen a selection of hand painted stones and some art equipment. They were standing at the little till point, waiting to pay. It was a lovely sunny day but a bit blustery. Imogen suspected the boys wouldn't be able to sail beyond the headland in the wind and would most likely be back in the village for lunch. Imogen asked Bridie where she would like to go and eat, so she could text Hugh and let him know where they'd be.

The decision was made to head towards the Garansay Whisky Distillery building, which sat impressively at the foot of the winding mountain road leading to the eastern side of the island. They started to distil the water from the burn that gently trickled down the hillside about twenty years ago. The spirit produced by the peaty brown liquid had become world renowned. The building itself housed a visitors' centre and café on the second floor which boasted lovely views up the glen.

As they walked along the narrow village road, past the camp-site, Imogen kept returning to the same thought. She was no expert, but the handwriting on the note Michael showed them had struck her as similar to the sort of indecipherable scrawls that were written on the 'thank you' cards they used to receive at the kids' primary school, back when she was on the Parents' Committee. They used to get them once a year from the residents of the old folks' home in Maldon, after the school had hosted afternoon tea. It made Imogen think the inscription on the note was made by someone very old, who had perhaps seen Michael's photograph in the paper and recognised him. Imogen asked her brother the previous evening if he could identify the post mark on the envelope but he said he hadn't been able to read it. The letter might have been sent from anywhere.

'Look, Mum - there's Uncle Michael,' Bridie called out as she pointed towards the distillery car-park.

Imogen's older brother was emerging from the driver's seat of his German sports car and gazing about him. Imogen surmised that Michael must have driven back from Kilross via the 'North-End' of the island, in the hope he might hook up with them here in Port na Mara. Bridie and Imogen stepped up their pace and shouted over when they got closer.

Michael turned to greet them. That was when Imogen caught her first glimpse of Cameron Fleming, who was getting out of the passenger seat as they approached. Her initial thought, upon seeing the boy, was how very handsome he was. Cameron was tall and blond and athletically built. The young man was also extremely well-dressed.

His clothes were casual but they obviously had designer labels. He possessed the kind of tanned complexion which suggested a lifetime of expensive holidays spent in the sun. It was the type of skin tone which, even in a Scottish summer, would only require the hint of good weather in order to be 'topped up'.

'Imogen!' Michael cried out with genuine enthusiasm. 'I was hoping we might bump into you.' He gestured grandly towards his young companion. 'This is Cameron.'

The boy stepped forward and gave them a shy smile before holding out his hand. 'I'm so pleased to meet you,' he said politely. 'Michael has told me all about you. I can't wait to be introduced to Ewan and Ian and Mr Croft, of course.'

'They should be coming here for lunch soon, you are welcome to join us if you'd like?' Imogen tentatively suggested.

'Well, that was the plan,' Michael said and he took her arm as they entered the lobby of the visitors' centre.

Cameron and Bridie chattered away to one another and chose a table by the window whilst Michael and Imogen ordered some drinks at the counter. The boy actually seemed very sweet. Imogen could see why her brother had become so fond of him. But for some reason she was a little uncomfortable in his presence. Imogen found herself suddenly conscious of the shabbiness of her walking trousers and mac. Cameron had done absolutely nothing to make her feel this way, but she felt it nonetheless. Although it didn't make her proud, Imogen resent him for it.

While Cameron and Bridie discussed what they would like to do on Garansay during the holiday, Imogen snatched the opportunity to ask Michael some more questions about the mysterious note he'd shown them the previous night.

'I have a hunch,' Imogen told him, 'that the text of the letter was written by a very old person. I didn't get the sense it was someone deliberately trying to disguise their script, because then they would have just typed it - or cut out letters from a newspaper and stuck them on - or some other technique of that kind.'

'But if the note was written by a crackpot who saw my photo in the papers, it doesn't much matter how old they are, does it?' Michael remained unsure of where she was heading with this.

'Can you think of anyone - even from decades ago who you might have asked to do something for you and then, for some reason, you lost touch with them and never managed to repay the debt - or return the favour, or whatever it might have been. Because this person could have seen your picture all these years later and it reminded them to get back in touch with you again.'

'I will have a good think about it, Imogen, and see what I can come up with,' Michael said with genuine intent.

Their discussion was halted by the arrival of the boys, who were wet and windswept and full of talk about their sailing trip. In all the excitement of introductions and animated tales of the sea, Michael's unexplained letter was completely forgotten.

*

Hugh and Michael took the youngsters back out on the boat after lunch. They seemed to be hitting it off pretty well. Taking advantage of the free time, Imogen trolled down to the Port na Mara General Store to shop for a big family supper. When she'd surveyed what was on offer, she decided upon a fairly simple menu of beef stew with veg. Even in summertime on Garansay the evenings could be quite cool and you often needed to light the fires all year round, so Imogen picked up some logs and kindling too.

When the family finally returned to Lower Kilduggan Farm later in the afternoon, Michael showed Cameron up to his room and Imogen made a start on dinner. Hugh was looking sunburnt, but his wife could tell he had really enjoyed his day out on the water. He came up behind her whilst she chopped the vegetables, placing sleeveless arms around Imogen's waist, nestling his face into her raven black hair.

'So, what do you think of Cameron?' Imogen asked in a low voice.

'He's a very good sailor,' Hugh replied, quite unhelpfully.

'Thank you for your specialist insight, Professor Croft.' Imogen leant back gently into his embrace. 'Come on, you know what I mean.'

'Well, I like him. He's obviously had a fairly sheltered upbringing. He seems a bit young for his age perhaps. But that is only to be expected. He's been to a tiny private school in Dubai and presumably, his family only socialised within the small British ex-pat community out there.'

'But he was okay was he? Being back out there on the Kilbrannan Sound?'

'Yes, he seemed to enjoy it. I know what you're driving at Mrs Croft, but people deal with loss in different ways. Perhaps Cameron likes to be out there on the water. It may make him feel closer to his family.'

Imogen considered this and decided that Hugh was right. She had to concede she was in no position to judge others on the way they dealt with their grief. Imogen experienced some fairly conflicting emotions a couple of years ago when her own mother died. These things could affect people in lots of different ways.

Hugh started to nuzzle his face into her neck and Imogen put down the knife for a second and pressed herself into him, closing her eyes and giggling as his stubble started to tickle her cheek.

All of a sudden, their intimacy was cut short when a strident and confident voice booming from behind them declared: 'what's for dinner, Mrs Croft? Something most certainly smells good.'

They both swung around, like teenagers caught out in the act, to find Cameron, standing nonchalantly in the kitchen doorway, casually holding a magazine.

'Oh, just a beef hotpot. I hope that's okay?' Imogen jovially replied.

'Sure. That sounds great!' Cameron promptly disappeared in the direction of the sitting room.

Imogen turned towards Hugh and shot him an inquiring look. He gave a noncommittal shrug by way of a response. Although he had shown no sign of having taken offence, Imogen couldn't help but wonder how long Cameron had been lurking in the doorway, and just how much of their conversation he had overheard.

The family dinner proved to be very pleasant.

Because Cameron offered to clear away the dishes and wash-up, Ewan was pressurized into volunteering his services too. The young men seemed to be getting on extremely well as they divided the jobs out between them.

'I could get used to this,' Hugh declared loudly as he stretched himself out in the old armchair in the sitting room whilst Michael busied himself down by his feet, attempting to light the wood burning stove.

'Well, don't,' Imogen added acidly. 'Because I'm not going to cook for you all every night, I've not come on holiday to be your unpaid skivvy!'

Michael remained quiet while Hugh and Imogen enjoyed their playful exchange. Imogen's older brother then offered to pour the couple a drink and entreated them to sit down for a moment and listen, because he had remembered something he wanted them both to hear. The wood had really started to take now and was crackling away nicely, producing a strong flame which would gradually die down to leave softer, glowing embers. It was these that would provide the room with a steady, long-lasting heat. Drawn towards the blazing fire, Imogen and Hugh stopped joking around and settled themselves down, drams in hand, waiting in eager anticipation for what Michael had to say.

8

Michael informed them at breakfast the next morning that he had arranged for Cameron to have a tour of the lifeboat centre at Kilduggan Point. He wondered if the Crofts would like to join them.

'Cam's trustees have arranged for a modest donation to be given to the RNLI on his behalf. He has a card which he wants to pass on to all of the volunteers who helped bring him back to safety. I thought it might be good for Cam to take it there himself,' Michael explained.

Imogen moved over to sit at the kitchen table next to her brother. 'I'll ask the kids if they want to come along. I'm sure they will.' She laid a hand on Michael's arm. 'Do you think Cameron will be alright going back to the Kilduggan headland again, being so close to the place where his family was killed?'

Hugh nodded sagely while he finished a mouthful of scrambled egg on toast. 'I think it's a good idea. He may get upset but that won't be such a bad thing. He needs to get used to reliving the circumstances of his rescue so he becomes accommodated to it in his mind. The problems will arise for him if he blocks off the event and then begins to experience flashbacks later on that he finds overwhelming. This is what happens to people who suffer from PTSD.'

Imogen went over to re-fill Hugh's coffee cup. She was perfectly happy to accept her husband's judgment on this because Hugh was considered to be something of an academic expert in the field of Post-Traumatic Stress Disorder. His second published book was all about this terrible condition. Hugh had interviewed dozens of sufferers, mostly ex-servicemen, over a period of several months. His aim was to establish some recognisable trends in the patterns of behaviour created by the disorder. As a result of the conclusions Hugh had reached in his study, he had been interviewed on national television as an authority on the subject and had even been called as an expert witness in a couple of high profile criminal cases.

'That's decided then,' Michael stated. He abruptly stood up to take his plate and cup to the butler sink.

Michael seemed to Imogen to be subdued today, possibly because the evening before, he had provided them with a possible explanation for the strange anonymous note he had received back in January. His sister had asked him to think very carefully if there could have been a time in his past when he might have got himself indebted to someone, perhaps without even fully realising it.

As they gathered around the wood burner late the previous night, Michael told them about an intriguing incident he had remembered from his youth.

In the late 1970s, a couple of years after their father had died, Michael left Garansay to study for a degree in Engineering at Robert Gordon

University in Aberdeen. This was the career path he felt was right for him at the time. The University back then was closely linked to the oil and gas business. This was the industry Michael had seen himself moving into. Imogen recalled so clearly the day her beloved older brother left home for the first time. Their mother had been particularly upset, as Michael was such a support to her after their father had his accident. But the family was also pleased for him, of course, and Isabel Nichols would never have dreamt of standing in his way. It was interesting for Imogen to hear Michael talk about his early student days because she couldn't recall him ever mentioning before what he had done during that period of his life.

Throughout the seventies, Aberdeen was at the centre of the 'scramble' for North Sea oil and gas. This was the decade in which most of the major rigs were constructed, either there or in the turbulent seas off Shetland. Michael's interest in Chemistry and Engineering made this the most obvious career route for him to take at that time. But as his course went on, he started to realise this might not be the right profession for him.

At the start of the second year, he began a work placement at one of the major gas companies in the city. Michael said it was a dynamic time for the business, with new developments and discoveries becoming commonplace. The 'big' money didn't start rolling in from North Sea Oil until the eighties, but some executives were already making comfortable profits. One of these men, the CEO of the company where Michael had his placement, was called Roger McKilvenna. He also happened to be the father of Miriam McKilvenna, the girl who, a few years later, was to become Michael's wife.

Michael first met Miriam when there was a huge office party to celebrate the company's tenth anniversary. There was a barbecue and marquee set up in the garden of the McKilvenna's impressive Aberdeen home. Positioned high up on a hillside, just to the north of the city, the elevated lawns looked out over the iron grey sea, from the depths of which, all of the McKilvenna's conspicuous wealth had been provided. Michael told us that when he caught sight of Miriam at the event, with her shoulder length copper hair falling in perfect curls onto a full length emerald green evening dress, he knew straightaway she was the one for him. Although she was a couple of years younger, Miriam was already engaged at that time to someone else - a chap called Fergus - who was an executive working at her father's company.

Imogen kept deliberately quiet during this part of the tale. She was dying to chip in, as in all these years Michael had never once mentioned this before, but she did not. Imogen was learning that sometimes it is best to just let people talk.

Michael made the mistake of declaring his admiration for the boss's daughter to another student on the placement, a chap called Keith. Imogen's brother intimated that Keith was a bit of a 'jack the lad' type. As soon as Michael told him what he thought of Miriam he immediately wished he hadn't. Keith kept encouraging him to ask her out to dinner and send her flowers. This was never Michael's style.

Then, a circumstance arose which meant Imogen's brother might meet Miriam again. One of the directors of the business was retiring and there was to be a big bash for him in the ballroom of Aberdeen's premier hotel. Of course, Michael knew that Miriam would undoubtedly be accompanied by her fiancé, so there wouldn't be much of an opportunity for him to speak with her. He said as much to Keith one night after work, when they were having a pint together in the pub next to the Company's premises.

When the evening of the retirement party came around, Michael found to his great satisfaction that Miriam was there alone. He got his first chance to have a proper conversation with her. In fact, they seemed to get on pretty well. It must have helped that Michael was tall and dark with almost film star good looks back in those days, Imogen thought. All of his female contemporaries on Garansay had been dying to go out with him.

Keith and a couple of their other student mates turned up late and fairly drunk. It was only then Michael found out the source of his good fortune. Keith declared, quite proudly, that they had taken Fergus to the pub after work for a 'quick' drink. Miriam's fiancé had been rather keen to join them, probably because he was going out with the boss's daughter and had previously found himself excluded from the easy camaraderie which existed between the other young men in the office. Keith and his cronies proceeded to get Fergus blind drunk. They bought him whisky chasers, plied him with spirits and then left him there, slumped in the corner of the public bar, in a kind of alcohol induced stupor. It turned out that Fergus was really quite unwell but a kindly fellow drinker called an ambulance. He spent a night at the town's infirmary. There was no long term damage, but Michael had no doubt there could have been. It was lucky Fergus had passed out when he did and hadn't been tempted to drink any more.

Imogen finally decided to interject. 'So, this Keith character thought you wanted him to get Fergus out of the way for the evening. But that wasn't what you had actually meant.'

'No, not at all. I was just sounding off about not getting a look-in with the girl of my dreams. It was adolescent stuff really.'

'But you and Miriam *did* get together in the end. What happened to this Fergus fellow?' Hugh asked.

'Well, no one ever worked out that his drunken exploits were a set-up. He and Miriam were together for a few more months before she called off the engagement. In the weeks that followed we started to see more of each other. If I am honest with myself, I would have to admit that it did all start with the evening of the retirement party. Fergus went on to marry someone else. He now has two grown up children and lives in Inverness. We had no further contact with him for decades. Then, when Miriam died, he came to the funeral in Aberdeen. We've kept in touch ever since.'

'So it worked out okay for everyone in the end,' Imogen added. 'But you think this Keith chap might believe you owe him a favour because of what he did for you?'

'I wouldn't have said so, but you did ask me to plumb the depths of my past to see if I could come up with anything. This was the only scenario I thought of. The trouble is, I can't remember what his surname was. I'm sure he hailed from Fife or thereabouts. He could live absolutely anywhere now, especially if he went into the oil and gas industry. He could even be out working in the Middle East.' Michael sat back in his seat, looking tired.

Imogen left it there, but in lots of ways the story did seem to fit. Although, Imogen's original theory was that the letter writer was elderly. If Keith was Michael's age or even a few years older, he would be sixty now at most, which wouldn't be quite right. With these unresolved thoughts still ticking over in her head, Imogen had put down the empty whisky glass and gone to bed.

*

When they reached Kilduggan Point, the strong westerly wind of the previous day was still blowing in from the Sound. The warmth they should have been feeling from the bright August sun was having to battle against the bitter chill biting through the brisk breeze. Imogen had to force Bridie to put on her fleece as they walked towards the Lifeboat Centre. Their daughter had always been reluctant to wear anything more than a tee-shirt during the summer months. Imogen often had to remind her that down in Essex the ambient temperature was a little higher than it was there.

Mae Millar was waiting for them at the entrance to the Centre. Mae was a neat and attractive woman in her late sixties. She worked as the volunteer archivist for the Garansay Lifeboat. She lived in a lovely little cottage just up the coast. She also happened to be a great friend of Imogen's late mother. Mae immediately moved forward to kiss Imogen's cheek.

'Thank you so much for meeting us here, Mae,' Imogen said with sincerity. 'I hope that you are keeping well?'

'Oh, aye, I can't complain. But I'm missing Isabel terribly you know. I think about her every Tuesday morning when we would usually have had our trip to 'The Port'. It's not really the same without her.' Mae said this so cheerfully that it didn't come across as at all maudlin.

Imogen was glad that Mae was able to talk about her mother so freely. Some people felt they had to shy away from the subject which simply meant Imogen's hardworking and feisty mother hardly ever got mentioned.

'Now, this must be young Cameron,' Mae switched topic and turned towards the only fair-haired person in the group, making Imogen suddenly realise just how obviously different he appeared from the rest of them.

'I'm very pleased to meet you Mrs Millar,' he replied with his usual politeness.

'Cameron has a card he would like to leave for the volunteers, Mae,' Michael prompted.

Cameron rather shyly handed over the envelope.

'I will certainly pass it on to them, my dear boy. Now, would you all like to come and have a look at the lifeboat? I might just be able to let you have a wee climb aboard.'

For the next hour or so they looked around the shed that housed Northern Garansay's inshore lifeboat. Mae gave them a potted history of the lifeboats on the island. Imogen told her that their Great Uncle, Ian Stewart, had been a volunteer at the station back in the years before the First World War.

'Well,' Mae responded, 'the first motorised boats were used by the RNLI as early as 1890, when they were steam powered, but here on Garansay the boat would have still been reliant on sails and oars. So when your Great Uncle Ian was taking to the water out there to save lives, the vessel would have been lowered down the slipway on huge wooden wheels. After that, the men would have had to use brute strength in order to row against the high winds and waves.'

'And it's hard enough to fight the weather when the lifeboat is powered by an outboard engine,' Michael supplied, with considerable feeling.

Imogen was fascinated by Mae's instruction on the history of the lifeboats, but as she gazed around the group, she suddenly noticed that Cameron was no longer standing with them. Not wishing to interrupt the flow of Mae's talk, she slipped out quietly, walking back through the centre, searching for the boy in each of the small rooms which led to the entrance.

Not finding him, Imogen stepped outside the building itself, instantly feeling the force of the wind on her face. Pulling her jacket tightly around her she turned and strode out onto the promontory of rocks that protected the huge concrete jetty. Climbing further along, Imogen saw the distant outline of a person, positioned westward and facing the Kilbrannan Sound.

The small figure was standing perfectly still and appeared to be right down by the water's edge, just inches from the crashing waves. Imogen made her way swiftly towards the waterline. The rocks were steep and slippery and the going difficult. When Imogen finally reached Cameron, the noise of the sea was so loud she was sure any words she uttered would be lost. Instead, Imogen gently touched the young man on the arm. He turned round abruptly, to see who was intruding on his grief. It was obvious he had been crying and his face was a mask of anguish. In that moment, Imogen offered the boy her hand.

Thankfully, he reached out and took it. Imogen led him back up the rocks to safety, with neither of them uttering a word.

9

The wind had finally died away. All the early signs indicated it would be a perfect summer's day. Imogen's two sons ambled self-consciously into the kitchen on this clear and bright morning. Ewan surprised his mother by asking if he and Ian could take packed lunches and go walking in the hills.

'Okay, that sounds like a great idea,' she replied cautiously. 'But what about Bridie? Doesn't she want to go with you?'

'She said she's not bothered about coming,' Ian answered. He poured himself an orange juice and popped a slice of bread into the toaster.

'Well, she might change her mind about that,' Imogen suggested, 'in which case, one of the adults will have to go along with you.'

'Alright,' said Ewan, taking charge of the discussion. 'But if Bridie doesn't want to come, then can Ian and I do the walk by ourselves? I'll take the map and we'll stick to the paths. We've done the route up to those hills loads of times before.'

'Just let me speak to your dad first, and what about Cameron? You'll need to find out if he'd like to go too.'

'I'll ask him, sure,' Ewan said good-naturedly. 'I just thought he might not be feeling up to it after yesterday.'

Imogen nodded her head to acknowledge Ewan's perceptive observation. She lowered her voice a little. 'He's bound to get upset every once in a while, but it might do him good to have some time with you boys. I'll just check with Uncle Michael first.'

Whilst the lads were upstairs digging out their walking gear, Imogen broached the subject of their expedition with Hugh over breakfast. Imogen was aware it might appear they were overprotective of their sons. However, they felt as if their circumstances were a little different from other families. Ian suffered from type 1 diabetes, which was diagnosed back when he was a toddler. This meant he needed an insulin injection every day. His diet and the timing of his meals had to be closely monitored. Because they had lived with his condition for so long, everyone in the family was used to making sure Ian was eating the right things at the correct time. They all knew the early warning signs of a possible 'hypo' attack.

Ewan in particular, was really switched on to the risks of diabetes because he helped his mother out so much with Ian when he was little. Being the older sibling, he had learned how to share the burden of responsibility at an early age.

'Ewan will have to make sure Ian eats his packed lunch and that they sit down and have a chocolate bar if he is feeling at all wobbly,' Hugh said firmly. His expression indicated he still didn't feel very comfortable with the idea.

Imogen sat down next to him and placed her arm around his waist. 'There'll come a time when Ian has to manage his condition by himself. We want him to have the chance to go to university like all his mates, don't we? So we need to start putting him on a longer leash.'

'I hear what you're saying. It's just Ian's at that difficult age. He's unpredictable and stubborn. It concerns me he might do something stupid.' Hugh sighed as he set down his mug of steaming coffee on the scratched surface of the old wooden table.

'That's where Ewan and Cameron come in. They are both pretty sensible boys. Ian is actually more likely to listen to them than he is to us.'

Begrudgingly, Hugh went off to help the boys plan their route and make sure they had enough food and equipment for the trek. It turned out that Cameron was keen to join the outing. As Ian had predicted, Bridie was happy to stay with the adults. She wanted to do some sketching from the meadow bank behind the farmhouse.

As the sun was climbing steadily up the glen ahead of them, the boys set off on their adventure, with backpacks and maps and mobile phones and promises that they would keep in touch at all times. They strode off with beaming smiles on their faces and Imogen felt suddenly very glad they agreed to let them go.

The house seemed oddly quiet without

the lads. Imogen wanted to stay at Lower Kilduggan while they were gone, just in case they needed them for anything. Michael had been quietly working in his mum's old study since first thing in the morning. As soon as the boys had left, he popped his head out of the little room and called his sister over. As Imogen leant against the door frame, she could see that Michael had a number of official looking papers spread out all around him on the old oak desk.

'These are the findings of the inquiries into Cameron's parents' helicopter crash,' Michael explained. 'He asked me to have a look through the documents so I could help him make some sense of it. Could you possibly spare a few minutes and give me a hand?'

Imogen went back into the kitchen and dragged one of the heavy dining chairs into the study. It was a bit of a squeeze, but she managed to place the seat next to Michael.

'There are two reports; one from the Fiscal's Office and the other from the Air Accident Investigation team at Farnborough. The Procurator Fiscal was investigating the sudden deaths of Richard, Isla and Lucy Fleming and of the pilot, Thomas Watson. The 'Air Accident' people were purely looking for the reason why the helicopter might have crashed into the sea.'

Imogen nodded to show she understood the distinction.

'The Fiscal's report was driven by the relatives of the pilot, who were keen to ensure he was not blamed for the accident. Apparently, Tom Watson had been flying helicopters for over fifteen years and had an unblemished safety record.'

'It must be awful for his family,' Imogen said, resting her head in her hand as she leafed through some of the papers.

'Yes, he had a wife and two young children. There can be a tendency for aircraft manufacturers to try and put the blame on 'pilot error' rather than mechanical failure in the aftermath of an accident. This would be made easier for them by the fact that Tom is no longer here to defend his actions.'

'But the Air Accident report is supposed to be totally independent?'

'Exactly. In this case they couldn't recover the Black Box Recorder as the Sound is very deep and the currents on that night were so strong. This has hampered their analysis. The report itself is a bit technical. Cameron was struggling to understand the details. I think I've finally grasped the gist of it. The helicopter was a Gravar A160 and had been in operation for three years. Tom Watson worked for a private hire aviation company which flew out of Glasgow Prestwick Airport. The maintenance reports for the Gravar were completely up-to-date at the time of the flight last December. Tom was one of their best and most experienced pilots. All of the debris from the flight was salvaged and taken to Farnborough airfield where they were painstaking examined by the

Inspectors; piece by tiny piece. Fortunately, the cockpit was almost completely intact. I saw that myself when we sailed out to the wreckage on the night of the accident. These newer helicopters have floats built into their landing skids so they are designed to stay upright if they put down on water. What the report concluded was that there were no obvious mechanical problems with the Gravar when it crashed. The tail rotor and the swash plate were both intact and functioning well. They ruled out the in-flight failure of these crucial components which, apparently, can be a common cause of helicopter accidents.'

'You told me at the time, that Cameron said they experienced violent juddering and shaking just after they flew into the storm. Could they account for that?' Imogen enquired.

'The report couldn't find a technical reason for it. They suggest it could simply have been the force of the wind on the rotors. From Cameron's first-hand account and the readings taken from the cockpit computer, it seems the helicopter just suddenly and catastrophically lost height. This happened when they were about two kilometres out over the Kilbrannan Sound. It resulted in the aircraft hitting the water. What is also clear from these findings is that the Gravar pitched forward just before it struck the sea. The investigators thought this was unusual. The accident report says the pilot should have been trying to keep the helicopter upright at this point. They cannot explain why he suddenly ditched. A few suggestions are put forward by the experts. One of which is that Tom lost control of the Gravar in those last few seconds, for reasons that remain unknown. But Cameron's testimony doesn't really support this theory.'

'Cameron thinks Tom was fighting to keep them in the air, right up until the last minute?'

'Yes, but there's something else that doesn't quite seem to tally either. The Air Accident Investigators are adamant in their summary that the passengers of the flight, and the pilot himself, must have, at some crucial point, removed their safety belts. This could have happened either before or after impact. But it must have occurred at some stage, otherwise their bodies would not have been washed away by the sea before the wreck was discovered.' Michael sounded genuinely puzzled by this aspect of the report.

'I can't see them taking their belts off during the flight. Might it be possible they survived for a short while after the helicopter crashed?'

'It's certainly feasible. If they did they would have wanted to get out of the chopper before it sank. It's designed to stay afloat for a short time, but it would have eventually capsized in those high seas. I wouldn't be surprised if they had then drowned, because conditions were absolutely horrific out there that night. Or, they might have been clinging to the wreckage, like Cam did, but

71

then they succumbed to hypothermia and just slipped away into the depths.'

Imogen sat very still for a couple of minutes before she could hold back no longer from declaring, 'so how come Cameron survived and they didn't?'

Michael said nothing for a while but eventually, misinterpreting the meaning of her remark, he wistfully replied, 'yes, and that is the question the poor boy is going to have to wrestle with for the rest of his days.' Imogen's brother sighed with great feeling and carefully began to gather up the various documents into a neat and ordered pile in front of him.

The weather was so lovely that they decided to eat lunch out on the patio in the back garden. Afterwards, Bridie and her mother took a leisurely stroll down to the Kilduggan Shore, where Imogen sat on the sand and watched her daughter glide back and forth through the almost tropically clear water. They remained on the beach for a couple of hours before meandering up the path towards the farmhouse. Bridie immediately rushed upstairs to take a shower. Imogen wandered into the sitting room, looking for Hugh. She found him lounging in a garden chair, a little beyond the open French windows, contentedly reading a book. Imogen was just about to ask him if he had heard from Ewan yet when there was a sudden, violent hammering at the door.

Hugh jumped to his feet. They both instinctively ran to the kitchen. When they get there and discovered the source of the noise, Imogen's hands flew up to her face in horror. Cameron was standing stock-still just within the side entrance. He was silhouetted against the glare of the afternoon sun, with his features in shadow. Imogen could clearly see he had a streak of blood down the front of his tee-shirt. From his hands a thick, sticky liquid was slowly dripping down onto the stone floor.

In desperation, Imogen scanned the path behind him for a glimpse of Ewan or Ian. Realising the boy had returned alone she screamed, 'Oh my God! What the hell have you done to my boys?'

10

Michael came running into the kitchen a few seconds after Imogen's uncontrolled outburst. He took hold of Cameron by the shoulders, steering him over to the table and sitting him down on one of the heavy dining chairs. Hugh had to take hold of his wife in an upper body grip, pinning down her arms, to prevent her from going for the boy's throat.

'What's happened?' Michael instantly commanded, taking Cameron's face in his hands and looking him squarely in the eye.

Upon hearing the older man's voice, Cameron seemed to snap out of his reverie. He started to shout, 'it's Ewan - his leg is caught in some kind of trap. We decided to go off and explore for a bit, when we were on our way home. Ewan suddenly ran off, he was only a few metres ahead of us, in the undergrowth, but then he just collapsed and started yelping.'

'A man-trap?' Imogen screeched, in utter disbelief, 'on Garansay?'

'Where are they? Is Ian okay?' Hugh urgently demanded, releasing his grip on Imogen so he could run to fetch the phone.

'Ian stayed with him. I thought it would

be best. I didn't want him to get tired out as I knew I would have to run the whole way. We made a tourniquet with Ewan's sweatshirt. There were some paracetamols in the back-pack. He's had a couple of those. I think we stopped the bleeding. But I just couldn't get the horrible thing to release.'

'You've done the right thing,' Michael said calmly. 'How far are they from here? Can we get him back to the house?'

'I think so. They're below the loch but we went exploring rather than coming straight back down. The boys are about a mile and a half off the path, towards the north-west,' Cameron explained.

'They're probably closer to Colin Walmsley's farm than they are to here,' Michael suggested. 'It might be best to take him down to Loch Crannox and wait for an ambulance there.'

They called the emergency services. The decision was quickly made that Imogen would stay with Bridie and drive over to the Walmsley's farm. Michael and Hugh would go and find Ewan and Ian, bringing them there to meet them. All Imogen could do was stand and watch as her husband and brother pulled on their hiking boots, grabbed the medical kit and with Cameron as their guide, strode off along the footpath.

If they were heading north-west they would need to follow a bearing that crossed the section of hillside which lay within their own property. Beyond that, the route Cameron had outlined passed over the boundary fence and into the pasture land which belonged to Colin's farm. Ewan and Ian had to be somewhere within that area.

Imogen needed to remain calm for Bridie's sake, but her stomach was turning over and over. Bridie didn't seem to have fully grasped what had happened to her brother. She was keeping her mother sane by chattering away in the car all the way over to Loch Crannox Farm. Luckily, Bridie had not seen the blood on Cameron's tee-shirt. Otherwise she might not be quite so cheerful. Imogen had given Colin a call on his mobile before they left. He was waiting for them as Imogen manoeuvred the car up the steep tarmacked road that led to the single story building Colin used as his offices.

The farming operation was on a much larger scale there than had ever been achieved at Lower Kilduggan. In fact, after Imogen's mother died a couple of years back, Colin had been keen to buy the farm from them, so he could expand even further. There were absolutely no hard feelings when they decided not to sell. The Walmsleys had been friends with the Nichols for a long time. They'd been through a lot together. Imogen felt they were fortunate to still be neighbours.

As soon as she climbed out of the car, Colin said briskly, 'Imogen, I wish we were seeing each other again under better circumstances. Come on, you can wait in the farmhouse.'

Imogen said nothing but took Bridie's hand as they followed him towards the side entrance of the old stone house. He directed the girls straight into a pleasant, country style kitchen.

'Can Bridie go and watch T.V or something?' Imogen asked as he automatically filled up the kettle.

'Of course.' Colin stepped into the hallway. To Imogen's surprise, he called out, 'Julia!'

A tall, slim woman, who Imogen would have said was in her mid-thirties at most, appeared from one of the ground floor rooms.

Colin said to her, 'could you please take Bridie into the lounge and show her how to use the television in there?'

The woman smiled, putting an arm around Bridie's shoulders and without any fuss, whisked her away.

'Thanks,' Imogen muttered. As soon as her little girl was gone, she slumped down onto the table. Colin came across and rested his hand on her arm.

'He'll be okay.'

'There was so much blood, Colin.'

'I've seen plenty of farm injuries over the years. I know it's of no comfort to you now, but they always look worse than they really are.'

Imogen lifted herself up onto her elbows and looked directly at her neighbour and friend. 'I thought he'd done something to them. When I saw the blood, it was the first thing that crossed my mind. I screamed at him and I would have gone for him if Hugh hadn't -' the rest of her words were lost as a sob rose up into Imogen's throat.

'Cameron?' Colin replied, obviously puzzled.

Imogen didn't get a chance to explain any further because at that moment everything seemed to happen at once. The ambulance arrived. Imogen and Colin ran into the car park to meet it. The paramedics then spotted Michael and Hugh stumbling down the hillside, with Ewan being carried between them and the two younger boys following along behind. Very quickly, the medics got Ewan into the ambulance and somebody shouted, 'come with us, Mum. The rest of you can follow on behind.'

Imogen looked frantically around her before jumping aboard, but was reassured when she thought she could hear Colin's distant voice saying, 'we'll take care of Ian and Bridie. You just stay with Ewan and don't worry about a thing.'

*

The paramedics gave Ewan a shot of morphine on the way to the Kilross Accident and Emergency Department. Michael and Hugh had managed to prize the foothold trap from his ankle but it had been a horribly painful process. By the time they arrived at the hospital, Ewan was drifting in and out of consciousness. The doctor was waiting in the lobby. He allowed Imogen to stay whilst he examined the injured leg. They had to show him the 'man trap' itself; a medieval looking contraption which seemed to have no place amongst the modern medical equipment that surrounded them.

Doctor McKelvie had grown up in a farming community in the Highlands. He informed Imogen sombrely that he hadn't seen anything like it for many years. To her great relief, the doctor pointed out it was a so-called 'humane' trap, in that it did not possess the nightmarish spikes which would usually be associated with these brutal mechanisms. But the spring was still very strong, with the metal having been sharp enough to slice through the flesh of Ewan's lower calf, almost cutting it to the bone.

Imogen was now sitting with her son, whilst he slept soundly in his hospital bed. He seemed peaceful enough. There was no sign yet that the wound had become infected, which was what Dr McKelvie was most concerned about.

The medics were going to keep an eye on Ewan for the next couple of days, making sure there was no nerve damage to the leg. Ewan needed to build his strength back up after all the blood he had lost. For the moment, Dr McKelvie was confident they could treat him on Garansay and his wound wouldn't require surgery. He told Imogen they tried to avoid a transfusion if at all possible. He stressed that Ewan was young and fit and should make a good recovery.

Imogen didn't manage to get a wink of sleep the night before and was just dozing off in her chair when Hugh arrived for visiting time.

'How's he doing?' He asked in a low voice as Imogen opened her eyes to find her husband perched on the edge of Ewan's bed.

'He's recovering really well,' she said, propping herself up. 'They still need to do some tests to make sure the nerves of the leg haven't been damaged, but the wound is already starting the healing process.'

'He looks so pale.' Hugh delicately lifted Ewan's hand and burrowed his face into the palm. He sat like this for a few minutes, until Ewan shifted over into a more comfortable position and Hugh laid their son's arm gently back at his side.

'Where are Ian and Bridie?'

'They're with Michael. He's driven them over to Kilross Castle, to keep their minds off things for a few hours.' Hugh shifted around uncomfortably. 'The police arrived to question Colin. Not long after you left in the ambulance. Apparently, it is illegal to have man-traps on your land. It has been since 1827.'

Imogen sat bolt upright. 'But Colin hadn't put it there, had he?'

'No, and he was appalled at the very suggestion of it. He pointed out to the P.C that his farm is mostly arable. He doesn't have any game to protect and if he put mantraps on his land they would most likely damage his own cattle. It wouldn't make any sense.'

'What did the policeman say to that?'

'He agreed. But he said they were obliged to investigate as someone had been seriously injured. It turns out there have been some problems with poaching on Garansay in the last couple of years. He said the police can't allow farmers to take the law into their own hands.'

'I see, so did the police have any idea where the trap might have come from? My brothers and I played on those hillsides for decades and I've never seen anything like it before.'

'The P.C said that they are back in circulation again. Rural poverty is on the rise and what with the price of food going up too criminals are starting to turn their hand to poaching fish and game from the big estates. He said there hasn't been an incident here on the island, of landowner's using man-traps to deter theft, but there have been cases up in the Highlands. The local station had been told to be on the look-out.'

'Well, there's been a case now. Although, I don't believe for a second Colin would be involved. I've no idea how it got there. The trap itself was a museum piece. It must have been a least a hundred years old.'

'These old relics do turn up from time to time. Let's just be thankful that Ewan is recovering. He's given us both a bit of a fright,' Hugh said, with deliberate understatement.

Imogen turned towards her son, placing

her fingers just beneath his mouth and nose so she could feel his warm, rhythmical breath on her skin, just like she used to do when he was fast asleep in his cot. Imogen felt the tears prickling at her eyes. Sensing his wife's change of mood, Hugh slipped his arms around her. Imogen rested her head against his chest and allowed herself to be comforted by her husband until the nurse popped her head around the door to tell them the time had come for him to leave.

11

When Ewan's girlfriend heard about his accident, she was keen to come over to Garansay as soon as possible. Chloe cut short her work placement at a chemical company in Manchester and was due to arrive at Kilross Harbour on the late afternoon boat. Imogen had spoken to this young woman more often in the last couple of days than in all the time she and her son had been together. Ewan was not very good at communicating with his parents about his love life. Imogen had only now discovered, for instance, that Chloe's parents moved fairly recently to Dubai. Imogen suggested that she and Cameron would have plenty to talk about when she got there.

Ewan was now out of hospital and back at Lower Kilduggan Farm. His leg was strapped up and he had parked himself decisively on the old but comfortable sofa in the sitting room. He had to take a cocktail of pills, most of which were to reduce the risk of infection. But primarily, he had been prescribed plenty of rest. Imogen was pleased to see him sitting up, reading his magazines and fiddling with his smartphone. She kept coming up behind him and running her hand through his thick curly hair, something he had not permitted her to do for many years. Imogen was determined to make the most of it.

They had given Ewan the option of returning home, to their house that looked out over the River Blackwater in east Essex. But Ewan said they might as well stay on here. He suggested he would find the car journey more comfortable when his leg had the chance to heal up a bit. So they were carrying on with the holiday and attempting to settle back into normal life.

Bridie and Ian appeared perfectly happy in his company, but Imogen had been doing her best to avoid Cameron. She was sure he must have heard her accuse him of doing goodness knows what to the boys, after he had shown up at the back door on that fateful afternoon.

Just after Ewan returned from the hospital and the dust was beginning to settle on the event, Hugh questioned her about the outburst. He said he thought it was peculiar for Imogen to immediately imagine Cameron had deliberately done Ewan or Ian harm.

'It's just that Michael had been telling me about the accident report into the helicopter crash, earlier that day,' she had tried to explain. 'A couple of the facts didn't make sense. I couldn't understand how Cameron could have survived when none of the rest did. Because it now looks as if at least some of them were still alive after the helicopter hit the waves yet Cameron claims he can't remember anything about it. If there were others in the water with him then why doesn't he recall any of it? I would have thought it would be pretty damned memorable.'

'He was unconscious when he was rescued. Perhaps he'd been out cold ever since the impact,' Hugh suggested.

'But that makes it even more incredible that he survived. Why didn't he slip off the skids into the sea and drown?'

'It happens that way sometimes, Imogen. There are certain people who just happen to be fitter and stronger than the rest. Perhaps he was conscious enough to grip on to the float but because he wasn't wide awake and panicking he didn't succumb to hypothermia. Whatever happened out there, it certainly doesn't mean he killed them all. If that is what you are hinting at,' Hugh added with an amused glint in his eye.

'Of course not. There's just something about him I don't like. It's as simple as that. And I'm not at all sure it's clear yet what actually went on inside the helicopter before it crashed.'

'Well, as a psychologist I would have to conclude that these wild suspicions say more about you than they do about him.' Hugh chuckled to himself. 'On a serious note, we have to remember that Cameron's quick thinking after Ewan stood on the man-trap probably saved his life. If he hadn't put on the tourniquet and run back to get help Ewan could have bled to death.'

'I know,' Imogen replied guiltily. 'Look, just humour me, will you? Michael has asked you to chat to the boy and help him come to terms with losing his parents and sister. While you are doing that, see what his responses are like. If you come back and tell me that he is a perfectly normal young man who is grieving for his family in a perfectly natural way then I will crawl back under my rock and say no more about it.'

'Fine. But I'd just like to say, for future reference, that the misuse of a psychotherapist's position can lead them to be struck-off or in extreme cases, to their imprisonment at her Majesty's pleasure.'

Imogen laughed at this and they ended the discussion there. However, she knew her husband was only half joking and was sending her a warning. He was reminding her that they should not abuse his training by utilizing it for the wrong reasons. Hugh was absolutely right. Nonetheless, Imogen's instincts were telling her she should find out some more about this young man. If it turned out he was going to become a permanent fixture in her family's life then she felt perfectly justified in doing so.

It was pouring with rain as Chloe made her way along the pier at Kilross Harbour. It was not the best of conditions in which to gain your first glimpse of the island. All the highest hills were under a cloak of grey cloud. The water in the bay looked dark and uninviting. Ewan's girlfriend, however, seemed to have been blessed with a sunny disposition. She talked good naturedly about her journey and family on the drive back to the farm.

Chloe was a rather petit girl, with short, bobbed brown hair which she wore in a sweep across her forehead. Clearly recognizing them as her most striking feature, her large brown eyes had been encircled with thick, black liner and her lashes were exaggerated by copious amounts of dense mascara. This was the fashion for girls of her age, Imogen knew. Apart from her heavily painted eyes, she was make-up and piercing free.

Imogen was touched by the way Chloe greeted her son when they arrived at Lower Kilduggan. She carefully placed her soft bag down in the wide hallway and rushed into the sitting room, throwing herself into Ewan's arms. They lounged together on the sofa, excitedly showing one another messages and images on their phones before settling down to watch a movie. Imogen felt immensely relieved that Ewan would have someone so obviously caring and sweet to pass his convalescence with.

As a result of the dreich weather, they had a fairly quiet day. Cameron disappeared up to his room. Bridie had spread herself out at the kitchen table, with her sewing box and a half-finished embroidered blanket lain across it. Hugh's mother, Kathleen, had taught her granddaughter many of the skills required for the various types of fabric craft which were Kath's great passion. It was a joy for Imogen to watch the gradual development of their wonderful creations. The only drawback seemed to be the cost of the materials needed for this hobby, which Bridie had to find from her own pocket-money. Hugh and Ian were sitting opposite one another in the kitchen snug playing monopoly. Imogen assumed Michael must be holed up in their mum's study, either working his way through Cameron's papers or tinkering with one of his latest building designs.

Imogen found herself with a rare moment of solitude. She went upstairs to the guest-room that she and Hugh shared, gazing out of the bay window, across the distant strip of water to Carradale. The cloud was lifting over the Sound and Imogen predicted they may yet have a pleasant evening in western Garansay. She let the stresses and preoccupations of the past few days lift from her shoulders. As she did so, Imogen was suddenly reminded again about Michael's strange letter. Having an idea, she quietly closed the bedroom door. Sitting on the edge of the eiderdown, Imogen took her phone and a notebook out of the bedside drawer. Quickly scrolling through the contacts she stopped at the one she was looking for. Without thinking for too long about it, Imogen dialed the number.

The mobile phone she was ringing buzzed for a while. Then a voice answered that Imogen immediately recognized. It belonged to Stuart McKilvenna, Miriam's older brother.

'Hello, Stuart? It's Imogen Croft, here. Michael's sister.'

'Well, hallo Imogen, how wonderful to hear from you!'

'Are your family keeping well?' She enquired politely.

'Oh aye, we're grandparents now, you know. Impossible to believe it eh? And how's that brother-in-law of mine? We don't see as much of him as we'd like to.' Stuart McKilvenna was now the chief executive of the oil and gas company that was once run by his father. It was a long shot, but Imogen hoped he might be able to provide her with some information.

'That's why I'm calling really. Michael's been trying to get in touch with an old friend of his. He'd like to be able to invite him to Sarah's wedding. This chap used to work with Mike at the company. They did a placement together about thirty years back. We think he carried on working in the oil and gas trade, but we aren't sure.' Imogen thought it sounded flimsy, even to her. 'I haven't got much to go on, I'm afraid, which is why Michael didn't want to bother you with it.'

'Tell me what you know and I'll pass it onto my PA. She will have a look through our system. It might take a couple of days if that's okay?'

'Of course, there's no rush. Sarah and Ross haven't even decided on their venue yet!' Imogen added, trying to keep it light.

'This chap's name was Keith and he did a student placement at your firm in 1978. Michael is convinced he carried on working for you after that time. Keith would be about sixty years old now. He came from the Fife area. Sorry, that's all I've got.'

'I'll see what I can do and Imogen, please keep us posted on the wedding preparations. Tell Michael we want to help out in any way that we can.'

12

The fine weather had returned. Ewan had graduated from his position on the sitting room sofa to sprawling himself across one of the sun loungers in the back garden. Chloe was lying languidly next to him, sunbathing in her shorts and tee-shirt on a beach towel laid out on the grass. As Cameron stepped out of the French Doors to join them, Imogen was gratified to see that his perfect grooming and striking, almost Nordic good looks did not appear to have any obvious effect upon her son's girlfriend. Chloe remained engrossed in the novel she had positioned above her face in order to shield her eyes from the glare of the sun.

'Would anyone like a drink?' Cameron asked in his gentle Scots accent.

Ewan turned towards the passage at the side of the house, where he knew Imogen was tidying up the flowerbeds. He called out, with his unmistakably estuary English twang, 'could we have a beer Mum?'

It was the middle of the afternoon and Imogen couldn't think of a good reason why not. But she immediately worried that Michael may not approve. This niggling doubt made her hesitate. 'What did Dr McKelvie say about drinking whilst you're taking medication?'

'I've finished my course of antibiotics. I only

take the painkillers if my leg is giving me trouble,' Ewan replied, quite reasonably.

'I'd love a beer too, Mrs Croft. I think there's some in the fridge left over from the barbecue yesterday evening,' Cameron chipped in.

Imogen made her way down the shadowed passageway and out into the bright sun. Pulling off her gardening gloves she finally capitulated. 'Okay. You can have two cans each - but then that's it, alright?'

'Sure, thanks Mrs Croft, I'll go and fetch them.'

Cameron headed off towards the kitchen and brought back the cans of lager along with a jug of lemonade and some glasses. The cold, slightly tart drink provided Imogen with very welcome refreshment. She carried on with the weeding for another half an hour until the heat drove her back inside the cool, shady house. Imogen left Chloe and Cameron discussing their experiences of life in Dubai while Ewan pored over one of his favourite motoring magazines.

Michael and Hugh had taken Bridie and Ian out for a beach walk. They were following the route to the 'King's Caves', which lay up the coast to the north, just beyond Kilduggan Point. It was a flat and fairly easy trek, where they would be feeling the benefit of a fresh sea breeze. Imogen was beginning to wish she'd joined them. Though in the end it turned out to be fortuitous she did not. While wandering through the bedrooms, picking up discarded clothing and trying to restore some order to the kids' personal domain Imogen heard the phone ringing downstairs.

'Hello,' she answered breathlessly, after jogging to pick it up.

'Imogen? Hi, it's Stuart McKilvenna here,' replied a business-like voice that made her think the man must be calling from his office. 'Sorry it's taken a few days to get back to you. We're a bit snowed under just now.'

'No problem at all.'

There was a shuffling of papers on the other end of the line before Stuart continued. 'Okay, I think we may have identified the chap that you're looking for. His name was Keith Bennett and he worked for us from 1978 until 2009.'

Imogen noted Stuart's use of the past-tense and felt immediately disappointed.

'Keith was based in our Aberdeen office for about fifteen years. Then he moved to Abu Dhabi and spent his remaining career working for us out there on our Middle Eastern operations. He was married with two children. Unfortunately, he died when a Chinook went down en route to one of the rigs out in the Arabian Gulf in 2009.' Stuart paused here to allow the information to be absorbed.

'That's awful,' Imogen added, turning the facts over in her mind.

'But look,' Stuart said, adopting a more serious tone, 'Michael didn't know this Bennett fellow too well, did he?'

'No, not at all. I mean, the last time Michael had any contact with him was back when they were both students.'

'Good, because at the time of the crash it seems as if Bennett was under a bit of a cloud. It turned out he was being scrutinized by an American agency called the Department for the Investigation of Industrial Fraud and Criminality, or the D.I.F.C. as it is commonly known in the business. It's a blot on our copybook actually, because we should be able to pick up on these things internally, before any outside agencies need to become involved. So it's probably a good thing that this Keith chap won't be coming to Sarah's wedding after all,' Stuart said this with a note of finality. But Imogen wasn't quite ready to end it there.

'This helicopter crash happened before the investigation into Keith had been completed. Was there anything suspicious about it?' She pressed.

'The accident you mean? Regretfully not. It's an accepted part of the job that you will be travelling back and forth to the rigs. We all know there are certain risks involved. It wasn't one of our choppers that went down but I am led to understand a thorough review followed the crash. It concluded the cause was some kind of mechanical failure. Sadly, these things do happen.' Stuart really sounded as if he would like to wrap up the conversation then and there.

Imogen thanked him profusely for his time adding, just before he rang off, 'perhaps it would be best not to mention any of this to Michael. He didn't know I was searching for Keith. As the man has passed away there seems no need to upset him unnecessarily.'

'No, quite so,' Stuart replied, in a thoroughly heartfelt manner. They ended the exchange with this shared resolution.

As Imogen carried on with her jobs, she mulled over what Michael's brother-in-law has just told her. It was clear the anonymous letter could not have come from Keith Bennett. However, Imogen was struck by the similarity between the fate of Bennett and that of the

Fleming family. Both men had worked in the Middle East and been killed in a helicopter crash over water. If she were being rational, Imogen would have to accept that the parallel between the two cases ended there. Richard Fleming was a banker and had no obvious connection to the oil industry. The two accidents took place thousands of miles and several years apart. In addition to this, helicopter crashes in the oil trade were, unhappily, a relatively common occurrence.

Imogen was distracted from her train of thought by the sound of raised voices outside. She moved over to the small window of the bedroom Ewan and Ian shared and looked down into the garden below. The sun loungers that Cameron, Ewan and Chloe had formerly occupied were now empty. The only evidence which remained of their presence were a few used beer glasses and cans, lying strewn across the patio table and scattered about the previously immaculate lawn. Imogen's eyes then moved up the meadow bank and along the ridge above it. She couldn't see any sign of them there. Sensing something was wrong, she rushed down the stairs.

When Imogen reached the kitchen she could see that Michael and Hugh must have returned from their walk because a set of rucksacks and rain jackets lay discarded along the wall of the snug. Imogen strode out of the back door and along the gravelled footpath, making her way up into the glen. As she approached the first stile, she finally caught sight of her family.

They were huddled together in a group, with

Ewan positioned in the centre of them all. He was hunched uncomfortably over his crutches. When Imogen got to within earshot of this strange cabal, she began to get a sense of what was going on.

Michael's face was red with rage. From this vantage point, it appeared that Ewan was hanging his head in shame. Chloe, however, was standing straight as a rod. Her posture seemed in resolute contrast to the bent figure of Imogen's eldest son. She had her arm around his waist. Imogen was suddenly extremely glad Chloe had been there in her absence.

'I'm sorry, Hugh, but I really feel this is an abuse of my hospitality.' Imogen could hear Michael saying.

'All I can do is to apologise for my son's actions. I promise that Imogen and I will be having very strong words with him,' Hugh was replying. His facial muscles looked taut.

As Imogen climbed up to join them she broke the uncomfortable silence by asking warily, 'What's happened?'

Imogen's brother turned towards her. In a barely controlled tenor, he explained, 'I'm afraid that Ewan and Chloe have brought cigarettes with them on this holiday. We just came across the two of them puffing away up here in the meadow. This unpleasant discovery was made because Cameron, who has never had a cigarette before in his life, passed us in the kitchen. He was on his way to find somewhere suitable to be sick.'

It was probably because of the two cans of beer he'd drunk earlier in the afternoon, Imogen reflected guiltily, but certainly did not say. 'Okay,' she replied instead. 'Thank you for letting us know what has gone on. Hugh and I will take it from here.'

Imogen walked over to Chloe and asked her if she would kindly return to the farmhouse and tidy up the garden whilst she and Hugh had a private conversation with Ewan. Thankfully, Chloe got her meaning straightaway and hurried off at some considerable speed through the overgrown meadow, to dispose of the evidence before Michael got back down there. Unfairly, Imogen snapped at Bridie and Ian. Telling them they must return to the house immediately and find themselves something quiet to do in their bedrooms for half an hour. Michael turned and marched stiffly down the path after the children, presumably to check on how Cameron was doing. Imogen could sense that Hugh was fighting hard to control his anger. As soon as they were finally alone with their nearly grown-up son, Imogen took the lead.

'Ewan, can you explain yourself please?'

When the lad lifted his head up she could see he was crying. 'I'm so sorry, Mum. I don't even smoke that much. I just have the occasional fag if I've had a drink, you know?'

Imogen flashed him a warning look.

'Chloe brought a packet over when she came. But please don't blame her. It was *my* idea for us to come up to the meadow and have a cigarette. I only offered Cameron one out of politeness. He *is* nineteen. I thought he would just refuse it if he didn't smoke.'

'Don't make excuses Ewan Croft. You have really embarrassed us in front of your Uncle Michael. He has been extremely generous since

97

we've been here,' Hugh said tersely.

Ewan slumped over his crutches again and started to sob, muttering quietly, 'I'm sorry, Dad.'

This prompted Imogen to put her arms out to support his weight. 'Could you help me to get Ewan back to the house please Hugh?'

No one said any more until Ewan was in his room and Imogen had propped up several pillows and cushions to make her son comfortable on his bed. Hugh left them alone to check on the others. Imogen sat down on the padded quilt next to Ewan and rested her hand on top of his good leg.

'Look, these things happen. But what you get up to at Uni is a very different matter from what you do when you are at home with us, okay? I'm just cross that your brother and sister had to hear it all. You wouldn't want either of them to take up smoking would you?'

Ewan looked appalled at this suggestion. 'Of course not. That was why we went up into the meadow to have a fag. I would never have smoked in front of Bridie and Ian,' he added sheepishly, 'it was Dad and Uncle Michael who brought the kids up the hillside and then started giving us chapter and verse.'

Imogen agreed with her son. She was starting to think that Michael and Hugh couldn't have handled the situation much worse.

She sat passively next to Ewan for a few more minutes, during which time he worked up the courage to say, 'and another thing, Mum. Why is Uncle Michael acting as if this house belongs just to him? Kilduggan Farm is as much yours and Uncle Allan's as it is his - isn't it?'

Imogen silently acknowledged that Ewan was absolutely right. In fact, the mention of her middle brother Allan suddenly put some perspective on the whole episode. She could just imagine what his reaction would have been to the way they barracked a twenty year old university student for having a sneaky fag. He would have laughed in their faces. The type of stuff Allan was getting up to in his younger years was in a whole different league. Then, quite unusually, Imogen found herself wishing he was there with them.

This thought made her start to giggle. Ewan asked what was so funny and Imogen replied, 'it's just I was beginning to long for your Uncle Allan to be here with us, in order to provide the voice of reason,' she chuckled as she plumped up his pillows, 'which just goes to show that something around here must have gone very, very wrong.'

To her great relief, Ewan broke into a smile too and took hold of his mother's hand, giving it a tight and extremely reassuring squeeze.

13

There was an uncomfortable atmosphere at dinner that evening. Imogen carried a tray of food up to Ewan in his bedroom. Chloe had chosen to eat up there with him. They had certainly not been banished from polite company, but it just seemed like the right thing to do for the time being. Imogen chatted to Michael and Hugh perfectly politely about their walk to the King's Caves, but this was mostly for Ian and Bridie's benefit. In reality, she was feeling quite angry with them both. Imogen took her leave of the post-dinner conversation early, claiming to be very tired after the heat and excitement of the day. Imogen retired to their bedroom, pausing along the way to check on Ewan and Chloe.

Hugh came up to join her about half an hour later. Much sooner, Imogen noted, than he would usually have done. She was still awake, reading a book, propped up in bed with the table lamp switched on. Neither of them uttered a word until Hugh had completed his ablutions and slipped into bed next to his wife.

'I take it you don't agree with the way I handled the situation with Ewan today,' Hugh said resignedly, turning to face her and resting his head in his hand.

Imogen did not reply for a moment or two but then placed her novel down carefully on the bedside table. 'I would like to remind you of the kind of activities we got up to when I was in my second year at university. You and I had just started going out. I accept that you were a couple of years older than me, however, we were both drinking and smoking. I certainly do not recall our parents knowing anything about it or of anyone tearing us off a strip for acting like regular young adults.'

Hugh kept his eyes steadily upon her. 'If my Mum and Dad had known about it they would have been, quite rightly, rather upset. The real issue for me is that Ewan had taken advantage of
Michael's hospitality.'

Imogen shifted around, so that she could look Hugh straight in the face. 'But that's exactly it. This isn't Michael's house. It's *all* of ours. He has no business to suggest my children are abusing his good will. They have as much right to be here as he has.'

'Imogen, you were over the moon when Michael said he was going to spend more time at the farm, especially after finding out the truth about his relationship to your parents.'

'That was before he started acting as if that boy was more important to him than his own family.' The statement came out more forcefully than she had intended.

'Ah, so that's it,' Hugh added triumphantly, daring to lay his hand on her thigh.

'Did you see Cameron at dinner? There was absolutely no sign he was feeling unwell. He polished off the meal pretty quickly and then he had dessert too.'

It irritated Imogen to see that Hugh was smiling broadly at this. 'What exactly are you

101

suggesting?' He started to move in closer, emboldened by the fact Imogen had not yet removed his hand.

'If you must know, I think the 'young and innocent' Cameron Fleming deliberately got Ewan and Chloe into trouble. If today was the first time the boy has had a cigarette and couple of cans of beer then I'll eat my hat.'

Hugh began chuckling quietly as he manoeuvred himself so that his body was pressed up against his wife's. 'Okay, that is your assessment of Cameron Fleming,' he said with finality. 'But I have just one more important question for you, Mrs Croft. I would like it to be answered with absolute and total honesty.'

Imogen looked at him with curiosity.

'How could you possibly know that the kids had been drinking beer?'

Imogen lifted up Hugh's redundant pillow and started hitting him over the head with it. They collapsed in giggles onto the bed, their disagreement over the boys temporarily forgotten.

*

The collective mood at Lower Kilduggan Farm had much improved, but no one was quite yet back into the holiday spirit. Ewan and Chloe were spending a lot of their time alone together, up in the boys' room. Hugh and Imogen hadn't said more than a couple of words to Michael over the course of the morning.

The Crofts were discussing what to do with the remainder of this gloriously sunny day when there was a knock at the front door. Imogen left it for Michael to answer, knowing he was working in the study across the hall, but she had half an ear cocked to hear who it was.

Imogen could just make out the sound of a deep male voice. The tone of the exchange made the subject sound serious. She put her head around the sitting room door to see what was going on.

Standing in the hallway was a uniformed police woman. Next to her was an untidily dressed man who Imogen assumed must be her superior. The gentleman twisted round in her direction and Michael was prompted to introduce them.

'Detective Inspector Zanco, this is my sister, Imogen Croft. She is visiting Garansay with her husband and children.'

The Inspector took her hand in his firm grip.

'We have come bearing some difficult news for Cameron Mrs Croft, but it is heartening so see he has so much support around him. The lad is going to need careful handling when we tell him what we have found.'

'My husband is a psychologist,' Imogen said to this. 'If Cameron doesn't object, then I'm sure Hugh can spend a little time helping him to make sense of things.'

'That would be extremely beneficial, I'm sure,' Zanco replied, breaking into an uneven smile. 'Now, if we could find somewhere quiet, where we will not be disturbed, I would like to speak with the boy.'

They set up Ewan's tablet computer in one of the upstairs bedrooms and showed a movie for the kids. The rest of the adults, along with

103

Cameron Fleming, gathered around the scratched old kitchen table. Imogen glanced quickly across at Cameron. The youngster's expression was difficult to read but her sense was that the boy was working hard to keep his emotions in check. Michael seated himself next to Cameron at the table. Imogen experienced an unpleasant jolt of surprise to see her brother automatically take hold of the boy's hand.

Detective Inspector Zanco proceeded to inform them, with as much tact as possible, that a body had been recovered from the sea. They believed it to be the remains of Cameron's father, Richard Fleming. As this information was delivered, Imogen watched the young man's face very closely. She observed his muscles go immediately rigid at the mention of his father's name. Imogen was no expert in body language, but somehow she didn't feel that Cameron was expressing the reaction she might have expected. Shock, or even relief may have been a natural first response to this news. But the overwhelming emotion that was radiating from the boy was quite unmistakably, one of fear.

Michael broke the resultant silence by asking the Inspector some questions about where the body was found and if it would be possible now to make arrangements for a funeral. Zanco told them the 'remains' of Richard Fleming were washed up on a beach which lay on the eastern side of the Mull of Kintyre. They were discovered by one of the locals who happened to be walking his dog along that stretch of sand late last night.

Cameron turned towards the policeman and said in a quiet and distant voice, 'was it near the lighthouse? Because we used to go there when I was really young. I loved lighthouses, you see, so

Grandad liked to take us to the Mull of Kintyre. It isn't manned anymore. It's actually run from Edinburgh, but there's a little museum where you can learn about what life must have been like for the Keeper. I used to think it would be the best job in the world. All alone for months on end, looking out and knowing absolutely nothing lay between you and the vast ocean beyond.'

The rest of them sat tongue-tied and useless during this melancholy tale. When the boy fell silent again Hugh seized the initiative.

'Perhaps Cam would like to come for a walk with me and Michael - just to get a little fresh air?' Hugh didn't wait for a reply but marched straight out into the hallway to fetch their coats. Cameron offered no objection to the idea, so the two men hustled him protectively out of the back door.

Imogen found herself suddenly alone with the police officers. 'Will Cameron have to identify the body?' She enquired.

'Thankfully, that shouldn't be necessary, Mrs Croft. We will perform a DNA test on the remains. Just to be certain it *is* Mr Fleming we have found. Cameron's father had to provide the police with a sample of his DNA when he was involved in a minor incident several years ago. We have his profile on the national database.'

'Does the discovery of the body throw any new light on the investigation into the crash?' She probed.

'Its early days on that one, I'm afraid. We have some tidal experts looking at the place where the body washed up. I didn't want to mention this in front of the boy, but the cadaver

105

was not completely intact, if you catch my meaning. It had been in the water for a very long time and the rocks around that headland are treacherous. It is more a case of identifying the clothing and shoes and hoping we can extract a decent amount of DNA for analysis.'

'I see.'

Realising they had not even offered Zanco and his assistant so much as a cup of tea, Imogen jumped up and asked if they would like any refreshments. The officers politely declined her belated proposition.

While she was escorting them through the hallway towards the front door, Zanco paused for a second, turning around to face his host. 'This will be very difficult news for Cameron to take on board. It will have come as something of a shock so long after the crash itself. It would be helpful if you could keep an eye on him and make sure his mood doesn't deteriorate.' Then, as if the idea had only this minute crossed his mind, he added, 'and if you do notice anything about Cameron that happens to concern you, please don't hesitate to get in contact.' Zanco placed his card in the palm of her hand and was gone.

The Inspector's final words had appeared, on the surface, to be motivated by a natural concern for Cameron's welfare. However, something about the way he looked at Imogen, when they stopped briefly in the hall, had encouraged her to interpret his request in a slightly different way. Imogen was beginning to wonder if Detective Inspector Zanco might possibly possess the same misgivings about the Fleming boy as she did.

14

While Hugh spent the rest of the afternoon counselling Cameron, Imogen took the opportunity to mend some bridges with Michael. She proposed they take Bridie and Ian for a stroll on the beach. Thankfully, her brother agreed. Packing one of Imogen's mother's baskets with a flask, cakes and a blanket, they made their way down the overgrown, sandy path to the Kilduggan Shore. Michael and Imogen positioned themselves on the picnic rug while the kids ran off exploring along the rocky waterline. Imogen did her best to steer the conversation away from contentious issues by asking her brother how the arrangements for Sarah and Ross's wedding were progressing.

'They're still looking at venues, I'm afraid. So we don't have a date yet. Everywhere they've seen has some kind of disadvantage. All the very best places are booked up for years in advance,' Michael explained disconsolately.

'Did you have any further thoughts about hosting the wedding here at the farm?'

'That idea was a little fanciful, I fear. Sarah appears to have her heart set on a grand hotel for their 'big day'.' Michael sighed.

'That's a shame,' Imogen lamented. 'Because if you put up a marquee in one of the fields at the front of the house, with their fabulous views out across the Sound, I think it could be the perfect location.'

Their discussion came to a natural end, but as they continued to sit for a while, in a mutually companionable silence, Imogen caught sight of a couple of figures approaching in the distance.

They were wandering along the beach a few hundred yards to the north. When the pair stopped to talk to Bridie and Ian down by the shore, Imogen realised the male walker must be Colin Walmsley.

Michael and Imogen made their way over to join them. As she grew closer, Imogen could see that Colin's companion was the tall, slim lady who looked after Bridie at Loch Crannox Farm on the day Ewan had his accident. On this occasion however, Colin introduced them properly to this attractive lady, who managed to look glamorously chic even in a fleece and walking trousers.

'Imogen and Michael, this is Julia Laing. She is my clerical assistant up at the farm, and also my girlfriend.'

Julia put out an elegant hand and kissed them on each cheek. The children rapidly lost interest in this adult greeting ritual and dashed off to play on the taller rocks at the headland. The four adults sauntered across the pebbly shingle after the youngsters. They naturally fell into two pairs, with Michael and Julia leading the way and Colin and Imogen ambling along behind.

'She seems like a very lovely girl,' Imogen said to her companion.

'Yes, she is. Julia came to work for me about eighteen months ago. We just hit it off straight away. Things haven't been easy for her in the last few years. Her husband died very suddenly and tragically young, so it has been particularly difficult for her to start over again.'

'My goodness, the poor thing,' Imogen replied inadequately and they walked along in silence for a little. In a change of subject, Imogen hushed her voice in order to say, 'do you remember what I mentioned to you in your kitchen, on the day Ewan stepped on the trap?'

'About Cameron?' Colin responded, equally quietly.

'Yes. Well there was an incident at the farm yesterday. Ewan and his girlfriend did something really silly, but not malicious in any way. I'm sure Cameron deliberately tried to drop them in it with Michael. I can't prove it of course, and Hugh thinks I'm just imagining things.'

'I'm not the one who's the psychologist, Imogen, but if your suspicions are correct it wouldn't be too surprising would it? Cameron has lost the only family he had. Now the one person he has left in his life is Michael. He probably feels a little jealous of you lot turning up. Perhaps he wants to keep Michael for himself,' Colin suggested.

Imogen hadn't considered this possibility. It made Cameron's actions seem much less sinister and far more understandable. Encouraged by Colin's insight on this subject, she dropped her pace right back and told him, in the lowest tone that would still be audible, about the letter Michael received back in January. Imogen explained how it arrived at Lower Kilduggan Farm just after they rescued Cameron from the helicopter crash and all of the media attention

109

that had gone with it.

'So, you think the person who sent this letter had seen a photograph of Michael in the press, remembered he still owed him money for something and got in touch again,' Colin summarized. 'But Michael has no clear idea of who this person could be?'

'No, that's right. Or it could simply be a crackpot, of course.'

'All I can suggest,' Colin said, as they grew ever nearer to Michael and Julia, 'is that perhaps it is a case of mistaken identity. I mean, if the person who wrote the note was very old, they may have thought Michael was someone else. It may not be as obvious to you Imogen, as it is to other people, but the Nichols all share a very distinctive look. The letter-writer might have got mixed up. Perhaps he thought it was your father he saw in the photograph rather than Michael?'

They had to end their discussion as Imogen and her neighbour caught up with the rest of the group. Bridie demanded that they watch her jump from the tallest of the boulders down onto the soft sand below. They cheered and clapped as she landed squarely on her feet, raising her arms in a pose she had learnt at gymnastic club. Colin and Imogen didn't get another chance to talk before going their separate ways but he had certainly given her plenty to think about. Colin had provided Imogen with the invaluable perspective which can only come from someone outside the family. She realised now this was exactly what she had needed.

When they returned to the farm later, Imogen found that Ewan and Chloe were up and about. She was pleased to see her elder son appearing much more mobile than he had in previous days.

They were both sitting at the kitchen table, happily playing board games. It was Ewan who was getting up periodically in order to heat the kettle on the stove.

Cameron was in the same room as them, but sitting slightly apart, in the depths of the little inglenook, reading a paperback novel, rather than joining in with the others. Imogen made a point of asking him if he was feeling okay before heading off to locate her husband. Hugh was out in the back garden, removing the crisply dry washing from the line. Imogen crept up behind him and slipped her arms around his waist.

'This is an impressive picture of domesticity,' she whispered into his ear.

'Well, the clothes have been dry for several hours now so it seemed cruel to keep them dangling for very much longer,' Hugh replied lightly as he turned to reciprocate her embrace.

Something in his tone was uncharacteristically downbeat. Imogen lifted her face up to his and asked, with real concern in her voice, 'is everything alright?'

Hugh didn't reply but left the laundry where it was and took her by the hand. He led Imogen through a gap in the garden hedge and then about a yard or so up into the wild flower meadow, where he finally stopped.

'I had a long talk with Cameron this afternoon, after the police had left.'

'How is he handling things?'

'I think he may have been trying to confess something to me.'

Imogen immediately blurted out, 'what do you mean? What has he done?'

'It's not him who has done anything at all. But I suspect that his father might have done things to them - to him and his mother and sister. Whether it was violence or a different type of abuse I just don't know,' Hugh clarified.

'I see, what exactly did Cameron say?'

'I was asking him about how he felt, now that he would finally be able to lay his father to rest. It took a little while, but he eventually admitted that he felt guilty, because his primary reaction was relief, to have received the proof his father was really gone. I pressed the boy on what he meant by this. He just kept saying that his dad had been a very difficult person to live with and it was his mother and sister whom he really loved and missed.'

'He didn't admit to anything concrete, then.'

'No, but the implication was that he didn't feel much love for his father at all. I got the sense he wasn't even sorry he was dead. I found that a little shocking to be honest with you.'

'It's funny, because after you and Michael had taken Cameron out for some fresh air this morning, the Inspector told me that no one would need to come and identify Richard Fleming's 'remains'. This was because they had his DNA on the police database. He said Cameron's father had been involved in a 'minor incident'- is what he called it - a few years back.'

'The incident must have been here in Scotland then, rather than out in the Middle East. What kind of offence would you have to commit for your DNA to be taken? Zanco didn't suggest it was anything to do with domestic violence, did he?'

'No, he didn't say any more than that. If Cameron and his mother and sister had experienced abuse of some description, it might explain the lad's odd behaviour,' Imogen said, almost to herself.

'It certainly would,' Hugh responded. 'So when we go back into the house, we will all try to be as kind as possible to the boy- yes? After all Cameron has been through in his short life I think the least we can do is to tolerate a certain amount of minor mischief-making, don't you agree Mrs Croft?'

Imogen nodded, lightly pressing herself into Hugh's body and resting her head against his chest, listening to his reassuringly steady heartbeat. Imogen could understand her husband's sympathy for the boy. To a certain extent, she shared it. The knowledge that Cameron had a troubled relationship with his father certainly would account for some of the strange behaviour he had displayed whilst staying at Lower Kilduggan Farm. However, she couldn't help but feel this information might also throw new light upon the circumstances surrounding the helicopter crash. If Cameron hated his father and felt no love for him, this may have provided the boy with some kind of motive to want him dead. She immediately shook away this fanciful notion and placed an arm firmly around Hugh's waist, quietly accompanying him back to the farmhouse.

15

As part of Hugh's campaign to cheer Cameron up, he had organised another day of sailing up at Port na Mara. After much pleading by their older son, it was decided Ewan was fit enough to join them, as long as he didn't try to do too much. Michael and Hugh had hired a large, 22 foot yacht to take out onto the Kilbrannan Sound. The plan was to sail along the western coast to the southern tip of Garansay. It would be an ambitious venture, but the weather conditions were excellent. They wanted to make use of the whole day, perhaps mooring up somewhere in Kintyre to have lunch. Imogen volunteered to remain on dry land, so she was free to meet them somewhere en route if anyone got fed up or Ewan needed a rest. All of the kids, including Chloe, were confident on the water. Imogen hoped her services would not be required for the rest of the day. She was planning to keep her mobile phone close to hand, just in case. As she stood on the gravel driveway at the front of the farmhouse to wave them off, Imogen felt a guilt-tinged sense of anticipation. If Michael and Hugh knew her own plans for today they would not approve. This knowledge was not going to deter her. When the cars had disappeared from sight, Imogen returned to the house through the kitchen door.

Since the previous night, Imogen had been

reflecting on what Hugh told her up in the wild flower meadow. Just before bed she asked Ewan if she could use his tablet computer the following day. Her son wrote down his passwords and showed his mum how to access the internet through his account.

Armed with the appropriate gadgets, Imogen fixed a pot of Hugh's strong coffee and took it with her into the sitting room. She sat down in one of the armchairs by the bay window. According to Ewan, this place received the strongest WIFI signal.

Last year, when Imogen was conducting some research into their family tree, she had used a number of research websites. As a result, she knew how to look up the Scottish newspaper archives through one of the Glasgow Library databases. Imogen still possessed her log-in details. The objective this morning was to search through their files to find any reference to Richard Fleming's criminal record.

Now, Imogen knew for a fact that Fleming must have been found guilty of an offence for the police to have taken his DNA. She was sure of this because a couple of months back Imogen helped Ian to plan for a class debate on the National DNA Database. He had to discuss the ethics of the state keeping hold of people's profiles for unlimited periods of time. In the course of their research, they discovered that in Scotland, a sample of DNA was only taken from people who were actually charged and convicted of a crime. This had surprised her, as in England and Wales you needed only to be a suspect in an investigation to have your biological identity recorded indefinitely by the authorities.

Imogen had determined last night that if Richard Fleming committed a crime in Scotland it was most likely to have been *before* the family moved to Dubai. It seemed the most logical conclusion. The family had moved to the Middle East in 1997 and the DNA database was only set up in 1995. So in order to make the hunt more manageable, Imogen decided to focus on the three years between the start of '95 and the end of '97.

As Imogen waited for the results to process, she noted how much easier it was to investigate the past misdemeanours of men than it was of women. They were much less likely to have changed their name through marriage in the intervening years. Her thoughts were interrupted as the database offered up a short list of potential matches. The article she was seeking had proven to be very straightforward to find.

Imogen clicked on a link which took her to a short piece in the Glasgow Herald which was published in January 1997. It comprised a thin column of text within the news section and provided a brief outline of what D.I. Zanco described as the 'minor incident' involving Cameron's father. It reported that Glasgow businessman, Richard Fleming, had pleaded guilty to a charge of 'common assault'. The case had been heard in the Gallowgate Magistrate's Court the previous day. It appeared that, a couple of months earlier, Fleming had been embroiled in a scuffle at a restaurant in the financial quarter of the city.

During the course of the affray another party, unnamed, had been struck across the face by Fleming. The other individual had chosen to press charges against Cameron's father who was then obliged to attend a court hearing and put in a plea. Richard Fleming received a fine, three months of community service and a criminal record, although it was noted by the magistrate that at no time had he denied his involvement in the assault.

Imogen sat back against the comfortable but threadbare seat. She placed a half-full cup of coffee to her lips and gazed out of the large, angled windows. A sparse covering of cotton wool cloud formed a wispy scrawl across an otherwise clear blue sky. As the tall poplar trees that lined the farm's steep driveway bent in the brisk westerly breeze, she imagined Hugh's sailing boat scudding decisively through the distant emerald waters of the Sound. When Imogen glanced at her watch she realised it was already lunchtime. Logging-off the computer, she carried the coffee pot and cup into the kitchen.

Imogen prepared a sandwich and took some time to consider this new information. It would seem that Richard Fleming was the type of chap who was capable of violence after all. He had a criminal record to prove it. Imogen wondered how his bosses had reacted to this incident back in 1997 and the adverse publicity which must surely have accompanied it. Then Imogen had a thought. What if Cameron's father had fallen out of favour with the bank as a result of his conviction? What if that was the reason why he was packed off to a Middle Eastern posting for the next sixteen years of his career? Did Richard Fleming make the decision to relocate to Dubai willingly, or was it forced upon him?

There was no actual evidence that Fleming had ever been violent towards his own family. Cameron was the only person who had ever suggested this. Although, it did appear Richard Fleming had quarrelled with various family members over the years. His wife's mother didn't seem to be grieving much for his loss. Nevertheless, Imogen was acutely aware that Cameron's father was not around to defend himself and remained reluctant to jump to any conclusions based purely on the boy's word alone. Imogen had this unshakeable feeling that Cameron was trying to manipulate them in some way, although to what ends she was still not sure.

Imogen found she'd been sitting at the kitchen table for ten minutes in front of an empty plate. She was jolted back to the here and now by the freshening wind, which knocked over one of the flowerpots out in the courtyard. It rolled around aimlessly in circles until finally settling itself against the corrugated iron door of one of the outhouses.

Shaken out of her reverie, she decided to make good use of the rest of the day. Imogen would clear away the mess left by the workmen at the side of the farmhouse, where the narrow passageway met the public footpath up to the glen. She rummaged through the kitchen drawers until locating a roll of black bags. Imogen pulled on her old wellies and a pair of rubber gloves which were still lying amongst the dusters and cloths under the sink.

As Imogen methodically shifted the small bits of wood and masonry that had been overlooked by the contractors, she mulled over the nature of Richard Fleming's assault charge. The newspaper excerpt had recounted that the fight took place in a restaurant in what sounded like an up-market part of Glasgow. This must have been a pretty unusual occurrence. The Herald did not mention the name of the injured party in its report but she considered the possibility it was someone who Fleming already knew. A work colleague perhaps? Sadly, Imogen had no way of finding this out now. Cameron must surely have been too young at the time it happened to remember anything much about it.

Imogen stood up from her labours, placing both hands on her hips and stretching her back. Shielding her eyes from the sun, something prompted Imogen to look towards the footpath that wound its way into the peaceful valley beyond. It was a fabulous day to be out trekking in those hills. Although in recent years, this path had become less well used by walkers, who tended now to stick to the organised trails around the village of Kilross rather than venturing this far west.

As if to deliberately contradict her thoughts, a figure appeared on the path. It remained perfectly still and was positioned high up along the ridge. This solitary person was silhouetted against the glare of the afternoon light. It was impossible to accurately make out their features. He or she seemed to be staring intently at the farm buildings below. Imogen decided they were probably assessing whether or not there was a right of way through the property. Imogen resumed her task, resolving to try and make the footpath more obvious to visitors. When she glanced up again, to see if the walker had identified the correct route, they had gone.

Imogen carried on for another hour or so until the worst of the debris had been cleared. She dragged the full and heavy black bags over to the shed where they kept the bins. As she unlocked the wooden door and shifted the rubbish sacks over to make room for more, Imogen suddenly heard a shuffling noise coming from outside. Before she had time to straighten up and turn round something gave her a powerful shove forwards. Just before pitching into the shadowy darkness, Imogen's fall was broken by a thick, strong arm which clasped itself in a vice-like grip around her throat.

All of Imogen's body weight was pressing down onto her windpipe. She was desperately struggling for air. Imogen was also completely off balance and this left her powerless to get free of the man's grasp. She could feel hot, sour breath on the side of her face. A croaking, almost inhuman voice rasped, 'you tell him I want what's mine. I did exactly what he asked. I found the boy and I dealt with the woman. It caused big problems for me, make sure he knows that. If he thought he could come back now and I'd be dead and buried, he's got that very wrong. I won't rest until I've got my money - understand?'

Imogen did her best to nod, although this caused an acute pain to shoot through her neck. Just as she sensed his grip finally loosening, Imogen received a blow to the back of the head. Everything seemed to move in slow motion and she had a distinct impression of falling through space, but after that there was nothing.

16

When Imogen opened her eyes, she was surrounded by blackness. Gradually tensing each limb in turn she regained an awareness of her immediate environment. Imogen was lying on top of one of the bin-bags. It was thankfully filled with household rubbish, rather than the hard, jagged debris she'd cleared from the passageway earlier in the day. Imogen assumed it must now be dark outside but had absolutely no idea what time it was. She attempted to turn towards the door of the shed but a dull pain throbbed across her temples and nausea swept over her like a wave. Imogen quickly lay back down again, until the horrible sensation passed.

Drifting into unconsciousness, her peace was cruelly interrupted by the relentless chiming of her mobile phone, which must still have been in the back pocket of her jeans. There was a distant sound of people talking. The noises seemed to be growing progressively nearer.

'The phone's in here,' declared a disembodied voice. 'Christ, Mum! Are you alright? Oh my God - someone call an ambulance!'

Imogen sensed there were people gathered all around. A warm hand smoothed the hair out of her face. 'Imogen, can you hear me?'

Imogen managed a quiet grunt and made the

monumental effort to wriggle around a little, not wanting her children to think she was badly hurt.

'There's an ambulance coming, but do you want us to move you now?' Hugh asked. He was trying desperately to remain calm.

Imogen nodded as vigorously as she was able and instantaneously felt herself being lifted onto her back and then carried out into the cold night. When they reached the farmhouse, Hugh placed his wife gingerly onto the sofa. Fortuitously, someone had the foresight to bring in a plastic bowl which Imogen immediately vomited into. Bridie came running into the sitting room with her grandmother's eiderdown which she wrapped tenderly around her mum. She promptly snuggled up under it and whispered soothing words into her ear.

Feeling stronger, Imogen said to her husband, as forcefully as she could, 'make sure everyone's inside the house. Lock all the doors and then call the police.'

*

Hugh insisted his wife was thoroughly examined by the paramedics before the police had a chance to speak with her. Imogen's neck was badly bruised. She had a small contusion on the back of her head, but nothing that would require stitches. Imogen had not been sick a second time and the ambulance crew were still debating whether or not she should spend the night at the Cottage Hospital, when a young police constable put his head around the door.

'Can we have a word with the patient yet?'

'Yes, please come in,' Imogen answered,

before anyone else got an opportunity.

The officer pulled over one of the smaller armchairs and took out his notebook. Hugh sat down on the remaining seat, while Michael discussed his sister's state of health with the medics out in the hallway.

Imogen told the youthful policeman as much as she could remember about the attack. She explained how he pushed and grabbed her from behind so at no point did she get a chance to see the man's face. Imogen described his voice and everything she recalled of the words he spoke to her.

'Did the assailant have an accent at all?'

'It was a sort of mixture, if you know what I mean. I'm sure he was Glaswegian but he also sounded a bit Irish as well,' she explained. 'His voice was very distinctive. It was croaky, like he had emphysema. The strange thing was that he sounded really old, but his grip on me was incredibly strong.' Imogen shuddered at the memory.

'And you're sure you didn't recognise him?'

'Absolutely not. But I think he has contacted us before - well, contacted my brother that is.'

The policeman looked puzzled. Imogen explained to him about the anonymous note Michael received back in January and how that too had demanded money.

'We are going to need a copy of that letter, Mrs Croft. So when this man asked you to pass on a message to someone, he was referring to your brother, Michael Nichols?'

'Yes, I think he was. But I believe he may be mistaking him for somebody else. I don't think it is Michael who actually owes him the cash. Sorry, I'm not making much sense.' Imogen laid her head back on the cushions, letting her eyes close briefly.

'You've been very helpful Mrs Croft, just get some rest now. Please be assured we are searching the area for this person. The ferry has been alerted. No one will get off the island without us knowing about it. I will leave a uniformed officer here at the farm, so don't you worry about anything.'

It was finally decided that Imogen would stay put, with Hugh having to wake her up every three hours to check she didn't have delayed concussion. Michael ushered the youngsters upstairs to bed and ensured the house was peaceful and quiet. Hugh brought a duvet and pillow down and set himself up in the armchair for the night.

After sitting silently in the moonlit room for several minutes, he finally said, 'we should never have left you here all alone. I'm sorry.' He knelt down on the carpet and buried his head in Imogen's lap. 'I'm just so relieved you're okay.'

'And I'm just glad the kids weren't here. I'm truly thankful it was me and not them he attacked.' She ran a hand through Hugh's thick, dark hair.

He looked up and declared, 'why do you think it *was* you? Is there any reason to believe he might have waited until you were alone in the farmhouse?'

'Perhaps he'd seen the cars leave and thought the place was empty. Maybe his plan was to come and steal the money he so obviously thinks is his. Was there any sign he broke into the house while I was unconscious in the shed?'

'There's no sign of a break-in, but the police have dusted for prints everywhere, so we'll see what turns up. You told the PC you thought this man had mistaken Michael for somebody else, what did you mean by that?'

Imogen felt exhaustion flooding through her poor, battered body. She had to force herself to continue. 'It was because of something Colin Walmsley said the other day, when we met him and Julia on the beach. I asked his opinion about the letter and he said the Nichols all look very alike. He suggested that if this old man saw a photograph in the paper, he might have thought it was our father he'd recognised, instead of Michael.'

Hugh ruminated on this for a while. 'Then we need to explain to this thug that your father died the best part of forty years ago, so he needs to leave us all alone.'

'I don't think it's as simple as that. Michael may well be a Nichols and share the strong family resemblance, but Angus wasn't actually *his* father was he? Perhaps the person who is terrorizing us isn't searching for my dad at all, he may genuinely think he's found Michael's *real* father instead.'

'But nobody knows who Michael's biological father is,' Hugh said in a hushed voice.

'That's what we thought, but maybe somebody out there does. It was when he said to me, "I found the boy and I dealt with his mother". I just thought immediately of Michael and Aunty Mary.' Imogen sat bolt upright. 'Hugh, you don't think the man who attacked me today can have had anything to do with the death of

Mary Galbraith, do you?'

'That happened a generation ago Imogen, its past history now,' Hugh answered, but without any real conviction.

She was losing the battle to stay awake but managed to add, almost feverishly, 'can it be possible that he's been out there all these years; waiting and watching in the darkness, hoping that one day his paymaster would return?' And it was with this fanciful but disturbing image in her mind that Imogen finally succumbed to the blissful oblivion that had been gently, but unrelentingly tugging her towards its all-encompassing embrace.

17

In the cold light of day, the previous night's imaginings seemed far-fetched. The person who assaulted Imogen was a living, breathing human being. She knew that in order to help the police catch him she needed to keep a clear and rational perspective on things. Despite a thumping headache and a very sore neck Imogen felt surprisingly well. Her appetite had returned, which was always a good indication that a physical recovery was underway. They enjoyed a pleasant family breakfast. After Imogen reassured everyone that she genuinely want to hear all about the boat trip yesterday, the kids launched into a blow by blow account of their adventures.

They stopped and had lunch in a little fishing village on the Kintyre side of the Kilbrannan Sound, before completing their sail down to the southern tip of Garansay. Bridie sounded particularly impressed with Cameron's expertise on the yacht. Imogen wondered if she might have developed a little crush on him. She was glad to see Chloe and Ewan were enthusiastic about the day too. They appeared to have mended any broken bridges which existed between them and Michael's young ward. This was the great thing about youth. It was so much easier to forgive and forget at their age. Ewan had never been one for holding a grudge.

Michael volunteered to cook and was busily frying eggs and bacon at the stove whilst periodically making sure Imogen was furnished with a never-ending supply of hot, sweet tea. Hugh was unusually quiet. When the children had eaten up and dispersed contentedly throughout the house, the adults were left alone in the kitchen. Michael cleared away the dirty plates and sat down at the table. 'The policeman asked me to give him the anonymous note. He seemed to think yesterday's attack had something to do with it.'

'Yes, I told him about the letter because of what that horrible creature whispered to me. He wanted to pass on a kind of message. He didn't mention you by name, but this is what he said, and I'll try to repeat it exactly: "tell him I want what's mine" and then: "I did what he asked: I found the boy and I dealt with the woman and it caused big problems for me". Then, the very last thing he uttered - and it was really quite chilling, was: "I won't rest until I've got my money."' She sat back and sipped the hot, sugary liquid, as if to remove the foul taste of the words from her mouth.

Michael went quiet too. He was grey haired now and approaching his sixtieth year, but he still possessed the striking features and strong physical presence that made him so very handsome as a younger man. Michael appeared lost in his thoughts before finally saying, 'this must be something to do with my mother.'

They had rarely spoken as a family about the discoveries that were made a year ago concerning Michael's real parents. Imogen's brother never wanted to discuss it. He felt that the couple who brought him up was the only mum and dad he needed to know about. Imogen had always respected his decision. But her Aunt Mary, who was Michael's birth mother, had died in unpleasant circumstances. Sadly, Imogen had always felt that her unhappy life would return to haunt them some day.

Mary Galbraith died in the hills of Garansay over forty years ago. No one had ever been brought to justice for it. Indeed, there were still those who believe her death was an accident. But for Imogen that theory had never quite slotted into place. She always felt there was a piece of the puzzle they didn't yet have.

As Michael had raised the subject, Imogen took the lead by adding, 'I don't think it's actually you this man is referring to. This is only a theory but please hear me out. What if this old thug saw your photo in the paper or on the news. He's perhaps in his seventies or eighties and his mind isn't what it once was. He recognised your face straight away, but he was confused and muddled between the here and now and the past. So it isn't a person from the present day this man thinks he is seeing, but someone who he knew over four decades ago instead.'

'Somebody who he had been waiting for a very long time to come back,' Hugh chipped in.

'It must be a person who bears a strong resemblance to me,' Michael conceded, but without drawing any further conclusions.

The atmosphere in the room had become extremely tense. It was almost a blessed relief to hear the policeman who had been guarding the farm overnight come trudging across the gravel courtyard to the kitchen door. Hugh let him in. Michael poured out a large mug of tea which he handed to the dishevelled looking Constable, as soon as he stepped over the threshold. The man sat down heavily at the table and informed them they had scoured the surrounding area. Imogen's assailant appeared to be long gone.

'Has he tried to leave the island by ferry?' Hugh enquired.

'It doesn't appear so. Although we don't have a detailed physical description of the man so it's impossible to be sure. He might be lying low. We've informed all the local farms to check their outhouses for any signs of an intruder. We did find something strange though, when we were searching your land and the hillside beyond.'

Imogen leant forward, her interest suddenly piqued.

'My Sarge told me your boy got himself caught up in a snare a couple of weeks back. Well, last night we found some more. Right up the glen they were, sort of hidden amongst the undergrowth but pretty nasty nonetheless.'

'How on earth can they have got there?' Michael asked, totally nonplussed.

'We're looking into it, sir. It could be kids or it may be more organised than that. These contraptions we found yesterday were certainly vicious. They had great long spikes on them which were absolutely covered in rust. Make sure you keep off the hills for a few days, just until we've had enough time to clear the area.'

The Police Constable told them that a squad car would drop by every so often but if they saw or heard anything suspicious in the meantime to call the Kilross Station immediately. Hugh thanked him for his efforts and led him out through the front door, asking him to keep them informed of any developments in their search for Imogen's attacker.

As they watched him climb into his little jeep and drive away, Hugh announced that he needed some air. He and Imogen stepped out into the garden and wandered up to the line of hedges that marked the western boundary.

'Is everything okay darling? You seem very subdued.' Imogen slotted an arm through his.

Hugh turned towards her. 'I'm a scientist and I like to pride myself on being a rational thinker. But ever since yesterday evening I haven't been able to shake this terrible feeling of dread. It's a sensation I'm frankly not use to and I don't like it one tiny bit.' He clasped both her hands. 'Imogen, I want to take you and the children as far away from this place as I possibly can.'

'I'm scared too, but we can't leave Michael here alone. Look, let's get the kids into the car and head off for the day. We'll buy loads of silly knick-knacks and eat ice creams and have our meal out in a restaurant someplace. The police can keep an eye on the farm. Hopefully, by the time we get back they'll have found him.'

Hugh nodded his head, more in resignation than agreement. They proceeded back inside, adopting their most cheerful expressions and gathering together the troops for this hastily organised, last-minute trip.

*

It was dusk by the time they returned to Lower

Kilduggan Farm. Bridie was nearly asleep in the backseat and Hugh carried her straight upstairs to the little box room under the eaves. Ewan, Chloe and Cameron took themselves off to play cards in the kitchen snug.

Hugh fixed them a dram from Isabel's drinks cabinet in the cosy sitting room. Imogen asked Michael if there had been any word from the police. He'd heard nothing. When they were comfortably seated in the armchairs by the fire, with full glasses in their hands, Imogen asked her older brother another question.

'Do you remember Dad's letter? The one Allan and I brought over to your flat? You told us back then you didn't want to know what was inside it, but you gave me your blessing to read it, if I wanted to.'

'Yes, I remember.'

'I haven't ever opened it but keep it with me always, just in case you happen to change your mind.' Imogen sat forward, to place greater emphasis on her words, 'Michael, if the man who is menacing us has some kind of connection with our past, I believe the time has come to find out everything we can about your background. There might be crucial information inside that letter which could help us discover who our mysterious persecutor is.' Imogen slowly let out the breath she'd been holding in for the duration of the speech.

Michael polished off his drink and placed the heavy glass on the side table. 'You probably see me as a stubborn fool who wants to keep his head buried in the sand. It must be hard to comprehend why I wouldn't want to know the truth about my own parents,' he said this in a voice thick with sadness. 'I'm nearly an old man and I've only recently discovered I know absolutely nothing about my biological father. But I can tell you now that if this situation wasn't putting the rest of you in danger I would happily go to the grave without ever hearing another word about him.'

Imogen hadn't heard her brother so emotional since Miriam died. It pained her to be pushing him like this. She just knew it was necessary otherwise the past was going to keep haunting them forever. Imogen glanced towards Hugh, sending him a look which pleaded for some assistance.

'This is a perfectly natural reaction. Many people never have the slightest interest in finding out about their birth parents. It is the people who bring us up that really matter. But families are complicated and your circumstances were different. If children are taken away from their rightful home, for whatever reason, good or bad, it will always have far-reaching consequences.'

Michael nodded, knowing he was going to have to accept the inevitable. 'If you could bring down the letter, Imogen, I would like you both to stay with me while I read it.'

Imogen had kept the faded and stained envelope that bore her late father's handwriting in the pocket of her satchel for over twelve months. As she watched Michael carefully slice it open and unfold the pages which had been enclosed within it for half a lifetime, she felt a desperate need to hear her dad's voice again.

It seemed like purgatory waiting for Michael to read and digest every phrase. Although trying to relax, Imogen found herself steadily drinking her way through the bottle of single malt placed temptingly on the coffee table on front of them.

Finally, with a sigh of acceptance, Michael was ready to put his sister out of her misery. 'Angus appears to be asking my forgiveness for having lied to me about my true origins throughout my childhood years. But there are a couple of pieces of information here that I did not previously know. Angus writes a whole page about my mother, Mary. Then he tries to provide me with the few vague facts he'd been able to garner about the identity of my father. He says that many years earlier he had questioned his brother, Frank about who Mary may have been involved with around the time she fell pregnant. Frank told him how the family had taken in a young 'night worker', at some point in the mid-fifties, in order to bring a little more money into their impoverished household.'

'When I conducted some research into Glasgow tenement conditions last year, I discovered this was quite a common practice both before and after the war. The flat must have been terribly overcrowded already but families would occasionally take in lodgers who did shift work. The idea was that they used the tenement to bunk down in during the day but would be long gone when the family got home at night,' Imogen explained.

'Well, according to our Uncle Frank, this worker became very close to the Nichols. However, when it was felt he and Mary were getting a bit too friendly, our grandfather sent him packing. Frank said he thought the man might have gone off to sea, joining the Merchant Navy or something like that. There is no mention here of his name. A few months after this chap had left, Mary found herself expecting a baby.' Michael sat back in his chair and took a swig of whisky.

'So the Nichols *did* have an idea of who your father was after all,' Imogen muttered. 'Does Dad say anything else - if you don't mind me asking?'

'I don't mind at all and yes, he does. In the last paragraph of the letter he seems very keen that I should make contact with the remaining Galbraiths. He implores me to build a relationship with my half-brothers and make up for 'lost time', is how he puts it. He was particularly keen that I should speak with Mary's widower, Eddie. He says that now I know the truth about my real mother, he will be free to tell Eddie what Mary was really doing on Garansay the weekend she died. Angus emphasises the fact that Mary's husband had never understood why his wife had been on the island in the first place. He states here that it will be a huge weight off his mind to finally be able to tell his brother-in-law that Mary had come to Garansay to see *him*. He says the guilt of having to lie to Eddie and the police about it had really eaten him up.'

Imogen found herself choking back a sob. She knew her father could not have found it easy to lie about Mary's whereabouts on that fateful day in 1973 and here was the proof of it. Then she was struck by the tragedy of it all. 'But you never got the chance to do any of those things because after Dad had his accident, Mum didn't give you the letter as they had both planned. So Eddie Galbraith went to the grave without really understanding why Mary had died here on this island.'

'You do still have the opportunity to keep in contact with Alec and Andy. In that sense, it isn't too late,' Hugh interjected, being used to finding the positives in all manner of hopeless situations.

'You may both disagree with me, but I still believe Mum was right not to tell me the truth back then. I was too young to have coped with the knowledge. It would only have given Eddie Galbraith more pain to have known what Mary was really up to. I will concede that I am glad to know it now. Angus has expressed more fatherly sentiment to me in the pages of this letter than he did throughout my youth. I'm grateful you made me read it, Imogen, I really am.'

Michael submitted to the silent tears that had begun to trickle down his face. Imogen went over to him and placed her arms around his shoulders. That was how they remained for quite some time while Hugh collected up the empty glasses, cleared away the whisky bottle and dampened down the embers of the slowly dying fire.

18

Over the days that followed, the Croft's used Kilduggan Farm purely as a base from which to explore the island. They took an excursion to the Castle, with its impressive grounds that faced the Firth of Clyde. The children were also keen to visit the perfect sandy beaches and magical little coves that populated the southern peninsula.

In short, they simply took advantage of the good weather to stay out of the farmhouse for as long as they possibly could. Ewan was almost completely recovered from his injury. There were a couple of days when he and Chloe caught the 'hopper' bus from the end of the lane and explored the sights of Garansay on their own.

The police dropped by to see them every couple of days but Imogen's assailant remained at large. There had been something of a breakthrough, though. They received a phone call from Sergeant Dalkeith, whom they'd got to know quite well. He received a tip-off from the Strathclyde Constabulary. Apparently, a Glasgow man had been reported missing a couple of days earlier by his landlady. He'd been late with the rent. She had entered his rooms only to find them deserted. The lady said he'd not fallen into arrears in all the time he'd lived there, which was an extremely lengthy period according to her.

She'd thought it best to inform the 'bobbies' straight away.

Her lodger's name was Pat O'Connell. The landlady told the policeman on duty she thought he was probably aged in his eighties or nineties. When Strathclyde checked their database they discovered he had a list of convictions as long as your arm. It turned out his actual age was 72.

As far as Dalkeith was concerned, this Pat O'Connell fellow was the man they were looking for. O'Connell's record indicated he was a petty thief, an all-round thug and retired or not, he was at one time a thoroughly nasty piece of work. This fresh information had got Imogen thinking. The person being described by the police, despite his unpleasant past, sounded like an old man. Perhaps at one stage he was a force to be reckoned with but by now he must have been fairly harmless. Imogen recalled how she was deliberately shoved from behind. Although whoever it was had a very strong grip, he made sure she was taken by surprise and kept off-balance.

This fact made Imogen wonder if the man wasn't as physically powerful as she'd believed at the time. This bully-boy hadn't tried to take on Michael or Hugh, but waited instead until Imogen was left alone and vulnerable at the farm.

This theory gave Imogen some comfort, as she now considered it extremely unlikely that Pat O'Connell would come back to Lower Kilduggan whilst they were all there together. Hugh was not so easily mollified. He would have been happy for them all to get on the next boat off the island. But he was putting a brave face on it and trying to enjoy the holiday for the sake of the kids, who incidentally, were having a fantastic time.

Michael had been rather quiet but appeared to enjoy Cameron's company. Imogen felt she must begrudgingly acknowledge it was good the boy was there. Her brother seemed to feel a kind of empathy with the young man. Their friendship was giving him comfort.

They had invited Colin and Julia for dinner, returning home deliberately early from their day trip so Imogen could prepare the meal. Hugh had devised an imaginary boundary beyond which the youngsters weren't permitted to venture. They were allowed in the front and back gardens and the open part of the courtyard but that was about it. The young ones were going to eat an early tea, leaving the adults to dine in peace. Ewan suggested they have a take-away from the fish and chip shop in Port na Mara Bay. Hugh had volunteered to go and fetch it.

Imogen found herself surrounded by fish suppers, sauce bottles and rowdy children whilst attempting to prepare the simple pasta dish she intended to serve their guests later on. Imogen sipped at regular intervals from a large goblet of red wine. She allowed the teenagers to have a glass too. Michael appeared fairly relaxed about it.

'I hope you're leaving some for the rest of us,' Hugh joshed as Imogen stopped chopping to take a healthy swig.

She hurled a paper napkin in his direction. He laughed and began the job of clearing away the mess and re-setting the table. Now the children had disappeared from under her feet, Imogen found that everything was perfectly under control by the time Colin and Julia arrived.

Colin's girlfriend seemed to be a very agreeable lady. She told Imogen about her move to Garansay three years ago, just after her husband died. They had owned a house up near Oban. Because her late husband loved Garansay so much, Julia wanted to go there in order to feel closer to him and stayed on ever since. Now she had her job at Loch Crannox Farm, things had worked out very well.

Colin was planning more changes for his business. He outlined his ambitious proposals while they finished the main course. It appeared Colin was in the process of trying to obtain a significant piece of land in Ayrshire, but was currently locked in a bidding war with a rival developer, placing the scheme on hold.

Imogen took the opportunity created by a lull in the conversation to enquire after Colin's mother, Kitty, who was a resident in a nursing home on the eastern side of the island.

Before he got a chance to respond, Imogen put a finger up to her lips and shushed him.

'Listen,' she said in a loud whisper. 'Did you hear something?'

Hugh looked startled by his wife's rudeness but then, all of a sudden, they heard a very distinctive, low pitched whining noise.

'Kids! Are you still in the house!' Imogen shouted urgently.

'We're in the sitting room, Mum!' Ewan called back.

'It sounded like an animal,' Julia said, standing up to peer through the window.

'Maybe we should go outside and have a look around,' suggested Colin, glancing at Hugh and

Michael.

The three men got their coats and grabbed a flashlight. As Hugh pulled open the kitchen door, the terrible wailing sound came again. It was immediately clear the cry was coming from the direction of the hillside, from somewhere higher up the glen.

'Hang on,' Imogen said, before the menfolk proceeded any further. 'That noise is coming from beyond the farm. I think we need some kind of plan before anyone goes out there.'

'Imogen's right,' added Colin. 'It could be one of the Welsh Blacks. It's certainly an animal in pain. I'll have to locate it before I can ring the vet.'

'Michael and I are the most familiar with the terrain, perhaps we should be the ones to go and search?' Imogen supplied.

Hugh didn't appear at all happy with this proposal. 'We don't know if the police have cleared away all of the traps yet. I wouldn't say it was safe for any of us to go up there.'

'We can't leave the poor thing in agony. Look, Hugh, if we take walking sticks to beat the ground in front of us and each use a torch to scan the path, we should be okay,' Imogen replied.

No one voiced an objection to this. They gathered together what they would need. The plan was for Hugh and Julia to stay back at the farmhouse and look after the children. But as soon as they joined the public footpath which led to the first stile, Hugh strode up alongside his wife.

'I'm not going to let you go alone,' he stated

141

decisively. 'It's okay, I've left Julia and Ewan in charge.'

It was not yet completely dark. As often occurred when a cold evening rapidly replaced a warm day, there was an unseasonably damp mist lying on the ground. They decided that Hugh and Imogen would remain together, but Colin and Michael would each take a different section of the hillside to investigate. Their neighbour had opted to head straight in the direction of his field of Welsh Blacks, off towards the north-west. Michael took the fields down by the Kilduggan Shore as his search area.

Continually swiping their beating sticks to and fro within the undergrowth ahead of them, Hugh and Imogen headed up the valley and along the rocky track which led, ultimately, to the loch. As they scanned the landscape on all sides, they discerned that eerie and haunting cry again. It seemed somehow fainter and weaker now than it was before.

'It sounds as if it's coming from over there,' Hugh said, pointing towards the mass of heather and gorse that populated the hillside ranging out to the north of the official path.

'There isn't a proper track that way, so watch your footing carefully. The bank is steeper here than it looks. If you lose your balance, just grab the heather and hold on,' Imogen advised.

They began to deviate from their original course. Hugh was stepping slowly and cautiously through the dense scrubland. When Imogen turned back, she could see he had fallen some way behind. By the time Imogen reached the system of ditches that delineated this part of the hillside from Colin's arable farmland beyond, she could no longer see Hugh at all.

The trenches themselves formed a criss-cross pattern running all the way down the valley side, finally petering out when they reached the main road at the bottom. These dug-outs would be a natural place for an injured animal to take shelter, Imogen thought. She proceeded to follow the course of the ditch system, gently prodding her stick into the meandering line of dark crevices.

The light was rapidly fading and the torch only succeeded in illuminating a narrow strip of the ground in front of her. She slowed down a little, not wanting to stumble or twist an ankle, running the risk of becoming a liability herself. Despite taking extra care, Imogen stubbed her boot against a thick root and pitched over to the right, falling heavily into the bushes that lined the top of the trench. Unhurt, she shifted into a sitting position and felt around for the flashlight, which must have been dropped when Imogen automatically reached out to break her fall. She caught sight of the torch's beam just a few feet ahead. Before getting an opportunity to retrieve it, Imogen instinctively recoiled backwards as something seized her right ankle in its firm clasp.

She resisted the urge to kick at the hand that was holding her leg, sensing she was in no immediate danger. Imogen could tell that the strength of this person's grip was rapidly failing. She stretched forward and hooked up the flashlight. Leaning over the edge, she carefully scanned the interior of the pitch black pit. After a couple of seconds Imogen spotted him, lying, bent against the muddy bank of the trench, just on the other side of the bush from her. She immediately shook off his weakening grasp and jumped down into the hole next to him.

He looked like an old man bundled up in rags. His hair was matted and his wizened face grubby with dirt. He must have been sleeping rough out there in the mountains ever since the attack, Imogen concluded. Then, she caught sight of the blood. His lower leg was encased in the rusty jaws of a monstrous trap. A claggy, dark liquid was spreading out unchecked from the raw wound.

Imogen realised they didn't have much time left. As she reached down to locate her phone and call for help, the dying man turned towards the light that was pointing mercilessly in his direction. As soon as he got a glimpse of her face, the man visibly cowered. Putting his hands up to cover his eyes he began to quietly whimper and sob. 'You've come back.' He rasped and coughed, just managing to whisper, 'you have to know I never meant to hurt you.'

'I'll get help. I can call the Air Ambulance.'

'No, stay with me, I want to talk to you.' His resilient old hand shot forward again and this time took hold of her lower arm. The action was no longer a menacing one.

'I'm not who you think I am. Mary was my aunt, but I am Imogen. Listen, Pat - is that your name?' He nodded. 'Pat, tell me what happened. Why are you here?'

'I've been lying low in the hills. I've done it before, so I know how to survive - or I thought I did.' He paused in order to fight for breath. 'I needed to find him again because I've waited for so long. I'd finally done the job he wanted. But he never came back - not until now.'

'Who never came back?'

'The Captain. I didn't know him as anything else. I was a young man then and a bit down on my luck. I made a living doing jobs for people. It didn't much matter to me how unpleasant those jobs were.' He slumped down a little further. Imogen slid alongside him and took his icy hand in hers, leaning in closer, determined to hear every word.

'I first saw the Captain in a pub on the southside. He was like no one I'd ever met before. He was tall and handsome and had on a naval uniform. Of course, he wasn't a real captain that was just what I called him, although he may have become one later on, I don't know. He was searching for something otherwise he wouldn't ever have been in that godforsaken place. He was looking for his son. I worked for the Captain a good few years. He was as close to being a steady employer as I ever had. He knew who the mother of his little boy was, you see. She'd written and told him she was expecting his child and again when the wean was born. When he got back from sea, months and months later, there was no sign of any baby. The child wasn't with the mother or the grandmother or nothing - he'd just vanished off the face of the earth.' Pat fell silent and Imogen feared for a moment he might be unconscious. Then she heard him wheezing gently. 'When the Captain challenged the mother about where the boy had gone, she told him the baby was dead.'

Imogen gasped.

'But he never believed her. So the Captain paid me to keep tabs on Mary - his old sweetheart - as he thought she would eventually lead us to him. For years I followed her and was forced to witness her sorry excuse for a life. She even got married to some poor sod and had a couple of kiddies. But there was never any sign of another boy. I had to tell the Captain this every time he came back from a voyage. I even suggested once that she might have been right about the child being dead. But he wouldn't have it. I was being paid regular so it wasn't in my interest to complain.'

'Then, one day, she led you here,' Imogen said quietly.

'I was surprised, because she never normally left her regular haunts in the city. I sensed something was up. After getting off the boat she caught a bus out here. I found it particularly difficult to trail her, what with there being no one around to give me any cover. But I managed it, just about. It was when she walked down that path to the beach. I was hiding amongst the undergrowth. When I saw the kiddies playing on the sand I knew. The tall one, you see, he was the dead spit of the Captain. This is it, I thought, I've finally found him.'

'So what happened after that?' Imogen prodded, after he fell silent again.

'I was going to head straight back to the mainland. But I made the mistake of following her for a bit longer. These two fellas gave her money - lots of money, so I trailed her for the rest of the day. She went to a bar with one of the blokes. When she left she was so drunk I thought I would be able to take the cash from her, like candy from a baby. But it wasn't that easy. She was like a kind of witch, you see. I was only interested in thieving and drinking in those days but it was as if she'd put a spell on me. She led me up into those hills and started to remove her clothes and dance around in front of me, her dark hair flowing all about her. Of course it was all a trick. Mary wanted to know who'd sent me and like a bloody fool I told her. After I did she laughed. Jeered at me she did, told me that the boy had been sold and the Captain would never see his son again. It was like the spell had been suddenly broken. I realised I'd betrayed him - after all those years. Just for a few quid and a quick roll in the grass. So when she turned around to put her dress back on, I picked up a rock and hit her.

She fell straight into the water and floated there, nice and peaceful. I buried her clothes and pocketed the money.' His words were a barely audible whisper.

'Pat,' Imogen said cajolingly. 'What did you do then?'

'I knew I couldn't just go back on the boat. So I went off into the mountains. I slept in barns and outhouses for a couple of weeks, lived off scraps from the farms. Then I paid a fisherman to take me to Kintyre, no questions asked. It was several weeks before I got back to the city. By that time I reckoned I'd done the Captain a favour by getting rid of her. He would be free to go back and fetch his son. I left a message in our usual drop, telling him I'd found the boy at last. But I never heard nothing back. I waited for months, I even went to the docks and watched all the big liners and ships come in, seeing if he might step off one of them. But he didn't and years went by. Finally, I gave up hope of setting

147

eyes on him again in this lifetime.' 'Then   you saw his picture, in the paper.'

'He looked exactly the same. He'd saved some boy in a storm at sea. It was just the kind of thing the Captain would have done. I only wanted to tell him that I'd solved the puzzle. I'd found his precious son, so why hadn't he ever come back to me?'

Imogen didn't have the heart to tell Pat O'Connell about the mistake he had made. Despite the fact he was a killer and a thief. The life blood was seeping slowly out of the frail, hunched body beside her. It was leaching into the cold, hard earth of this lonely hillside. At this precise moment, Imogen felt that his wretched fate must surely be punishment enough.

Part Three

19

Imogen was lying on a sun lounger, on a tiny strip of privately owned beach. The sand beneath her sprawled body appeared almost white in the brilliantness of the bright, late afternoon light. She was gazing out at the glistening azure waters of the Arabian Gulf and about as far outside of her comfort zone as it was possible to be.

The story of how she got there was quite a simple one. After the death of Patrick O'Connell, Hugh and Imogen returned home to east Essex within the week. Imogen managed to persuade Michael to go back to his flat in Glasgow for the time being, giving her niece Sarah a call with the advice that she should keep her father there for as long as possible.

Hugh remained the only person Imogen told of the words Mary Galbraith's murderer spoke to her on that dark hillside. Surprisingly enough, her husband agreed they would not tell Michael anything about it. Hugh's reasoning was that if someone does not wish to seek out the identity of their birth parents, they must do their very best to respect the decision.

Normal life appeared to have resumed for them all. Cameron Fleming went off to visit his grandmother in Dunkeld and then returned to his rented flat in Glasgow, declaring that from this point onwards, he would be searching for a suitable job.

The Crofts still had a couple of weeks remaining of the school holidays. One morning, a couple of days after they had arrived back from Garansay, Ewan came to talk to his mother, whilst she was busily tidying the study. He had just been speaking with his girlfriend, Chloe. It transpired that he had been given the task of passing on her parents' gratitude for welcoming the girl on their family vacation. After delivering this message, Imogen's eldest son lingered for a while, looking a little sheepish.

'Come on then, is there anything else?' Imogen enquired, eyebrows raised.

'Well, you know how Chloe's parents have just moved to Dubai?'

Imogen nodded her head, thinking she might have an idea of where this was heading.

'Their house is a few kilometres out of the city, but Chloe's dad has been offered the use of one of his development company's five star villas on the coast for a few weeks. The thing is he's asked if I want to come out there and stay.' Ewan did not elaborate on the statement but waited instead to assess his mother's reaction.

'Okay,' she said, putting down the cloth. 'So you and Chloe would travel out there together, is that the plan?'

'Yes, and Chloe's parents have offered to pay for the flight and everything. It shouldn't cost me a penny.'

'We would be happy to help out with the money, Ewan. This could be a trip of a lifetime for you,' Imogen replied, not wanting to appear totally mean-spirited.

Ewan's face absolutely lit up at the realisation

she might actually be amenable to the proposal. He stepped forward and gave Imogen one of his rare hugs. She took the opportunity to ruffle his mop of dark hair.

'Of course, they did invite the rest of you to come as well. But I declined on your behalf. I put it very politely, don't worry about that. I just explained how you don't really like flying and the heat would be a bit too much for you - it can be over forty degrees at this time of the year, you know. I simply explained how it wasn't your kind of holiday at all.'

Having received the answer he was angling for, Ewan gave her a brief peck on the cheek and without pausing for a reply, strode straight out of the little office.

But Imogen had halted his retreat by calling out, 'Ewan! Could you please send a message to Chloe's parents? Would you inform them that we are extremely grateful for their very generous offer and on behalf of the entire Croft family, I would be absolutely delighted to accept their kind invitation.'

*

Although it was approaching six o'clock in the evening, it was still extremely hot. Imogen tossed her paperback novel down onto a beach towel and padded back inside. The Princes' luxury villa was sculpted from a beautiful, pale cream local stone. The interior was impeccably decorated with natural materials designed to complement the holiday home's stunning setting. It was one

151

of a long line of exclusive properties that swept along this frond of the famous Palm Jumeirah Island. Shaped like a giant palm tree, this man-made land mass stretched out from the city centre of Dubai and had doubled the length of its coastline.

This, according to Chloe's father, was the 'raison d'être' of the incredible project. Sheik Mohammed Maktoum realised that in order to reinvent Dubai as the 'go-to' resort for the rich and famous, the city's 70km expanse of exquisite beaches was not going to be enough. So a huge development programme was initiated nearly a decade ago. A significant element of its ambitious strategy involved expanding the tiny Emirate out into the clear waters of the Arabian Gulf and creating a mind blowing archipelago of artificial islands.

Howard Prince was the co-director of a building company which had been taking advantage of Dubai's stellar growth over the past few years. With the housing market back home remaining in stagnation for so long, Howard and his partner had been doing business in the Middle East for quite some time. In the last six months the Princes decided to make the move out there on a permanent basis. Liz Prince told Imogen and Hugh how their house was situated in a gated community about 15km outside of the city. So to be spending some time on the Palm Jumeirah was as much of a novelty for them as it was for the Crofts.

Howard's company owned a number of villas within this property hot spot. Several of them currently sat empty while they made money purely from the increase in house prices on the island since they were bought four years ago.

Imogen could certainly see how the family was tempted to relocate there from the rain prone suburbs of greater Manchester.

Like her daughter, Liz Prince was a petite and attractive lady. She had short and expensively styled dark brown hair but unlike Chloe, she had already cultivated an impressively deep tan. Since arriving the previous evening, all they had seen of the smallest of the seven United Arab Emirates was what was visible during the taxi journey from the airport. It was certainly clear that Dubai was still very much a work in progress. As they drove along the six lane highway that connected the Palm Jumeirah to the mainland, there appeared to be building sites all around them. However, one could still observe the sheer largess and grandeur of the place, not least when Imogen suddenly caught sight of the Burj Al Arab hotel, emerging with its distinctive, sail-like shape, from out of the bluey-green surf of the Gulf itself.

Ewan was quite right when he said this wasn't the type of holiday the Crofts would usually take. It was particularly fascinating to Imogen, who grew up on an island which took millennia to evolve out of the slow development of its natural environment, to witness firsthand these incredible man-made structures that appeared almost to defy their physical location. Indeed, without the huge artificial break water that shielded Palm Jumeirah from the prevailing currents of the Arabian Gulf, the entire edifice would, most certainly, be washed away by the sea.

Hugh had been to Dubai before. He came on

a trip with his parents many years previously, before he and Imogen were married. Kath and Gerry had relatives living and working out there. Hugh said it had changed significantly since then, although there was still that sensation of being somehow isolated from the rest of the world. Not simply because the city was surrounded by hundreds of kilometres of desert, but also because there was almost an 'unreality' to the lifestyle.

Liz and Howard had organised a small gathering that evening for some of the ex-pat couples Howard knew through his work. Imogen was hoping to get a snapshot from them of what it was like to live in this seemingly remote Middle Eastern outpost.

The villa they were staying in was vast. Although the boys were sharing, Bridie had a guestroom all to herself. Hugh and Imogen had an enormous suite. As Imogen made her way up the twisting marbled staircase leading to the first floor she was relieved to note how much cooler it was in here than out in the blistering heat of the secluded beach. Hugh was seated on a chair in front of the open doors of their small terrace, gazing out at the simple panorama of sea and sky, punctuated only by the houses and hotels that vied for their allotted portion of this paradise island.

'It's very beautiful, isn't it?' Imogen said, moving up behind him and lightly draping her arms around his shoulders.

'Yes it is. Although the children have got so much planned for the next few days, I don't think we'll get an opportunity to just laze on the beach.' He lifted one of her hands and placed it against his warm lips.

'I've had a few hours of sun worship this afternoon and that's probably enough. Not wanting to complain or anything, but it's simply too hot for me out there.' Imogen moved over and poured a glass of iced water from a jug on the small palazzo table.

'I have to confess. I was a little surprised when you decided we should take the Princes up on their offer,' Hugh added, and not for the first time since his wife informed him about the trip less than a week ago.

'Well, I must concede that the Garansay holiday was not quite the success I hoped it would be. We had some lovely days, of course, but I wanted us to have a proper break before school and university started up again. I just thought a week in the sun would be the perfect antidote to the constant drama that seems to surround my family.' Imogen sat down on the seat next to her husband, absorbing the extraordinarily relaxing vista.

'Have you heard from Michael in the last few days, how is he doing?' Hugh asked, with genuine concern.

'I gave him a call before we flew out. He's fine. Cameron has been over to visit a few times and so has Sarah. He seems to think that with the death of Pat O'Connell the whole business is over and done with.' The little cubes of ice jingled as Imogen lifted the cold glass to her mouth.

'It is isn't it? O'Connell must have been the only one to have still been alive from the whole sorry episode,' Hugh said, reluctantly drawing his vision away from the mesmerizing view.

'Yes, of course. But I would like to know what

155

happened to Michael's father. I'm sure that if I did some digging I could probably find out which of the Merchant Ships he'd served on. I've got enough of the relevant dates, I think. Then I might actually be able to come up with a name for him.'

'Imogen, if Michael doesn't want to know any more then you have to leave it there. At least we know he didn't pay O'Connell to kill Mary Galbraith. That was what I was most worried about,' Hugh pointed out.

'That's true. In fact, it sounds as if he was a decent person. He just wanted to find out where his son was. It's heart-breaking he never got the chance to meet Michael. What do you think happened to him?'

'He must have died somewhere at sea. Either his ship went down or he contracted an illness during the voyage and didn't survive long enough to make it back to port. He seemed so keen to locate his child that I cannot believe he simply settled down in another part of the world and forgot all about the search. But we'll never know, Imogen. It will have to remain purely conjecture - okay?'

Imogen nodded her head as she slowly sipped the refreshingly cool liquid, staring dreamily out towards the distant horizon once again.

20

Howard and Liz had organised an informal cocktail party for their guests. The silver trays filled with canapés and drinks were being expertly transported around the room by a team of uniformed, predominantly Filipino waiting staff. The presence of this troop of domestic helpers made Imogen feel a little uncomfortable. As did the pointed warning Howard gave at the start of the evening. He reminded them it was perfectly fine to drink alcohol within the private grounds of the house, but they must not take their glasses out into the street, as this was against the law in Dubai. Howard had a special liquor license issued by the government in order to entertain his clients and contacts. Otherwise they wouldn't have access to alcohol at all.

Observing first-hand how the ex-pat lifestyle worked out here, Imogen found herself having to give Cameron Fleming some credit. He had actually always been very willing to help out with domestic tasks when he was staying with them at Lower Kilduggan Farm. Knowing he could have relied on servants back home showed he was fairly well brought up to chip in with menial tasks himself. Or perhaps the Flemings were not quite as well off as the Princes. Imogen didn't know enough yet about their existence in Dubai to be able to say.

The youngsters had formed a rowdy group out on the terrace. Some of the children of the other guests had gone out there to join them. The evening was still very pleasantly warm.

Hugh and Imogen chatted to an Australian couple called Steve and Anna, who informed them they had lived in Dubai for four years. Steve worked for an international bank in one of the high rise office buildings in the city centre. Anna worked for an estate agency which catered predominantly for the ex-pat community. Life out there appeared to be treating them very well. They were both golden skinned and heavily adorned with expensive watches and jewellery. Anna told them they lived in a top floor apartment in the heart of the city. She entertained Hugh with some extraordinary anecdotes about the high profile celebrities and business people she had helped to buy homes and apartments for over the past few years.

Whilst Hugh and Anna discussed the price of real estate, Imogen took the opportunity to ask Steve about the banking industry in Dubai and why he chose to come out to the Middle East from his previous home in Melbourne.

'As you can see,' Steve explained, sweeping his hand in an arched motion to indicate their opulent surroundings. 'The quality of life can be pretty good out here. I reckon that before we settle down to have kids, we should enjoy what Dubai has to offer. But if you're asking about specifics, then I can tell you the job is pretty interesting in the UAE. A great deal of money flows into this country and then flows out again. Oil and gold have been the mainstays of the economy for the past few decades but when the oil reserves run out, the Sheik's looking towards westerners and their expensive tastes to plug the gap. At least once a week I might take clients to see the horse racing or to a polo match. The rest of the time we treat them to lunch in restaurants and hotels. There are more celebrity chefs here in Dubai per square metre than you'd find in London or Sydney.' Steve took a sip from his lethal looking cocktail.

'These trips come out of the bank's expense accounts do they?' Imogen ventured, figuring that Steve may let down his guard a little.

'Oh yeah, we wouldn't be able to do it if the bank didn't pay. But some of my erstwhile colleagues have partaken a tad too much in Dubai's expensive attractions.'

Imogen smiled, saying nothing. She hoped Steve was loosened up enough to elaborate without any need for prompting.

'There's an awful lot of cash coming in and out of this place,' Steve continued, warming to the subject, 'most of it is legit but a small amount isn't. We've all been approached at one time or another by a client who wants to offer us an incentive to process funds that can't be legally accounted for.'

'What do you mean?' Imogen asked in her most innocent voice, gazing up at him with an expression of rapt interest.

'Well, I'm not saying the criminals come from here - quite the opposite. The Dubai authorities are very keen to stamp this kind of thing out. These organisations make their money out of buying and selling something illegal, such as guns or drugs, or even people. These funds come into the Emirates from places like South America

159

or Eastern Europe but they need to be legitimized. The gangs offer people huge pay-offs in order to provide them with a 'front' for their cash. We can usually tell when it's happening because someone lowly starts driving around in flash cars and indulging in the lifestyle a bit too much.' Steve started laughing and laid his hand on Imogen's arm.

Anna moved towards them, looking distinctly unhappy.

Imogen made their excuses and led Hugh in the direction of the terrace.

'What on earth are you up to?' he whispered, as they weaved through the guests with pleasant smiles painted onto their faces.

When they finally reached the privacy of the pretty walled garden Imogen stopped to explain. 'I was just trying to find out what it's like to work in the banking industry here. Steve was a bit tipsy and became indiscreet about some of the dodgy practices that go on. I'm not surprised, really. Where there's money there is always corruption.'

'But why are you so interested in that?' Hugh asked. Then he broke into a humourless smile as realisation dawned. 'I see. You agreed to come to Dubai so you could find out some more about the Flemings, didn't you? I should have bloody well guessed it!'

'Hugh,' she placed a hand on his upper arm, as if to prevent him walking away. 'I swear that was not my original plan. I said yes to Ewan for all the reasons I told you. When we arrived here I just thought it wouldn't do any harm to discover what kind of life Cameron and his family had lived in Dubai. My motives aren't sinister you know. I actually want to be able to understand the boy a bit better. But whenever I've suggested doing any investigating recently, you always seem to be arguing against it.'

Hugh led her over to an elegant bench that had been smoothed out of the stone wall which enclosed the veranda. 'I don't actually mind you exercising your brain a little whilst we are here, but I would appreciate it if you would let me know what you're up to. We used to be quite good at puzzling these things out together.'

'Okay, from now on I am going to tell you exactly what is going on in my head.'

Hugh shifted around, his lips finding hers. They remained in an embrace for quite some time, until the sun had completely set over the horizon and the Prince's guests had at long last returned home.

The following day, Liz and Howard volunteered to take the girls to see the sunken aquarium at the Atlantis hotel, which was situated on one of the outer fronds of the Palm Jumeirah resort. Imogen had seen pictures of it in the guidebook. It looked like it had been transported straight out of Disneyland. Imogen knew Bridie was going to absolutely love it.

The rest of the family decided to visit the Deira Creekside, where they could have a look at how the traditional 'dhow' boats were built and perhaps take a trip across the creek on one. Imogen was certainly keen to see the historic centre of Dubai and gain a sense of its origins as an ancient trading port.

There was a pleasant breeze rolling in off

161

Dubai's busy inland waterway which made the heat of the day easier to cope with. Imogen couldn't even imagine what it must be like out in the desert when the temperature was like this. Ewan and Ian seemed happy simply to enjoy the incredible sights that surrounded them. The Dhow Wharfage was thronging with tourists and the area provided them with their best opportunity yet to observe the vivid contrasts that existed within this diverse city. Expensive motor cruisers were moored alongside traditional wooden passenger boats. Many of the locals could be seen wearing their white kandoora robes. Yet western dress also appeared to be common attire amongst people of all nationalities. It struck Imogen, as they strolled along the quayside, what a tolerant society Dubai must be, in order to absorb all of these different cultures and yet remain such a safe and relaxed place to be.

Imogen was not convinced that Britain had managed to attain this type of social harmony, even though both countries had had fifty or sixty years in which to achieve it.

Perhaps the difference there was that the people of Dubai had to accept western influence as necessary in order for their isolated society to survive. Liz told them how the Arab community managed to maintain its own customs and religious practices even within Dubai's climate of rapid and almost overwhelming change. Liz believed this was accomplished through their community's awareness that the family unit was more essential for happiness and fulfilment in life than the acquisition of material wealth. Imogen wondered then what the local Arab people must make of the ex-pats who came out here to live and work, often leaving their own families behind, thousands of miles away.

Hugh broke into her thoughts by taking his wife's hand and asking if they should find somewhere to stop for lunch. As they ambled towards the Souk Area of the quayside and the myriad of restaurants that proliferated along this section of the wharf, Imogen said, 'I still can't work out whether Richard Fleming came to work here by choice, or whether his company forced him to re-locate.'

Imogen told Hugh, after retiring to their bedroom last night, about the newspaper article revealing Richard Fleming's criminal conviction back in the January of 1997. In the spirit of being more open with one another, she also informed him of her suspicion that his employers could have actively encouraged him to make the move out to the Middle East.

'If the bank wanted to get rid of him, they would simply have sacked him. These city institutions aren't exactly known for their compassion. Richard Fleming must have been making them lots of money otherwise they wouldn't have kept him on after a scandal like that.'

As they sat down at a table outside a small bistro and lifted up the menus Imogen replied, 'You're probably right. It just seemed a major coincidence that the Flemings came out here so soon afterwards.'

Whilst the boys loudly discussed their food choices, Hugh leant forward and advised, in a lowered tone, 'the only way to find out how the Flemings felt about living here in Dubai is to ask

163

somebody who knew them. They were based in this city for sixteen years. There must be plenty of people who had dealings with the family. It's simply a case of finding a way to locate some of them.' Hugh promptly shook out his napkin and began to counsel Ian on his lunch options.

Imogen selected her own meal, settling back to enjoy the warmth of the day and to watch the hectic quayside scene being played out in front of them. But in her head she was devising the best possible way to put into practice her husband's simple but rather brilliant suggestion.

21

After spending a couple of days in this fascinating city, Imogen was already finding the intense heat of the daytime left her completely drained of energy. By the evening, all she wanted to do was sit out on the tranquil terrace, enjoying a lingering after dinner drink. Thankfully, Chloe's parents were excellent company. They were content to join their new friends, watching as the glow of the deep orange sun finally melted away to nothing in the cool, sapphire waters of the Arabian Sea.

Imogen asked Liz how she was enjoying living out there.

The woman sat back in her seat, taking some time to answer the question. 'If I could watch a sunset like that one every night of the week, I would probably tell you I adored it,' she laughed. 'Our new house is gorgeous don't get me wrong, it's just that I'm beginning to feel a bit isolated within our accommodation complex. That's why we love it when family and friends come to visit.'

'It must take a while to make meaningful connections,' Imogen tentatively suggested.

'I know. Howard tells me I've got to give it longer. There are plenty of clubs and societies in Dubai for expats to get involved with. I will have to make more of an effort to join some of those. Howard has got his work, you see, but I'm stuck at home most of the time.'

Imogen was surprised to hear Liz speak in this way. She went on to confide that it was lovely while Chloe was there, as it was just like a family holiday, but when her daughter returned to Manchester, Liz could feel really quite low. Imogen pointed out how difficult it was when a first born child left home for college, let alone if you re-located to a new country at the same time. She laid a hand on Liz's tanned arm and reassured her it would get easier, although she could offer no guarantee of this.

Imogen mulled over their conversation, slowly sipping a gin and tonic. An idea came to her. 'Liz, why don't we attend one of the ex-pat clubs together whilst I'm here? It's always easier to go to these things with someone else.'

The woman turned towards Imogen, a distinct glimmer of excitement crossing her face. 'Really? Are you sure you wouldn't mind? There's not much in it for you, but I'd really appreciated it if you could.'

'I'd love to Liz,' Imogen replied, clinking her glass down decisively on the table. 'It would be absolutely no problem at all.'

The following morning, Imogen was acutely aware they only had a few days of the holiday left. If she was going to discover anything significant about the Flemings, she needed to get a move on. So when Liz shyly suggested over breakfast that they attend a British Club afternoon tea event that day, Imogen jumped at the chance.

'Hugh, why don't you and Howard take the kids out on the water? They're dying to visit the Sailing Club before we leave.'

'Bridie might want to come along with you

Mums,' Hugh added lightly as he absentmindedly buttered his toast.

Imogen flashed him a warning look.

'That's a bit sexist isn't it sweetheart?' Imogen replied, adopting a jovial tone. 'You know how much Bridie loves a trip out on the boat. We wouldn't want to be guilty of excluding her from all the fun, would we?'

Suddenly realising his wife must have some kind of plan in mind, Hugh speedily backtracked, 'of course, she won't want to be standing around all afternoon with a group of middle aged ladies sipping tea.' When an awkward silence greeted this remark he quickly added, 'although I wasn't meaning you two.'

Imogen and Liz burst into gales of laughter. 'You'd better go upstairs darling and see if the boys are up yet - before you dig yourself into an even bigger hole.'

After a pleasant lunch outside on the villa's shaded terrace, Liz drove them in her smart little jeep to the Emirates Country Club, where the afternoon tea was being hosted. The Country Club lay to the south of the city and was situated near the Race Course and not far from the Sailing Club where Howard and Hugh had taken the children. As soon as they pulled onto the sweeping gravel drive Imogen could tell this was the part of Dubai where its elite residents spent their leisure time. Not least because of the impressive array of extremely expensive, high performance vehicles that populated the Club's landscaped car park.

167

Imogen wasn't sure how to dress for this event, so plumped for a full length halter necked summer dress and high-heeled sandals. She even put on the pretty ruby stoned necklace that Hugh's mother had bought for her last Christmas. Imogen very rarely wore jewellery of any kind, but the aim today was to blend in amongst the wealthy ex-pat community as much as possible. Imogen had to admit the deep red gems complemented her pale skin and ebony hair beautifully. She made a mental note to put it on more often.

Liz also looked lovely, in a knee length green silky skirt and blouse set which show off her petite figure perfectly. Despite her immaculate appearance Imogen could tell she was nervous. They linked arms and entered the main dining room together.

The huge space was light and air-conditioned. About a dozen finely appointed tables were arranged in a circular pattern in the centre. As soon as they stepped over the threshold, a young waitress presented them with a pretty array of steaming tea cups, carefully laid out on an ornate, gold inlaid tray.

Furnished with their refreshments, Liz and Imogen were ready to begin the serious business of circulating the room. When Imogen's companion was comfortably ensconced in conversation with a woman who, it turned out, lived in the same housing complex as the Princes, she broke away, proceeding to mingle amongst some of the intimate groups that had begun to form in the room.

Imogen joined a gaggle of ladies discussing the varying fortunes of the polo team that one of them coached. When she found an opportunity,

Imogen introduced the topic of the Fleming's tragic accident. Her plan was to allege she was a friend of the family from back home in Scotland and claim she was trying to help Cameron get in touch with some of his school pals in Dubai.

None of the polo ladies seemed to have heard of them. As soon as a chance arose, without being too obviously rude, Imogen moved on to a new little clique. This pattern continued for another hour or so with little success. Imogen did find one woman, called Sally, who had known of Isla Fleming. But all she could tell her was how Cameron's mother was a quiet person and the family had kept their lives very private.

It was while Imogen was having a break from her investigations that she finally turned up something of interest. Imogen headed over to sit with Liz for a few moments, at one of the treat laden tables. She was just reaching across for an extremely tempting looking scone, smothered in jam and cream, when a voice behind her said, 'I hear you are looking for someone who knew the Fleming family.'

Imogen twisted around to see who had spoken these words. She discovered a tall woman with straight, shoulder length blond hair towering above her. Getting to her feet, Imogen put out a hand.

In a cut-glass southern English accent the woman explained, 'my name is Stella Hargreaves. The Flemings were my neighbours for about five years.'

'Very pleased to meet you, I'm Imogen Croft,' she replied, adding disingenuously, 'I was a friend of Isla's from back home in Dunkeld. It's

169

absolutely tragic what happened to the family, we are all still in a state of shock about it.'

'Did you come out to visit Isla while they were living here? I don't recall them *ever* having family or friends over.'

Imogen kept her cool. 'No, sadly we never did. I have three children, you see. They were only little for most of the time Isla and Richard were here. Now they're older, we've finally made the trip out to Dubai. But of course, it's come too late.' For some reason Imogen also decided to add, 'and, just between you and me, my husband didn't really get on with Richard Fleming all that well.'

Stella Hargreaves relaxed the guarded look that up to now, she had been stubbornly adopting. In a lowered tone she replied, 'I had a similar problem myself. I was quite good friends with Isla for several years but then we had a little 'incident' with her husband. After that, we just drifted apart.'

Imogen remained quiet, waiting for Stella to explain.

'Jim and I threw a dinner party for a handful of local couples, including the Flemings. As soon as she arrived, Isla warned me that her husband was having a difficult time at work and was in a foul mood. He seemed okay over dinner but then, later on, when we were having drinks outside, he took offence at something one of my friends' husband said to him. I really thought he might attack the guy, but Jim managed to smooth it over. They left pretty soon afterwards. As we were saying goodnight I had this horrible feeling that Richard was going to take it out on Isla when they got home. She'd just seemed terribly on edge and fearful. The thought of what might be going on behind closed doors really haunted me for a while. There's not much you can do with these domestic things - is there?'

'No,' Imogen agreed sympathetically, 'especially if there's no real proof of it. Cameron did suggest to my husband that his dad had made life very difficult for them. Regrettably, he didn't go into any specifics about it.'

'Cameron?' Stella declared with disbelief. 'He was nearly as bad as the father in my opinion.' She took a sip from her dainty cup.

Imogen stood stock still and then enquired, in as neutral a tone as she could muster, 'what do you mean?'

'Well, the dad was a bully really, always putting Isla down and criticising poor little Lucy too. But Cameron was like that as well. I suppose the exclusive private school our boys attended might have encouraged him to become quite full of himself and look down on other people. That may explain the way he behaved. He used to speak to Isla as if she were one of the domestic staff. I found it quite uncomfortable to be in their house if Cameron was at home. I often thought if my son started acting in that way I'd have to take a horse whip to him or something else as drastic!' Stella began to laugh. Imogen tried to join in with her but it was proving difficult, because her mind was racing.

Then Stella qualified this by adding, 'of course it is heart-breaking for the lad to have lost his family like that, don't get me wrong, I do feel for him. It's just when I first heard the news about the accident and found out Cameron was the only one to be rescued - I know this will sound absolutely awful - but I just thought how sad it was that it hadn't been Isla and Lucy who survived, because they were the only truly decent people in that whole family.' Stella immediately put a hand up to her mouth, as if she realised she had admitted to something she really shouldn't. 'Oh dear, perhaps it would have been best to keep that to myself?'

Imogen leant over and placed a hand on her arm, 'not at all Stella. It sounds as if you knew the Flemings better than most. I suspect you are probably quite correct.'

22

Liz had made some new contacts from their afternoon at the Country Club and seemed very pleased with how things went. Hugh and the rest of the group don't return to the villa until quite late. As they finally piled through the large and imposing front door, Ewan proudly announced that they stopped for burgers at a hotel bar somewhere off the highway on their way home.

Everyone appeared exhausted, especially Bridie, who immediately excused herself and retired to bed. Even the boys were subdued. Rather than their usual evening stroll along the beach, they parked themselves on the leather sofa to watch the Princes' huge cable T.V. Imogen glanced towards the kitchen. Chloe and her mother were chatting happily, propped up at the solid granite breakfast bar.

Imogen took the opportunity to steer Hugh outside onto the terrace, out of earshot of the house. 'How was your day?' She asked, hooking her arms around his neck and brushing her lips across his lightly tanned cheek.

'Pretty wonderful, actually. There was just enough of a breeze for us to have a decent sail. The kids jumped off the boat and swam in the creek for a while after lunch. It was quite magical. It's a shame you missed it, darling.'

'Well, Liz has made some new friends, so I think it was worth the sacrifice.'

Hugh placed his fingertips underneath her chin and tilted her face up to meet his. 'Come on then, Mrs Croft. Don't leave me in suspense. What have you found out?'

'It was hard going at first. There didn't appear to be many people at the Club who had known the Flemings at all. But then I was approached by someone who had lived next door to the family for over five years. She told me something very interesting.'

'Oh, yes.' Hugh was becoming intrigued.

'She confirmed what we had suspected about Richard Fleming. Stella, her name was, said she thought Richard might be beating up his wife 'behind closed doors', is how she referred to it.'

'Well, that definitely corroborates what Cameron told me on Garansay.'

'Yes, but that is what was strange. Stella suggested, in no uncertain terms, that Cameron was just as bad as his father. She said he treated his mum like a servant and he was a 'bully' just like his dad.' Imogen waited for Hugh's reaction to this.

'That isn't the impression the boy has given us, and especially not Michael,' Hugh stated, obviously unsure of what to make of this new testimony.

'No, he hasn't. But I must confess that ever since I first met him I thought Cameron was putting on a kind of act for our benefit. I don't think we've seen anything yet of his true character.'

Hugh remained silent for a short while before proposing, 'he could be trying to re-invent himself. Perhaps he knows how obnoxious he was before the crash and guilt has forced him to change his ways. People can alter their behaviour, very often for the better.'

'I'm willing to bear that in mind, Hugh. However, I also want you to consider the possibility that Cameron Fleming is an extremely manipulative young man. I can certainly accept he has attempted to re-invent himself, I'm just not convinced his motives for doing so are quite as innocent as you are suggesting.'

They both took a step back from one another, while still maintaining steady eye contact. Hugh ended the temporary stand-off by saying, 'Let's try and find out some more. But until then, I'm prepared to keep an open mind, as long as you are too.'

Imogen's face broke into a broad smile. 'I do believe, Mr Croft that we have finally come to some kind of an agreement.' Moving forwards once again, she slipped comfortably into her husband's waiting arms.

Before arriving in Dubai, Imogen had spent some time looking into the backgrounds of Isla and Richard Fleming. Imogen found it actually quite amazing what you could discover about people from the internet. Of course, there had been a great deal of column inches devoted to the Flemings in the weeks following the helicopter crash. These newspaper articles were Imogen's starting point. They allowed her to build up a basic picture of their lives from which she could go on to do a little digging of her own.

Isla Fleming, née Cook, grew up in the little town of Dunkeld in Perthshire. Her mother,

Nancy, still lived there, but her father died six years ago. One of the newspaper pieces mentioned that Isla had a younger sister called Annie. She now lived in Inverness with her husband and two teenage sons. Imogen assumed this must be the family who had, at some point, fallen out with Richard Fleming.

Dunkeld was a pretty little place. Hugh and Imogen drove through it once when they took the scenic route up to Aberdeen, back when they were first married and living in East Lothian. They stopped to look at the Cathedral which sat on the banks of the River Tay. Imogen thought it must have been a lovely town to grow up in.

Richard Fleming hailed from the larger, nearby city of Perth. His parents, Lillian and Alec both died over ten years ago. It was Michael who told his sister that Richard had an older brother, called William, who now lived in Canada and had done for many years. Perhaps Richard's brother would travel to the UK for the funeral, when it finally took place, but this remained to be seen. Isla and Richard had grown up within fifty miles of one another. They must have met, somehow, because of this geographical connection.

Imogen knew they got married in 1990 and that Isla was 48 years old at the time of her death and Richard was 53. They were only five years older than Hugh and Imogen were. Poor wee Lucy had only been a few months older than Bridie. Being in Dubai, so close to where the family had lived, Imogen was beginning to feel the tragedy of their deaths more acutely than she had done back in Britain. They were starting to seem more like real people. She wanted to be able to better explain why their lives were ended so abruptly.

It was easy for Imogen to pin-point the location of Richard's workplace in Dubai. In fact, she'd marked it on her tourist map before they even arrived. The bank that employed Richard Fleming had its own high rise office building, not far from the Dubai World Trade Centre. Imogen had a hunch that Richard's job held the key to understanding the dynamic which existed within the Fleming family. She sensed his banking job, in some way, could have precipitated their deaths. It might simply have been that the pressures Cameron's father was experiencing in his career caused him to be such a difficult, volatile person at home. She was just not sure yet. Imogen also had no clear plan of how she might find out about Richard's working life. She couldn't just walk straight into the office building and start asking questions.

They only had a couple of days left in the Middle East. When the already hot sun rose on the penultimate morning of their trip, everyone seemed to have an idea about what they would like to do. Ewan, Chloe and Ian were desperate to visit the Burj Khalifa, which at that point in time, was the tallest building in the world. There was a viewing area at the top of the building from which the panorama promised to be spectacular.

Luckily, Howard was keen to give them the guided tour. He proudly announced that you could see all of his company's property developments from the summit of the tower. Imogen believed he'd take great pleasure in pointing them out to the youngsters when they finally got up there.

Hugh and Imogen decided to take Bridie

shopping. They needed to buy some gifts and the shopping malls of Dubai were reputed to be something incredible to behold. The jaunt proved a more pleasant experience than Imogen was expecting. The malls were all fully air-conditioned and it was fascinating to browse in the windows of the many luxury stores. Every product on display was coated in jewels and possessed a price tag with at least three noughts attached.

It was as they gazed in disbelief at a display of diamond encrusted mobile phones that Hugh commented, 'it's an amusing novelty for us to look at this kind of merchandise on holiday. But if you lived amongst this largesse every day, it might make you develop tastes you couldn't afford.'

Imogen nodded in agreement. 'It's the expectation of wealth beyond one's means which encourages people to start taking back-handers. Like the people Steve told me about at the cocktail party.'

Hugh gave her arm a playful squeeze. 'You may have picked up some useful information at the Princes' soirée, but I wasn't totally happy with the tactics you employed to extract it.'

Imogen exhaled a chuckle and added, 'I'm afraid I don't possess the resources of the police. There are times when I need to improvise a little bit. Speaking of which, Richard Fleming's office building is just around the corner from here. I wouldn't mind taking a look. Would you treat Bridie to lunch somewhere nice? I'll meet you both later.'

'I'm perfectly happy to escort my daughter to lunch, darling,' Hugh said, with a steely edge to his voice. 'Go have a look and see what you can find out certainly. But just try to rein in the improvisation for today, okay?'

Imogen provided her husband with a reassuring smile, quickly pecking him and Bridie on the cheek, before turning on her heels and dashing off towards what the tourist map informed her was the city's financial district.

23

Similar to the cities Imogen had visited in the United States, the centre of Dubai wasn't really designed with pedestrians in mind. Although she didn't actually have to cross one of the sector's five lane highways, she still found it tricky to reach the dazzling, mirrored exterior of the Anglo-Gulf Bank on foot.

Upon entering the building, Imogen cast a look around the cavernous, minimalistic lobby. A vast, twisting staircase led up to a mezzanine level of open-plan offices. But it was the long line of elevators stretching the entire width of one wall which provided the principle means by which staff and visitors accessed the floors above. To make herself less conspicuous, Imogen browsed through a pile of leaflets about overseas investment which lay on a glass table surrounded by brightly upholstered sofas and chairs. She spent a little time observing the staff and customers coming in and out of the revolving doors, taking particular note of the distinctive orange lanyards that all bank workers had hanging around their necks.   When there was no more for Imogen to see, she picked up a couple of brochures and walked back out onto the street. Intense heat enveloped her, as soon as she was beyond the air conditioned environment of the bank's reception. Sweat began to prickle along the surface of her skin. Imogen put on her sun glasses and gazed around at the neighbouring premises, noticing that the hotel across the street was part of a well-known chain and had devoted it's ground floor to a busy looking bar and restaurant.

Imogen set herself up at a table near the entrance, ordering a sparkling water and a club sandwich. As she had hoped, a significant proportion of the lunchtime clientele appeared to be employees of the Anglo-Gulf Bank. Once she had finished the snack, Imogen carried over the glass of water and hopped on a stool next to the bar.

When a group of middle aged men, all displaying their orange identity cards, came to stand next to her, Imogen decided to seize the opportunity. As the bank employee beside her placed his over full glass of lager on the bar top, Imogen swiveled around on her stool, deliberately knocking the drink with her arm. She lunged forward to set the glass back up again, but half of it had already spilt.

'I'm so sorry!' Imogen said loudly, over the noisy chatter of the restaurant. 'Let me buy you another one.' She took out her purse and began to gesture energetically to the serving staff.

'No problem, love,' the man next to her replied. 'But if you insist on getting me a drink. I'm not going to stop you.'

Imogen ordered another beer and the man introduced himself as David. They chatted for a few minutes about the attractions Dubai had to offer. Then Imogen asked him if he worked for the Anglo-Gulf.

'I certainly do,' he replied, swinging his lanyard like a fairground hypnotist. 'Been

181

working over here about ten years now. I was in London before that, as you can probably tell from the accent.' He was, most likely, in his early forties, although his hair was noticeably thinning and this made him seem older.

'Oh,' she said, with surprise in her voice. 'You might know a friend of mine who used to work at the Bank - Richard Fleming. Well, it was his wife who was my friend really. It was absolutely tragic what happened to them.'

'Oh yes, I knew Richard all right. I don't reckon there was anyone at the Bank who didn't.' David took a swig of his pint. 'No one would wish that fate on another living soul, but as I'm sure you know, he could be a bloody difficult person to be around sometimes.'

'I often thought Isla had to be a saint to put up with it. But I always wondered why his employers tolerated him. I heard there was some kind of scandal back in Scotland, before they even moved out here to Dubai,' Imogen rambled on innocently.

'I don't know about that. What I do know is he made shed loads of money for us. For a long time it was with no questions asked.' He gave her an exaggerated wink.

'Was he involved in anything illegal then?'

'It probably wasn't against any laws when Fleming started his career. Back in those days you took every bit of business you could get. But Richard had a reputation for being a bit free and easy with the checks on where the biggest funds were coming from. He wasn't the only one up to it, by any means. Times have certainly changed. The yanks and the F.C.A are coming down on us like a ton of bricks nowadays. If these agencies find out you're 'aiding and abetting' criminal organisations, the bank gets fined millions and you get thrown in the slammer.'

'So Richard's style of banking was on the out,' Imogen responded quietly.

'I assumed it was one of the reasons he left Dubai,' David continued. 'Things were starting to get a bit hot - and I'm not talking about the climate, if you know what I mean.' He started to laugh and leant in a bit closer, his beery breath warming her face.

Imogen hastily excused herself and rushed out to the ladies toilets. She had to stand in front of the sink with both hands resting on the basin for several minutes before finally calming down. It felt as if she was close to unearthing something significant. Imogen was now wondering if she should perhaps be passing this information on to Detective Inspector Zanco, whose card was still in the bottom of her handbag somewhere.

After splashing cold water on her face Imogen walked out of the rest rooms and headed purposefully towards the hotel's exit. She remained close to the far wall and maintained a quick pace, looking down at the floor, just in case David spotted her trying to leave.

As Imogen passed a shadowy alcove, which must once have housed a public telephone booth, in the days before smartphones became ubiquitous, she was almost pulled off her feet when something gripped Imogen's lower arm, jerking her forcefully into the depths of the dark recess.

A hand was covering her mouth and an arm expertly secured her upper body in a firm, but not painful, hold. Imogen heard a low, transatlantic drawl whisper into her right ear. 'My name is Adam Frost and I work for the DIFC. I'm going to release you in a couple of seconds. Then I will show you my ID card, OK?'

Imogen moved her body in what felt like a nodding motion.

'When I remove my hand, I want you to remain very still and quiet, agreed?'

As soon as Imogen was released from his grasp she took in a long, deep breath, but did not utter a word. The man displayed a U.S government identity card and then asked her to accompany him to his car so they could have a talk in private. Terrified she may have got herself into serious trouble, she shuffled along beside him with her head bowed, like a disobedient child on their way to see the Headmaster.

He directed them towards a dark grey German executive car with tinted windows. Imogen was guided into the back. The suited man ducked into the front passenger seat and decisively shut the door.

He was youngish looking, perhaps in his mid-thirties at most. With his freshly shaven face and neatly cropped hair he appeared surprisingly clean-cut. He possessed a wiry frame that for some reason would never have made Imogen think he was a Federal Agent.

'As I told you back there, Ma'am, I work at the Department for the Investigation of Industrial Fraud and Criminality. I'm over here in the U.A.E with the rest of my team, working in conjunction with the local authorities. It's come to our attention that you've been asking a lot of questions about the late Richard Fleming.' He paused for a second, twisting himself around to address her directly. 'Can you explain why you have been doing that Ma'am?'

Imogen found herself squirming like a worm on a hook. Desperate to regain some kind of poise she sat upright and replied, 'well, it's a little difficult to explain. You see my brother has taken on the role of guardian to Richard Fleming's son, Cameron. In an unofficial capacity, of course. My name is Imogen Croft, by the way, and my brother is called Michael. But there was something about the boy I didn't like. Because he seemed to be playing such a significant part in Michael's life at the moment, I just thought, while we were here, I might find out some more about his family background...' Imogen let her words trail away as she sensed her explanation was sounding rather feeble.

'I know exactly who you are, Mrs Croft. You were born in Glasgow, Scotland in 1970. You now live in Essex, England, with your husband and three children. Your eldest son, Ewan, is currently studying Physics with additional Math at the University of Manchester.' When he saw her mouth drop open in surprise, Adam Frost continued, 'I am working as part of a very large operation, Mrs Croft. I have been in close contact with Detective Inspector Zanco of the Strathclyde Police. As soon as your family arrived here five days ago, there has been an agent keeping tabs on you, because of your connection to the Fleming case. When you began asking questions, it really shook things up back at my office in the States.'

'I don't actually know anything much about the Flemings at all. I was just acting on a hunch, really. I'm terribly sorry if I've caused your team any difficulties.'

Frost suddenly looked as if he was trying not to smile. 'If I tell you a certain amount of what we know, can I encourage you to leave things to the professionals from now on and take your family back home?'

Imogen nodded vigorously.

'OK, well you've stumbled into an investigation that's been operating for the last five years. The DIFC are primarily concerned with identifying institutions that have been allowing criminals to 'launder' their illegally obtained funds. Frustratingly, we have found that your UK banks are lagging behind in stamping this practice out. Are you aware, Mrs Croft that criminal gangs process £10 billion worth of 'dirty' cash through your banks and financial service providers every year?'

She shook her head, genuinely amazed by this statistic.

'The Government of Dubai is very keen to ensure that banks operating here are cleaning up their act. We have a dossier full of individuals who we believe have, either through negligence or deliberate felonious intent, allowed money to be processed, filtered and then 're-packaged', when in actually fact, it was earned through highly illegal activities. In several of these cases we have identified employees within the banking community who were willing to testify against the people paying them to legitimize their funds. This was in return for a lighter prison sentence, of course.'

'Was Richard Fleming one of those employees?'

'There have been three men over the past five

years who were ready and willing to give detailed testimony against these criminal gangs. Unfortunately for us, none of the cases that we carefully prepared for trial has ever reached a court-room. This is because each one of the three individuals who were primed to give evidence, is now dead.'

24

Imogen sat absolutely still in the rear seat of the US government vehicle, feeling numb. What had begun as a little harmless digging had led her to a place where she was completely out of her depth. While she was mentally chastising herself for her naivety, Imogen almost missed the rest of Adam Frost's explanation. He had already told her how two years ago, another financial services operative was on the verge of giving evidence against a large drug cartel. But then the chauffeur driven car which was taking him to a business meeting in Oman was involved in a head-on collision with a truck. There were no survivors of the accident.

Frost had just spoken a name that Imogen recognised. 'Sorry,' she interrupted, trying to remain focused. 'Who was that other man you just mentioned?'

'The very first witness who we managed to persuade to give evidence for us, worked for an oil and gas company in Abu Dhabi. His role had been to create false business credentials for a gang of people traffickers. Even his own bosses had absolutely no idea of what he was up to. We'd collected an awful lot of evidence against these people, who were part of a truly nasty organisation. Then the guy goes out to one of the rigs in a Chinook and it crash lands in the sea.

All of our painstaking work was for nothing. Keith Bennett the guy was called. We all thought it was simply a piece of incredibly bad luck. But now, with the Flemings an' all, it's beginning to look suspiciously like a pattern.'

Imogen decided not to admit to Adam Frost that she knew anything about Keith Bennett. In case he started to think that looked like a pattern too.

'These accidents must all have been thoroughly investigated at the time they occurred. I simply cannot see how these criminal gangs could have orchestrated them.'

'That is why no one made any connections between the deaths until a few months ago. We still don't know exactly how it was done. But we're certainly looking into it,' Frost explained. 'Mrs Croft, the various outfits we are trying to prosecute are run by very dangerous people. A great deal of money is a stake for them if we manage to uncover their networks and methods. I strongly recommend you take your family back to England on the next available flight. If we have picked up on your interest in Mr Fleming, then others will have noticed it too.'

Imogen nodded her head solemnly.

As she was about to open the car door, Frost brusquely added, 'just one more piece of advice before you go, Imogen - from one investigator to another. Your questioning technique requires a total overhaul. You need to take it a little more 'softly, softly' out there, otherwise you'll end up getting yourself into a situation it's gonna be damned tricky to get out of.'

Imogen gave Adam Frost a fleeting smile,

189

stepping out onto the empty pavement. She knew full well she'd just been provided with some extremely wise counsel. Although, she didn't think it would be possible for them to change their travel details at this late stage. They were leaving in 48 hours as it was. Surely they'd be safe in the meantime?

It was after dinner before Imogen got an opportunity to recount her brush with the US authorities to Hugh. She waited until they were standing out on the balcony of their guest bedroom and then provided him with all the details.

'It's certainly a remarkable story,' he whispered quietly.

'So, Inspector Zanco knew about Richard Fleming's involvement with the American investigation the whole time,' Imogen supplied.

'How on earth did these criminals manage to engineer the crash? It seems terrifying that they could have some kind of connection on Garansay. It makes you feel as if none of us are safe.'

'Exactly. I just wonder if Cameron knows anything about this. I did ask Agent Frost if he was aware Richard Fleming was most likely abusing his wife. He told me the men prepared to give evidence for them were often not very pleasant people themselves. Otherwise, they wouldn't have got involved with the gangs in the first place. His department needed to work with them so that the courts could bring even worse individuals to justice.'

'It's all relative, I suppose. So are we in trouble for meddling in official police business?'

'I don't think so, but I've definitely been

warned off. He told me to get on the next flight home.'

'We're going on Saturday morning. Is that early enough?'

'As long as we keep our heads down, it'll have to be.'

Imogen experienced a restless night as the facts she'd learnt about Richard Fleming swam around in her head. When she finally dropped off to sleep Imogen had an unsettling dream in which she was in a helicopter over water. It was one of those military style aircraft that drop supplies in war-torn countries. Suddenly, someone told her she'd got to parachute out. Imogen started arguing with everyone around her and then abruptly woke up, with her heart racing away inside her chest.

What she concluded, in the early hours of the morning, was that Fleming had probably been involved in his dodgy practices even when he was still based in Scotland. Imogen now believed that one of his colleagues back then must have been on to him. It would have been them who he got into a fight with in the restaurant in Glasgow. If that was true, Fleming most likely requested a transfer to the Middle East himself, before his activities were uncovered. But this remained supposition.

Imogen contemplated the nature of living in this remote and unworldly place. The Fleming family found themselves detached from their family back home in Perthshire and the pals they had made in Glasgow. Isla, certainly, would have been very isolated in Dubai, particularly as she was a shy woman who did not make friends easily.   These circumstances must have been a Godsend to a bully like Richard. Abusers thrived in situations where their victims were cut off from family and friends. Imogen was still unsure whether she felt sorry for Cameron or not. He, along with his sister and mother were innocently caught up in events beyond their control. They paid a terribly high price for Richard Fleming's actions.

It was the Crofts' last day staying with the Princes and their hosts had made plans for them. Howard announced a surprise over breakfast. He and Liz were going to take the youngsters up to the Dreamland Aqua Park, which lay several kilometres to the north-east. Hugh and Imogen were enthusiastically informed that Howard had arranged for them to have use of the company's motor cruiser for the day, which was moored at a marina further down the coast. Their offspring were so excited about the arrangement that Imogen felt they couldn't possibly refuse.

It was without the eagerness one might usually expect, that Hugh and Imogen set out for a day of luxury cruising.

'We're supposed to be keeping a low profile,' Hugh muttered, as they sat in the back of a taxi, on their way down the busy Al Jumeira Road, which ran parallel to the stunning Dubai coastline.

'We still can. Once we get out into open water, nobody's going to see us.'

When they arrived at the Sailing Club and caught sight of the boat, it became clear how tricky it was going to be to remain inconspicuous. The cruiser was absolutely huge.

The entire stern of the vessel had been devoted to a large outdoor dining area furnished with cream leather seats and shiny glass tables.

As they climbed aboard and slid their sun glasses on, Hugh commented through gritted teeth, 'Great, we are going to spend the day looking like international drug dealers ourselves.'

Imogen giggled, in spite of their predicament. 'Let's just cast off as quickly as we can. We could always head out towards the artificial islands they've just constructed. I'd be quite interested to have a closer look at those.'

Hugh took the helm whilst Imogen jumped down onto the jetty to untie the ropes. As she gazed back up at her husband, in his casual sailing attire and with his now deeply tanned complexion, she noted how handsome he still was. This was the first time they'd enjoyed a trip on their own together for over a year. It seemed a good idea to make the most of it.

Imogen padded along the wooden boards to the bow of the boat. When she'd pushed the vessel sufficiently clear of the pontoon, Imogen leapt aboard, immediately bending down to wind up the line which was tethering them to the vessel's mooring. Having completed the task, she arose from her crouching position and briefly rested her arms on the shiny silver rails that formed an arrow, pointing north-east towards the perfectly still expanse of sea which lay ahead.

Then, Imogen heard a splash from the starboard side of the boat, as if something large had fallen into the water. Instinctively, she ducked down below the gunwales. Keeping low, she edged her way, slowly but surely, towards

193

the stern.

Imogen could make out the sound of lowered voices, which seemed to be coming from inside the cabin. Resisting an urge to call out for Hugh, she felt above her for one of the small, rounded portholes and took a risk by raising her head up to get a look inside.

Two dark figures were rummaging around within the galley area. She dropped back down onto her haunches and tried to come up with a plan. They'd been travelling very slowly since they launched so she couldn't imagine the boat was too far out from shore. Imogen contemplated making a jump for it when she sensed the boat sway to the portside, as if someone else had just climbed on board.

The men inside the cabin must have thought the exact same thing, as they were beginning to move rapidly back up top. Knowing that danger was imminent, but not having any idea of how to evade it Imogen remained in her bent position, frozen with fear. She heard shouting and following this, the unmistakable sound of a single, piercing gunshot.

After an initial silence, the boat was filled with the clatter of heavy footfalls. Imogen could faintly discern muffled shouts and then realised she'd still got both hands clamped tightly over her ears. When she prised them away, the shouting became clearer.

'Mrs Croft, where are you, Mrs Croft?'

Imogen recognised the transatlantic drawl so she stood up slowly from her hiding place. From this position she could see Adam Frost, stepping unsurely across the cruiser's deck in her direction.   'Where is Hugh!' She hollered.

'He is receiving medical treatment on the

patrol boat. But don't be alarmed, your husband
will be absolutely fine.'

25

After being thoroughly reprimanded by Agent Frost for not having left Dubai as they were told, he filled them in on what happened. It appeared that Hugh witnessed very little of the events. As he was guiding the boat out of its mooring, holding the wheel and leaning out to the starboard side to gain a clearer view of the route ahead, he felt a sharp blow to the side of his temple. He lost consciousness straight away and tumbled overboard into the bay.

Luckily, the agent who was keeping them under surveillance immediately notified the local police patrol boat, which came up in their wake and pulled Hugh out of the water.

In the meantime, two intruders had gone down into the cabin of the cruiser. Frost said he believed they were looking for Imogen. It all occurred very fast, according to the agents. They managed to jump on board within minutes of the men and when one of them made a lunge for a local policeman, he was shot in the shoulder. Both of the assailants had now been apprehended and taken away for questioning.

'This is the first arrest we've had in this case for several months,' Frost added. 'We should be able to get valuable information from these men. But it is not safe for you to remain here in Dubai. This time, I'm going to escort you to the airport myself.'

'What did they want with us?' Imogen asked

quietly.

'They wanted you dead, Mrs Croft. You've been asking questions about their operations and making it look as if you know what it is they're up to. It wouldn't be in their interests to allow you to keep on doing that, I'm afraid.'

'Could you have someone go and pick up our children from the Aqua Park? I think I'd like to leave this place right now.'

'I'm very glad to hear it,' Frost retorted. 'I do believe that - what is it you English say? - the penny has finally dropped.'

*

The next couple of hours passed in something of a blur. The story Imogen told the Princes was that Hugh's mother had been suddenly taken ill and they needed to return to the UK immediately. They also had to explain away Hugh's bandaged head by saying he slipped on the boat and had to spend most of the day at the hospital.

Imogen felt terrible about having to lie to Chloe's parents in that way, but there seemed to be no alternative. Imogen made Agent Frost promise to keep a close eye on the Prince family, just in case her stupid actions had somehow made them a target for the gang. Frost agreed to put a surveillance team on them, but suggested Imogen's concerns were probably groundless. With their hastily packed bags and a group of highly disgruntled teenagers in tow, Imogen and Hugh said their farewells to Chloe and her parents at Dubai Airport.

Just as they were about to check in the luggage, Liz retrieved a folded up A4 sized envelope from her handbag. 'I nearly forgot. When I met up with some of the British Club ladies for coffee the other day, the woman you were talking to at the Country Club was there. She was asking after you and told me to give you this. Apparently, it's some letters and cards from Isla Fleming. Stella Hargreaves wondered if you would pass them on to Isla's mother, as they are no longer of any use to her.'

Imogen thanked Liz and stuffed the package into the large suitcase, just before it got hauled onto the conveyor belt. They had to prise Ewan away from Chloe, who was staying on in Dubai with her mum and dad until the end of the holidays. Then they ran at full pelt towards their boarding gate before it closed. When the plane finally lifted them high above the surrounding desert, Imogen was really quite relieved to be heading back home.

*

The drop in temperature was noticeable as soon as they arrived in England. Even though it was still the last few days of August, it already felt autumnal. The remainder of the weekend was spent preparing Bridie and Ian for their imminent return to school. Ewan decided to go back to his shared digs in Manchester a couple of weeks ahead of the start of term, so his travel plans needed to be arranged.

Imogen had very little time to think about the Flemings, or even her brother Michael over the following week. Then, one morning in early

September, when Hugh had left for work, taking the children to school on the way, she found herself in a peaceful house with time to reflect on the events of the previous month.

Their modern detached house was at the end of a bumpy track in the small rural hamlet of Cooper's End. It lay about a mile and a half from the pretty village of Mundon. The large windows that ran across the length of the living room and kitchen provided an excellent view over Cooper's Creek. The Creek itself was a sleepy and tranquil tributary of the River Blackwater, which reached a picturesque conclusion in the busy market town of Maldon, just a ten minute drive along the Mundon Road from there.

The days in which the late summer gradually transformed itself into autumn were Imogen's favourite time of the year. They were still treated to impressive sunsets out across the water to the west, but the whole of the Dengie peninsula became covered in a blanket of freshly fallen leaves of golden brown. If you could brave the muddier footpaths leading through farmer's fields, it was the perfect season for a brisk walk.

Before Imogen set out in her wellie boots on this crisp and sunny Monday morning, she decided to give Hugh's father a call. She had a couple of questions to ask him.

They'd had to confess to Hugh's parents about the little white lie they told the Princes in order to leave the UAE early. The youngsters had insisted on visiting their Gran immediately, in order to check she was okay. When the children were out of earshot, Hugh and Imogen told Kath and Gerry the full story about the Flemings and the investigation they'd been caught up in before their accident last December. Hugh did not inform his mum and dad of their close encounter with organised criminals, merely that they'd been advised to return to the UK at the earliest opportunity, for their own safety.

Gerry Croft had a long career as a bank manager before he'd retired just over ten years ago. Hugh's father provided them with valuable insights into the banking world that Richard Fleming was tied up in. Imogen now wondered if the fact Fleming had been involved in illegal practices at his bank might mean Cameron's inheritance would be affected. When he answered her call she posed her father-in-law that very question.

Gerry considered the point for a few moments before responding, 'I should think it probably would. Certainly whatever funds were in Fleming's current account and came from his earnings at the bank would very likely be seized. However, what you generally find with people who are up to their necks in dodgy deals is they put a large chunk of their money into bank accounts and property in their wife's name. If that's been the case here then Cameron will be able to inherit those assets directly from his mother.'

'I see,' Imogen replied thoughtfully. They chatted about the garden for a while and Gerry's plans to help them prepare their plot for the winter. With this joint resolution they ended the conversation.

Imogen put on her jacket and set out along the single track lane before turning left and joining up with St Peter's way, the public footpath that led along the coastline to the ancient chapel at Bradwell. Not intending to walk quite as far as that today, Imogen continued for a mile or so until reaching the now disused Anglo-Saxon Church of Mundon St Mary. It was a place Imogen always visited when she wanted to be able to think in peace.

Imogen often imagined it must be one of the most remotely sited churches in England. It lay a mile outside Mundon, buried away behind a copse of trees and down a long and winding track that seemed to be leading nowhere. You turned a little bend and there it was. Apparently, it once stood in the centre of the village but when the plague struck in 1665 the houses were moved up the hill to their current location, whereas the church stayed put.

The little chapel was in the middle of a piece of marshland. The boggy nature of the environment was blamed for the spread of the epidemic. This became the main reason why the survivors moved themselves away. The sodden terrain certainly meant the surrounding paths were often thick with sludge. A couple of horses in a field behind her turned their heads in mild interest as Imogen trudged past them, breaking the silence of this remote and lonely spot.

St Mary's Church had been recently restored by English Heritage and other charitable organisations. Because services were no longer held regularly there, the renovators had endeavoured to keep the chapel exactly as it would once have been. There was no electricity. As you entered the timber-framed building there was a sign advising visitors to wait a few moments until their eyes adjusted to the dim light before advancing any further inside.

Imogen sat at one of the wooden box pews. As a result of the remoteness of the building, along with its authentic interior, it felt as if she'd been transported back in time by at least a hundred years.

Imogen gazed at the modest altar that lay behind a pair of simple, oak rails. It was a great shame that more people didn't get the chance to experience the humble beauty of this place, she thought. Then it struck her. They had been so busy enjoying the luxury and glitz of the wealthy ex-pat lifestyle in Dubai, appreciating all the trappings that money and privilege could buy you out there. Yet perhaps witnessing all the glamour of the Emirates had caused Imogen to overlook what she believed to be the simplicity of most people's motivations.

When Imogen considered why Pat O'Connell came back to find Michael's father all those years later, she didn't believe it was ever really about the money. He'd taken Mary's cash when he killed her anyway. Pat needed to find Michael's dad, not necessarily to be paid, but because he wanted to tell him how he'd completed the job he was sent out to do. He desperately sought to gain the approval and gratitude of a man he had come to respect and look up to, even in his chaotic and lawless world. That much had been clear to Imogen when he had spoken of his beloved 'Captain' in that cold, black ditch on the hillside.

What if the Fleming case was somehow similar? When considering the fate of the Fleming family and the role of Cameron within it, Imogen had focussed almost solely on Richard Fleming's job and financial crimes. What if the money was just a red-herring, as it surely was with Pat O'Connell? Imogen was not sure how this could be the case or what other motives might have been be at play, but she suddenly sensed there was an angle they'd so far missed.

Imogen's thoughts trailed away as she abruptly realised how cold and damp she was sitting on this bench. Aware now of the dark and isolated surroundings she stood up and strode down the aisle of the chapel, exiting into the now harshly bright sunlight, carefully securing the sturdy wooden latch behind her.

26

The very next morning, Imogen was reminded of how the desire to promote a business ahead of its competitors could be a motivator of crime. This realisation immediately made her question the conclusions she drew yesterday morning in the chapel of St Mary. The desire for money could most certainly lead people to do terrible things.

Imogen received a phone call straight after breakfast from Colin Walmsley. She was surprised to hear from him and hastily imagined something may have happened to Lower Kilduggan Farm. But this was not the reason for him getting in touch. Colin was ringing to let her know that the police on Garansay had made a series of arrests in connection with the man-traps that had been placed on his land.

His tone was sheepish as he explained that the results of the forensic tests carried out on the snares revealed the prints of an individual who was already known to the authorities. The investigation had been stepped up a gear after the death of Pat O'Connell. A full team in Glasgow had been given the job of examining the evidence.

The Strathclyde Police brought the man in for questioning. He admitted to placing the traps on Colin's property. Because he was facing a manslaughter charge the suspect told them everything. It turned out he was in the employ of the development company who were Colin's rival bidders for a piece of prime brownfield land in Ayrshire.

'I had really been playing hardball over the negotiations. Because I was offering to use the land to create local jobs it looked as if my bid was going to be successful. So the competing developer decided to utilize some 'dirty tricks' to encourage me out of the game,' he explained.

'What on earth could they have been intending to achieve?' Imogen felt thoroughly aggrieved on her son's behalf.

'They claimed the intention was purely to create problems for my business, that's all. They thought it might maim a few cattle or get me into difficulties with the local police, which it very nearly did.'

'They must have known there was a danger someone would be badly injured.'

'The director of the company had told the hired thugs to cause difficulties for me by using whatever means they had at their disposal. He suggests they had no idea what these guys were actually planning. It turns out one of the henchmen had a load of ancient man-traps he'd discovered when they did over an old farm a few years back. They just thought they'd get some use out of them, I suppose.'

'Is this Director facing a manslaughter charge?'

'It's complicated because he's saying the traps were not his idea. But the police are certainly attempting to get something to stick.' Colin paused for a second before adding, 'I'm really very sorry, Imogen. I had no idea my plans would lead to something like this happening. I feel as if

I'm partly responsible for the terrible injuries inflicted on Ewan and that old man.'

'You couldn't have known, Colin. It's not a crime to want your business to succeed. I know that Hugh will feel the same as me. Try not to beat yourself up about it.'

'Thank you,' Colin replied quietly.

'How is Julia, by the way? It would be lovely to meet up with her again sometime.'

Colin hesitated for a moment, 'Julia found this whole incident with the traps very unsettling. I've given her a few weeks of paid leave. We are going to have a break from seeing each other for a while.'

'I'm terribly sorry to hear that Colin. It's a real shame.'

'Julia's husband was very work orientated. She always blamed the fact he suffered a heart attack so young on his driving ambition. I think she is reluctant to go down that road again. I certainly can't reproach her for that.'

'I see. How do you feel about it?'

'I'm sad and disappointed because we were having a good time together, Julia is a lovely lass. But I'm not heartbroken. I don't think she was the one for me.'

Imogen was inclined to believe him.

They ended the conversation with promises to remain in regular contact. She didn't think it was the correct moment to mention to Colin what they'd discovered about Richard Fleming. Imogen wasn't totally sure they were allowed to speak to anyone about what they'd learned.

When Hugh arrived home for dinner she eagerly explained how the mystery of the man-traps had at long last been resolved.

'It seems a real shame that Colin and Julia's

relationship didn't survive the episode. It can't be easy for Colin to meet someone when he's permanently based up in that remote valley,' Hugh commented.

'Come on, he's heavily involved with the local pub scene and he plays golf regularly. There will be plenty of local ladies who'll snap him up when they realise he's single again.'

'I suppose you're right. This incident might put Colin off his expansion plans and make him focus more on the Garansay side of his operations. Although, I don't believe he should be deterred, as none of this is actually his fault.'

'I quite agree and I told Colin you would too,' Imogen leant over and gave her husband a brief kiss on the cheek. She was certainly relieved to be back here at home, immersed in her daily routine and away from the dangers they'd faced in the last month. Hugh's head wound was now fully healed, but she felt as if the family had experienced a few too many close calls recently for her liking.

After carrying their coffees to the window seats in the lounge, Imogen shared some of the ideas she'd been forming over the previous few days. 'I know that the pursuit of wealth was the driving force behind this business with the man-traps, but I'm beginning to wonder if money really had anything to do with the fate of the Flemings at all,' Imogen said, whilst stirring the milk into her cup.

Hugh sat up a little straighter in his seat. 'What do you mean?'

'Well, I know Richard Fleming was tied up in all this corruption and criminality. But the

207

reason I was uncomfortable with the official account of the helicopter crash in the first place was because I didn't feel totally convinced by Cameron's version of events. Something just didn't add up when Michael showed me that accident report. I simply wonder if the whole thing had more to do with the domestic situation within that family than it did with Richard's financial dealings.'

'But the connection between the deaths of the other two men who were about to give evidence suggests that criminal gangs were involved in arranging these 'accidents'. That is the whole thrust of the international investigation into the fate of the Flemings. We know only too well what these people are capable of,' Hugh argued.

'I know that's the logical conclusion, but there was no evidence that any tampering had gone on within the helicopter. My question, when Michael showed me the details, was always why Cameron survived in those terrible conditions when the pilot, his parents and sister did not. I just think the key to this whole case revolves around something that occurred on board the flight - somewhere between it taking off from Kilross Harbour and when it pitched into the sea halfway across the Kilbrannan Sound.'

'This all comes down,' Hugh said, placing his empty cup decisively on the side table, 'to the fact you don't like the boy. The evidence categorically points towards foul play from an outside source. We may not yet know how they achieved it in technical terms, but Richard Fleming's paymasters had a role in causing that accident, I'm willing to bet money on it.'

'Stella Hargreaves told me that Cameron was a bully. She said he was arrogant and callous.

But that is not the impression he has been giving us. I know when someone is not being honest with me. Cameron Fleming is a liar and he's hiding something, I just don't know yet what it is.' Imogen sat back defiantly in her chair, staring out across the darkening expanse of motionless water.

'Have you stopped to consider, Mrs Croft,' Hugh added, with the mischievous glint back in his eye, 'that it might just be possible we are both right?'

27

Hugh had to leave early for a conference being held up in London. Imogen gave him a lift to the station, before dropping Bridie and Ian at school. Most of the morning had disappeared before she was able to make a start on any of the domestic chores.

The couple had ended the previous evening's discussion in reasonably good humour, mostly because Hugh now viewed the whole case as an interesting intellectual puzzle. He clearly believed that any role they might once have played in the events was completely over and done with. Hugh was probably right, but until she'd been given categorical proof of how the Fleming's aircraft ended up crashing into the sea, Imogen would always be searching for answers. Hugh did carefully point out, as dusk had fallen and they sat quietly in the resultant half-light, that they may never discover what really happened on that terrible night. But Imogen wasn't quite ready to accept it.

It was a mild but dull day, without the clear crispness one would usually associate with this time of the year. There was a melancholy mist hanging over the Creek. Imogen found herself unable to settle on any meaningful task. She finally made the decision to shift the empty suitcases back up into the loft, from where they had been temporarily stored in an unstable pile in the corner of Ewan's bedroom. As Imogen lifted the luggage out onto the landing she was abruptly reminded of the package that Stella Hargreaves wanted her to pass on to Isla Fleming's mother.

Imogen had been putting off the job of dealing with Stella's request as she was not sure if it would be tactful to simply send the envelope to Isla's mother in the post. Imogen thought perhaps it would be more sensitive to add an accompanying letter to explain things a little, but drew a blank as to what words she could possibly write to the poor lady.

Going over to the bedside drawer and lifting out the large envelope, Imogen turned it over in her hands. Not previously wishing to open a correspondence which was intended for someone else she hadn't really taken a proper look at the package since returning from Dubai. Now, however, she could see it was not actually sealed down but that the sticky flap had been left open. The front of the bundle carried no text or label. On a sudden whim, Imogen tipped the whole thing up and shook the contents out onto the bed.

The pile of letters and cards she was expecting did not appear. Instead, within the larger envelope were two smaller ones. Imogen picked them both up. There was a letter bearing the name of Mrs Nancy Cook which was bulging and heavy. She placed it down with care on the bedside table. The other note was thinner. Imogen was surprised to observe, when looking more closely, that it was addressed to her. Taking a few deep breaths to steady her rising heart rate, she sat back against the pillows and tore it open.

It was a letter from Stella Hargreaves, composed in a neat and clear script. It began with the explanation that she felt compelled to write to Imogen after their brief conversation at the afternoon tea party. Stella felt she hadn't given her the full picture about their relationship with the Flemings. In order to provide a more accurate account, she was now setting out the details of an incident which had taken place a couple of years back, while their two families were still neighbours and good friends.

Stella explained how it was certainly true when she told Imogen her husband fell out with Richard Fleming at a dinner party. But this, she said, would not have been enough in itself for her to end her relationship with Isla, whom she had always liked and would not have blamed for her husband's many shortcomings. Instead, their friendship faltered over an unpleasant episode that occurred several weeks later.

It was a very hot day during the school holidays. Isla had invited Stella and her son and daughter over to spend the day cooling off in their pool. Stella's children were the same age as Cameron and Lucy. The youngsters had always seemed to get on. The kids spent most of the day in the water or lounging on recliners at the poolside, sipping homemade lemonade. It appeared to be the perfect kind of arrangement. Stella admitted that she and Isla were sitting on the patio behind the house, slowly drinking chilled white wine for most of the afternoon, leaving the teenagers to their own devices.

A little later on, the children all disappeared inside. The ladies didn't hear very much from them for about an hour or so. Then, sometime in the early evening, when the heat had begun to recede and the shadows started to lengthen across the Fleming's arid garden, Stella's daughter had come running out of the house, promptly informing her mother she was ready to go home. The women had drunk a fair amount by this stage and were tired and frazzled by the heat so Stella had been a little short with her. But then she looked more closely at the teenager, who was now fully dressed and had the glistening sheen of tears in her eyes.

Quickly sobering up, Stella took her children back home, setting her son in front of the television and hustling her daughter straight upstairs. It took a little while to wheedle it out of her. The young girl finally told her mother that whilst they were listening to music in his bedroom, Cameron Fleming had held her down on the bed and tried to kiss her. She said it had started as a bit of a game but then he became too rough and she didn't like it. She'd kicked him in the shin and locked herself in the bathroom - shouting that she would tell on him if he tried to do it again. The girl then pulled up her sleeves and showed her mother the bruises on her arms, where Cameron had gripped brutally at her skin.

Stella questioned her daughter fiercely but the girl insisted he hadn't done anything else except try to kiss her. Ultimately, she accepted this was probably true, although Stella couldn't say what may have happened if her daughter had not got free of him. Unsure of what action she should take following the attack, Stella wrote that she simply did what most of us do in these types of situations. She broke off contact with the family and eventually, when the opportunity arose, they moved away. Stella never told her husband as he would have gone for the boy and got them into a worse predicament as a result. She added that Dubai was not a place where you wanted to find yourself in trouble with the police.

Stella concluded her account by declaring she felt duty bound to inform Imogen of what Cameron Fleming had done, particularly if they were going to remain in contact with the boy in future. As soon as Liz mentioned that Imogen had a daughter the same age as hers, Stella realised she had no choice in the matter. She suggested that if Imogen wanted to find out any more regarding the boy, she should speak with his old housemaster, who retired back to the UK the previous year. Stella supplied his contact details and added he was an honourable and decent man who always dealt very fairly with her own son.

When Imogen finished reading Stella's frank, carefully constructed letter she watched it drop from her hand and settle, still and harmless looking onto the duvet in front of her. It could be an extremely unpleasant experience to have one's suspicions confirmed and it offered no sense of satisfaction. Imogen sat in a kind of daze for several minutes, running through all of the occasions Cameron had been alone with her daughter. Despite replaying the whole of their Garansay holiday several times over, she couldn't think of any situation in which his behaviour towards Bridie was inappropriate. In fact, Imogen was far more inclined to imagine that her daughter had been keen on him and not vice-versa.

This information would continue to prey on

her mind. However, Imogen was fairly certain that nothing untoward had ever taken place between Cameron and Bridie. She had no doubt that if the boy had tried anything on with Chloe she would have let them all know about it pretty quickly.

Of course, during their stay at Lower Kilduggan Farm the place was always very busy. The opportunity to commit such an assault had never arisen. Cameron also appeared to have been on his best behaviour on the holiday, which she sensed was primarily for Michael's benefit. For this small mercy, Imogen supposed she should be grateful. The details of the assault that Stella described in her letter made it fairly certain abuse must have occurred within the Fleming family. Young boys simply didn't behave in that way unless they'd witnessed or experienced something similar themselves.

Imogen felt as if she now possessed almost all the pieces of the puzzle. A picture was beginning to form. Richard Fleming, at the head of the family, was a secretive man, difficult to get along with and sometimes violent. He was involved in financial fraud and the net was rapidly closing in on him. At the time he attended the wedding on Garansay, knowing he would soon have to give evidence against extremely dangerous men, he must have been feeling pretty desperate. His wife, Isla, was a weak and timid woman, bullied by both her husband and her son. She was isolated from family and friends. Her daughter Lucy was, most likely, her only solace. Lucy's character remained a mystery. Imogen sincerely hoped she was not herself a victim of her father

215

and brother. Regardless of that, the girl's life was undoubtedly cut far too short.

Which left Cameron.

Was he an abuser or a victim? Imogen was starting to think it possible he was both. She had seen with her own eyes that Cameron shed heart-wrenching tears of grief for his lost family. But perhaps his anguish was caused by something else. Could it have been triggered by remorse instead, or guilt even? How much did Cameron know about his father's crimes? Was the boy aware of just how much peril Richard had placed them in through his selfish actions?

Hugh may have believed they would never find out the answers to these questions but Imogen wasn't willing to accept that was true. Stella had handed her a line of inquiry to pursue. Imogen was going to do her the service of making sure she investigated it thoroughly. Imogen thought she had a good idea of what passed between the Fleming family on that brief and fateful helicopter journey but just needed a little more evidence to see if she was right.

28

Dr Barron lived in a pleasant little village called Wissington, which lay just on the border between Essex and Suffolk. Situated in the Stour Valley, the river meandered aimlessly past this sleepy hamlet. It seemed to Imogen like the perfect place to spend your retirement. It took her just over an hour to drive there, as the roads beyond Colchester were terribly slow. As Imogen pulled up outside a pretty whitewashed cottage, half-hidden behind an overgrown but attractive front garden, she felt the journey was worth it.

Dr Barron was a smallish man, neatly turned out and clearly quite bookish. At first, Imogen was taken aback by his unassuming demeanour. She wondered how on earth he was able to command the discipline and respect of a group of adolescent boys. But after speaking with him, she realised that his appearance belied a commanding presence. Once he had furnished them with a fresh pot of coffee, the retired teacher needed little prompting to provide Imogen with bountiful information about his former students.

'I'm surprised that no one had come to speak with me before now,' Dr Barron stated, as they sat in front of a small fireplace, where a large brown Labrador had spread itself out in front of the grate. 'As soon as I read about the accident and how young Cameron was saved, I expected the police to be knocking at my door, looking for a character reference.'

'I don't believe that was felt to be necessary. The inquiry focussed mainly on the technical reasons for the crash, Dr Barron.'

'Oh yes, I know that. It's just I had filled in so many damned forms about the boy and his really rather odd behaviour. I simply thought I might be required to elaborate on them. We spend so much time ticking boxes and writing up notes about these difficult students, I suppose it makes one develop the vanity of assuming they will actually be read and used by someone,' Barron chuckled to himself at this maxim.

'So you considered Cameron Fleming to be a difficult student?'

'Most certainly, and I wasn't the only member of staff who thought so. He was nearly excluded on several occasions. You probably wish to know how his behaviour manifested itself. If I were forced to sum it up, I would say he possessed a rather short temper and a proclivity towards violent outbursts.'

Imogen had been better prepared than usual for this meeting and brought along a pad and pencil. She jotted this information down, looking up and prompting, 'could you give me any examples, Dr Barron?'

Clearly used to addressing people who were at the same time taking notes, Barron adopted the practice of pausing every few moments, in order to allow his companion to catch up. As a one-time teacher herself, this idiosyncrasy made Imogen smile.

'Mostly they were trivial misdemeanours, like hacking another boy's leg in football matches or scuffles in the dorm. But once, there was a case of a first-former receiving a bloodied nose. That was the most recent incident which nearly got him expelled.'

'Why was he allowed to stay on?'

'I'm not a cynical person Mrs Croft, so I won't suggest it was the attraction of his father's money. Cameron was a bit of an oddity. He was inclined to these unpleasant episodes but at other times the boy could be delightful. He was a bright young man, sporty and very good-looking. He had won a great deal of honours for the school during his time there. The Headmaster wanted to give him one last chance, out of a genuine liking for the lad.' Barron sighed.

'I'm finding it hard to picture this school being out in the Middle East. As you're describing it the picture forming in my head is more like a scene from Harry Potter!' Imogen couldn't resist adding.

'That's an interesting observation, Mrs Croft. Other than the oppressive heat and a number of local students, we were in essence a quintessential English public school. The families who worked out in Dubai wanted it to be that way, you see. They yearned for their children to have the privileged educations they benefitted from themselves. The result was a set up that to the rest of the world must appear very artificial.'

'How did Cameron behave towards girls,' Imogen asked, as tactfully as possible. 'Could his conduct ever be viewed as *inappropriate*?'

'Now that is a question I cannot answer. I ran a single-sex House. Cameron was very much a boy's boy if that makes any sense. He was primarily interested in sailing and football and not much else as far as I could ever tell. Although he kept up with his studies well enough and gained himself a decent set of A-Levels at the end of it all. In fact, I taught him Senior Chemistry for a time and found him a good, solid student.'

Feeling that the retired Housemaster's insights were proving invaluable, Imogen decided to ask his opinion about something else. 'Dr Barron, what did you make of Cameron's relationship with his family? You must have had a reasonable number of dealings with them.'

'Ah, now therein lay the enigma of Cameron Fleming. His father, Richard was a truly dreadful man. He was always complaining about how we handled things and never willing to take responsibility for the boy's actions himself. He was a totally humourless chap as far as I could tell. His mother, on the other hand, was a sensitive and quiet woman. I dealt with her a great deal over the years Cameron was with us and I liked her. She was well-read and cultured. I counted her as a friend. I was deeply saddened by the news of her death and that of her lovely young daughter.'

Imogen thanked Dr Barron for his time and his help. As she proceeded along the cottage's uneven pathway towards the car, the old teacher surprised her by suddenly shouting from the doorway.

'Tell Cameron to come and visit me here some time. He's got the address and he knows that my boys will always receive a warm welcome.'

Driving back home through the winding, leaf

strewn lanes, past watermills and ancient ramparts Imogen mulled over this new testimony. Interestingly, she felt as if Dr Barron's description of the boy was the closest she'd heard so far to the Cameron who spent the summer with them on Garansay. Imogen could certainly recognise the contradictions embedded within the boy's personality. Barron clearly still held some affection for him and Michael and Hugh both identified a certain quality in Cameron that encouraged them to want to defend the lad, even at times to protect him.

The idea that Cameron was a product of his parents, with their vastly differing personalities, was an assessment she found extremely convincing. Oddly enough, Imogen had set out that morning expecting to receive proof Cameron Fleming was some kind of monster. Instead, she'd discovered he was a human being just like the rest of them, albeit a complicated young man who tended to divide opinion amongst those who had known him.

Later in the day, Bridie and Ian were unusually talkative about the onerous requirements of homework and the onset of GGCE courses. Their chatter cut through Imogen's thoughts. But it didn't much matter because she had already formed a plan. Imogen had been debating whether or not she should inform Michael about the incident that occurred between Stella Hargreaves' daughter and Cameron Fleming.

When she showed Hugh the letter last night he was adamant they should not. He felt it would upset Michael unnecessarily and that if Cameron really was trying to redeem himself, there would be little or no point in it.

After her meeting with Dr Barron, she'd decided not to be too hasty in denouncing the boy to her brother as this would most certainly end their relationship. Imogen would like to have a little more to go on before delivering that unpleasant piece of news and causing Michael any kind of upset. She would also like to have something more solid with which to approach D.I. Zanco of the Strathclyde Police who had, after all, told her to inform him immediately if she discovered anything untoward about Cameron Fleming.

So tomorrow morning Imogen was going on a trip. Kath and Gerry were prepared to mind the children for a couple of days whilst she headed back to the country of her youth. Imogen would need to begin the jaunt at the crack of dawn to reach her destination before nightfall because she was travelling to the pleasant but functional little town of Dunkeld in Perthshire, which was at least another hour's drive beyond Edinburgh.

It was a place she hadn't visited in decades and was set amongst the most stunning scenery. But it wasn't as a tourist that she was making this journey. It was to deliver a letter to Isla Fleming's elderly mother. A job entrusted to her by Stella Hargreaves and one she had a duty to undertake in person. There was another motivation to this apparently burdensome task. Imogen would be hoping to gain an insight into the personality of Cameron Fleming from his closest living relative; the only person still alive who knew exactly what he was like.

29

It was late yesterday evening when Imogen finally arrived in Dunkeld. She stayed overnight in a Georgian guesthouse, just beyond Thomas Telford's stone bridge over the River Tay, on the main northerly route out of the town. Imogen had a lovely double room. It felt extravagant to spend a night away by herself. She had arranged to meet Nancy Cook at 11 o'clock that morning for coffee. Isla's mother told her it would be better to come to her home. Imogen intended to explore the place for an hour or so before getting down to the real purpose of the visit.

Taking a stroll to the market place, Imogen immediately spotted the imposing Celtic cross which stood in the centre of this wide thoroughfare. Finding a small bakery across the street, she chose some little cakes to take with her. Imogen recalled that when she and Hugh were last here, they had visited the Cathedral. If she remembered rightly, the whole area was very significant to the early Christian church in Scotland. There was a monastery situated close by too.

This must have been a good place for Isla to grow up in. The town seemed to possess a friendly atmosphere. What a terrible piece of bad luck for her that she ended up marrying a person like Richard Fleming. Her life could have turned out so differently if she hadn't, or even if she'd had sufficient support around her to be able to leave him and start over again. There was no point in thinking like that now.

When it was time for her appointment with Mrs Cook, she looked carefully at the map and set off in what she believed to be the right direction. Isla's mother's house was situated in the middle of a modern terrace. Although small, it appeared to be neat and well kept. The lady who answered the door was petit and really quite frail. Imogen followed her into a tiny sitting room crammed full of photographs and ornaments. The old-fashioned television was almost completely obscured by a tall and leafy potted plant which was clearly far too big for the space.

Imogen offered to make the coffees. As she navigated her way around the unfamiliar but well-appointed kitchen, Imogen suddenly hoped that this lady had received a decent bequest from the Fleming's will. She made a mental note to ask Michael about it. Carrying a tray with two steaming mugs and a plate full of the pastries she brought with her, Imogen settled into an armchair in front of Nancy Cook and began to dish out the refreshments.

'So you are Michael's sister?' The elderly lady said in a lilting Scots accent. 'I can definitely see the resemblance.'

'That is certainly what people say.' Imogen had no intention of confusing this good natured lady by explaining her true blood connection to Michael. Instead she stated, 'Mrs Cook, while my family and I were on holiday in Dubai, we met up with someone who had been friends with your daughter.'

'Oh yes,' Nancy replied warily.

'The woman was called Stella. She gave me an envelope full of letters and cards belonging to Isla. She wanted me to pass them on to you, but if you would rather not have them I would perfectly understand.'

She took a few moments to react. 'I would like to have them, please. I have plenty of photos and cards from before the family went abroad. If I'm honest, I heard very little from them after they had gone.'

Imogen removed the package from her bag and handed it over.

Nancy placed it carefully on the coffee table next to her. 'Thank you, my dear, for coming all this way to give it to me.'

Imogen smiled, relieved that Nancy was not as distressed as she thought she might be. 'It must be of great comfort to you to have Cameron back in Scotland, after all these years.'

'Oh aye, it has been.' Nancy's face brightened at the mention of her grandson's name. 'I thought it would be the end of the road for me when I was told I'd lost Isla and Lucy. But Cameron has helped me through it. He came to stay a couple of weeks ago. Did Michael tell you?'

'Yes, he did.'

'He's tidied up the garden for me and decorated the spare bedroom. Cameron seems to like it here in Dunkeld.'

'Did Isla and Richard come over to visit much after they moved to the Middle East?'

'In the first few years they did. They flew over for a couple of weeks just after Lucy was born. I've got a photograph there on the mantelpiece which was taken during that trip,' Nancy

225

gestured towards a bank of frames, crammed into every available space.

Imogen located the picture she was referring to, taking a look at it whilst Isla's mother continued, 'but then the family came less and less often. Richard was a bit mean with the finances. He wouldn't let my daughter travel over by herself. I see a great deal of Annie and her boys. They're up the road in Inverness. They drive down every couple of weeks. There's always one child who you don't see quite so often after they leave home, isn't there? That seems to be the way for many of my friends.'

Imogen closely examined the photograph, whilst Nancy chatted away about the exploits of her other grandchildren. This was the first image she had seen of the Flemings. Isla was young here and extremely pretty. She was holding a new born baby in her arms and seemed completely happy. Richard stood next to his wife with an arm stiffly placed around her shoulders. He was solidly built but Imogen had to concede the man was rather handsome. Richard's other hand was resting on the head of Cameron, who must have been four or five years old and was absolutely angelic with his mane of shaggy blond hair and piercing blue eyes. They were a very good looking family, although Richard had barely managed to summon up a smile. His gruff expression spoiled what should have been a truly joyful occasion.

Nancy asked Imogen about her own children. They discussed their interests and achievements for a while. Imogen was pleased to see that Isla's mother was coping so well after her loss. She still had an interest in other people. Nancy appeared to have no concerns regarding the helicopter crash. She didn't mention it at all. Nancy had clearly accepted the event as an unavoidable tragedy.

'How do you think Cameron is coping, Mrs Cook, after the accident?'

'He seems okay to me, although he is quieter than he used to be. When he was a wee boy he would run around and around like a rocket. I used to think he'd end up cracking his head open. Och, but that's years ago.' Nancy's words tapered off. Her attention seemed to drift away from the conversation.

'I did observe him getting very upset once, but I agree, he has been extremely brave about the whole thing.' Imogen tried to encourage the lady back into the discussion.

'I was surprised, really,' she said, turning her face back towards Imogen. 'Just between you and me, Isla had been having real problems with the boy over the past couple of years. He got into terrible trouble at that boarding school of his, always in fights he was. My poor daughter was repeatedly summoned to speak to the Headmaster about his behaviour. She had to go all by herself of course, because Richard was too busy at work. That husband of hers was the root of all the problems anyway. He could be very rude to my lovely daughter. When Cameron witnessed that, he thought it was okay to do the same thing. So he didn't have much respect for his poor mother and *she* was the one who had to dole out the discipline when his father was away at work the whole time. That was always my theory as to what had gone wrong in the family. I'm not sure if it makes sense to anyone else.'

'It makes perfect sense, Mrs Cook,' Imogen replied with feeling.

'I told the man from the bank when he called that I didn't want a penny of my son-in-law's money. But then I thought about it for a week or two and decided to take it. I've put it into a savings account for my grandchildren - for Annie's boys, I mean. So they can use it to go off to college when they're older. I didn't want to penalize them just because of their old Gran's stubborn pride.' Nancy set her cup down with a flourish.

Imogen found she was warming to this lady very much.

'I wouldn't want to leave Cameron out,' she quickly clarified, 'but I reckon he'll be alright with his trust fund and everything. But Annie and Neil struggle a bit financially, although he's a good man and a great father to his kiddies.'

'Had Richard got any family left in this area Nancy?'

'Oh, Richard's parents died a long time ago. Dennis and I met them at the wedding, of course but we didn't have very much in common. They lived in a great big Edwardian villa in Perth. Richard's mother was involved in all these local societies and things. They moved in different social circles from us did Lillian and Alec. There was an older brother I think who now lives abroad. I don't even remember meeting him when Isla and Richard got married. My daughter did once say there was a sister, who died young. That must have been decades ago because it was never mentioned and there were no photographs of her in their house - although the whole place was a bit like a huge mausoleum.' She smiled a little at this observation but a shadow had passed across her face. It must have been the idea of Richard's long dead sister that triggered her grief.

Imogen swiftly changed the subject. 'Dunkeld seems like a lovely place. I had a walk around the Cathedral before coming here this morning.'

'Aye, my family had all been very happy here. Isla should never have left.'

Nancy looked across at Stella's package and said firmly, 'well, I'm getting myself upset now as it is, so we might as well have a look in this here envelope.' She patted the pack sitting on the table next to her. 'Would you mind staying a wee while longer? I wouldn't mind some company when I open it up.'

'Of course. I'll just take these cups into the kitchen, give them a rinse then come back in and join you.'

When Imogen returned to the cosy lounge a few minutes later, Nancy had spread the letters, notes and photographs out onto the small sofa. She was reading a Christmas card that her daughter must have written to the Hargreaves one year. There was a contented smile on the lady's face as she ran her finger over Isla's attractive, looping script. Imogen bent down to survey the scant array of memorabilia that remained to document sixteen years of the Fleming's lives. Her eyes temporarily rested on a photograph. It appeared to have been taken at a barbecue party, possibly at the Hargreaves' home. Isla and her children were the subjects of the shot, but the majority of the party could be clearly seen in full swing around them. Without asking Nancy's permission, Imogen snatched up the snapshot to take a closer look.

Despite the fact she was in the company of an old lady, Imogen immediately exclaimed: 'Bloody Hell!'

PART FOUR

30

Michael Nichols returned to his beautifully restored Victorian flat in the West-End of Glasgow to find Cameron Fleming busily preparing dinner in the small but functional kitchen. The young man was hurriedly chopping vegetables whilst checking every so often on a roasting dish emitting sublime aromas every time he levered down the oven door.

'What's for dinner?' Michael enquired, peering into the modest room on his way past.

'Moroccan roast lamb with seasonal vegetables,' Cameron called over his shoulder, without pausing from his labours.

'Sounds fabulous. I'm just going to change out of my work clothes.' Michael left his briefcase in the hallway and disappeared into the master bedroom.

An unspoken but regular pattern had gradually evolved between the two men since they returned from Garansay last month. About once or twice a week Cameron came to Michael's flat and prepared supper for him, often staying over in one of the apartment's grand spare bedrooms. The boy had been given his own key so that it didn't matter if his unofficially adopted guardian was held up at work and returned

231

home later than planned.

It had developed into a very pleasurable arrangement for both men. Cameron spent most of his days searching and applying for jobs online whereas Michael was at the crucial stage of an ambitious building project. As a result, these evenings were an important source of relaxation for the pair of them.

When the meal was finally ready, Cameron set up the small foldable table in his host's majestic living room. He and Michael sat down to enjoy some good food and a perfectly decent but inexpensive bottle of red wine.

'Anything interesting in the employment pages today?' the older man enquired.

'A few things, but it's just so competitive at the moment. I'm struggling even to get an interview for positions I'm over-qualified for in the first place.'

'It's a tough market out there for young people. My offer is still open to find you some work experience at my firm, but there's no chance they'll pay you for it. Times are difficult in almost all sectors.' Michael paused to take a luxuriant sip from his long-stemmed glass.

'Thank you, Michael. I am definitely bearing it in mind. It's not a question of the money, you know that. I'm simply not sure architecture is what I'm interested in. I just want to keep busy with an occupation I'm good at and find fulfilling. I did have an idea today about something I might quite like to try.' Cameron took a bite from his pot-roast, watching his companion's face carefully to gauge his reaction.

'Go, on,' Michael prompted.

'Well, what I love more than anything else is to sail.' He prodded at the joint with his fork. 'So,

I thought I might set up a sailing school on Garansay. I know you can hire yachts in Kilross and Port na Mara and be taken out on guided trips, but there's no one who will actually teach beginners how to do it properly. I thought I might ask Dad's trustees if they would release the funds for me to start up a business. If it goes well then I could always employ some locals too. You and Imogen are always complaining about how young people have to leave the island if they want to find work.' Cameron looked down sheepishly at his plate.

'I think that's a wonderful idea,' Michael said simply. 'I'd love to help you with the designs. You'll need to think about where to base yourself, but if you set up the school on the west coast then we would be able to see plenty of each other when I'm over at Kilduggan Farm. You could always stay with me while the building work is being done.'

The handsome young man smiled broadly. Suddenly regaining his appetite, he began to tuck enthusiastically into the impressive plate of food.

*

Over the next couple of weeks, Cameron's plans for the sailing school proceeded rapidly. He came up with a business proposal which he put forward to the trustees at his father's bank. They were surprisingly keen on the idea and informed the boy that someone from the finance department would be in touch with him to discuss a possible figure for the project.

He and Michael made a special trip to Garansay in order to check out potential locations, one of which lay about two miles north of the Kilduggan Shore.

The remains of an old jetty littered this remote spot. The once usable pier had now sadly become rotten and unsafe. But the site itself seemed as if it would be perfect for Cameron's purposes. After some research, the men discovered the land belonged to an English couple who had bought the accompanying boathouse a few years ago and renovated it at great expense to use as a holiday home in the summer months. They never had much interest in the rickety, ancient landing stage. They'd simply left it to decay into the sea. After some careful negotiation, it looked as if they would be willing to sell it to Cameron, as long as his building plans were sympathetic and didn't impinge on their privacy too much. Michael had been eagerly helping his ward to create the architect's drawings necessary to gain the appropriate planning permissions. This had led to him spending a fair bit of time back on the Isle of Garansay again.

Michael knew his sister was keen for him to stay away from their parents' farm, after the tragic incident with Pat O'Connell in the summer. But he believed she was being far too solicitous of his feelings. As far as Michael was concerned, the death of O'Connell drew a line under the whole unhappy affair. He was free to concentrate again on the organisation of his daughter's wedding and upon helping Cameron to realise his business aspirations. They were the only family he wanted to be focussing on at this point in his life.

The local police had cleared the hillsides of those vicious man-traps and discovered the source of their sudden appearance in this part of the island. As a result, there didn't seem to be any real reason not to return to the farm he had exercised so much of his energies bringing back to its former glory. But as Michael was now spending so much time away from his plush offices in the city centre of Glasgow, his partner asked him to give up the full-time personal assistant he had used for many years. He suggested instead that he take assistance when it was needed from the general secretarial pool. Finding himself facing looming deadlines and a mounting workload, Michael decided to call upon his neighbour, Colin Walmsley to ask if he could recommend anyone on the island who might be able to help him out for a few hours a week.

He had certainly not been looking to poach any of the staff at Loch Crannox, so Colin surprised him by replying, 'I don't know if Imogen has told you Mike, but Julia and I have split up. She was very upset about the trouble we had recently with the police and particularly by the death of the old man on our land. Perfectly understandably, she doesn't want to continue to work here any longer.'

'I'm so sorry, Colin. I had no absolutely no idea. Imogen and I haven't spoken for a few weeks,' Michael had responded.

'I'll give you Julia's number. She's very efficient and a lovely person. I'm sure she will be able to pick up on whatever is required of her. I'm more than happy to supply a reference.'

'That won't be necessary. She immediately

struck me as a very capable lady. I'm just sorry it didn't work out between you. It might purely be a question of giving it some time, you know.'

'Aye, maybe,' Colin agreed, 'but in the meantime it wouldn't be a good idea for us to work together. I'd feel an awful lot better if she'd got herself a new job.'

It turned out that Julia was very keen to take on some freelance work for Michael. She told him she had almost decided to pack up and leave her picturesque bijou Garansay cottage and return to the mainland. Office work was not easy to come by on the island and when positions did arise they tend to be located in the harbour town of Kilross, which was just too far for Julia to travel every day. The idea that another position would come up within a few miles of her home was more than this well-qualified lady could have hoped for.

With the additional administrative help, Michael was now free to regularly visit the sheltered little shingle cove Cameron was hoping to transform into his training centre for budding sailors. As he surveyed the crumbling jetty that would soon be converted into a boat yard and café, he truly hoped Imogen and Hugh could be tempted to come back to the island. Michael was worried that their holiday this summer had strained relations between them. He sincerely wished for this not to be the case and that Imogen could surmount the negative feelings he knew she bore towards Cameron Fleming. Sometimes he felt as if his little sister's finely attuned instincts could lead her to jump to the wrong conclusions about people.

His daughter, Sarah, certainly appeared to get on well with Cameron. She confessed to being relieved her father had someone close by who could keep an eye on him while she was back at home in Edinburgh. The search for a venue for the wedding, however, had sadly stalled. Sarah appeared to have a very definite picture of precisely what this special day would be like, although her long-term partner, Ross, was far more relaxed about it. They had both agreed on a civil ceremony, which was intended to broaden their choice of potential venues. However, several very lovely establishments had already been discounted for reasons that had seemed to Michael to be fairly trivial. In desperation, Sarah had asked her father if he would check out the hotels on Garansay to get an idea of the kind of packages they offered. This was yet another job Michael was going to have to get done within the next few weeks.

Just as Michael Nichols was becoming busy with the demands of his career and the seemingly never-ending developments within his immediate family, he suddenly found himself assailed by an unexpected and most unwelcome intrusion. Waking one morning in his bedroom at Lower Kilduggan Farm, on the beautiful western coast of Garansay, Michael's brief appreciation of the blissful tranquillity of this calm and peaceful spot was rudely shattered by the pealing of the rarely used and antiquated telephone in the downstairs hall.

Just managing to grapple with the receiver before it rang off, Michael was surprised to hear the broad accent of Detective Inspector Zanco of the Strathclyde Police delivering his greetings on the other end of the crackly line.

'I'm terribly sorry to bother you at such an early hour, Mr Nichols but we have had an important breakthrough overnight. It really couldn't wait.'

'Is this regarding the crash?' Michael enquired in his customarily measured tones. 'How may I assist you, Detective Zanco?'

'I'm afraid we will have to inconvenience you today, Sir. We would like to bring young Cameron into the Holland Street Station for questioning. I'd be most grateful if you would accompany him, as we feel he will need your support.' Zanco did not elaborate any further, but waited for Michael's response.

'Of course, Inspector. I would be happy to come along with Cameron. You are just going to have to give me enough time to get myself onto the morning boat.'

'No problem Mr Nichols, take as long as you like, we will be waiting. Simply let us know when you arrive in the City. Then we'll go straight over and pick the boy up.'

31

It seemed to Michael, as if the vast metropolis of Glasgow was trying to pull him back into its sprawling grasp. Not yet 48 hours since he had escaped its noise and crowds, here he was again, back in the midst of the indifferent lunchtime hustle and bustle of the city centre.

There had been no suggestion by the Detective Inspector that Michael could bring Cameron to the police station himself, so he was assuming he was expected to meet him there. Feeling uncharacteristically lacking in confidence, Michael Nichols was buzzed in by the Duty Sergeant on the reception desk of the Holland Street Police Headquarters.

From a side-door, emerged the shabby figure of D.I Zanco, wearing that crooked smile which had at one time appeared endearing but was now, to Michael's care-worn eyes, beginning to seem sinister. Standing next to the detective was another man, younger and in all respects providing a stark contrast to his older colleague. This policeman was extremely clean cut and immaculately dressed. Michael was immediately filled with a renewed assurance that the case might actually be in good hands after all.

'I would like to introduce you to Agent Adam Frost from the Department for the Investigation of Industrial Fraud and Criminality, or the DIFC for short. Mr Frost works for the American government. He has been heading up the international side of our investigation,' Zanco announced unexpectedly.

Caught totally off-guard, but not wanting to let it show, Michael held out an elegant hand. 'I'm very pleased to meet you, Mr Frost.'

'Likewise,' Frost drawled, also taken aback by the striking resemblance the man in front of him bore to Mrs Imogen Croft. The incredible likeness shocked him, even though he had just been told she was this gentleman's sister. Frost made no comment on it but instead continued, 'Cameron is waiting in interview room three. We are about to go in and begin our questioning. I'm afraid the boy has waived his right to have a lawyer with him, although we did advise him to have an attorney present. In light of this, we would like you to sit in on the conversation. You might just be able to help us out with a couple of things.'

Michael curtly nodded his head, following the two men into a small and airless space which had obviously been partitioned at some point. Cameron was already seated at a table in the centre of the room. He did not even look up as Michael entered but had his head hanging resolutely downwards, staring intently at the clasped hands placed in his lap. The confident and positive young man of just a few days ago appeared to be gone.

Zanco dropped down a bulging file of notes before pulling out his chair. The other investigator seemed to have brought nothing with him at all. After the usual provisos had been stated for the benefit of the tape machine, the British detective, at long last, began to ask his questions. 'We have some fresh information for you, Cameron, regarding your parents' accident. Are you happy for me to explain these facts for you now?' Zanco spoke the words slowly and carefully, as if addressing a small child.

'Yes,' the boy replied, without any hint of emotion.

'Firstly, I can confirm that the body we recovered from the Kilbrannan Sound a few weeks ago was that of your father, Richard Fleming. It will now be possible for you to go ahead and organise a funeral, okay?' Zanco said this more kindly and waited patiently for the young man to respond.

Michael placed his hand on Cameron's shoulder. The boy nodded his head, but did not yet look up and face the policeman sitting opposite him.

'The other issue I need to discuss with you also relates to your father, but in another way entirely. I'm afraid I have not been completely honest with either of you about the direction in which our investigation has taken us since last December.' The detective gestured towards his impassive colleague. 'Agent Frost and I have known for several months now that your father was involved in very serious acts of financial impropriety at the bank where he worked, Cameron.'

The lad sat bolt upright at this piece of news. To Michael at least, it appeared to have come as a total surprise to him.

'What do you mean?' Cameron asked.

'Have you heard of something called 'money laundering'?' Zanco looked at Cameron carefully. The boy slowly nodded. 'Well, your dad had been helping some very dangerous people to try and process their illegal profits in a legitimate way - does that make sense to you?'

'Yes, I understand.'

'The agency that Mr Frost works for discovered what your dad was up to about a year ago and they confronted him with it.' The policeman sat back in his chair and Frost took over. The switch was so seamless it made Michael wonder if they had planned it beforehand.

'Your father agreed to provide us with detailed testimony in return for a reduced custodial sentence. He also wanted to be able to serve his detention back home in a UK prison and not out in Dubai,' Frost explained. 'This all became part of the deal we struck with Mr Fleming, whilst you were still living out in the Middle East.'

Cameron's jaw dropped open. He seemed to be in a genuine state of shock.

'Your reaction is evident, but I still have to ask if you had any idea of what your father had been doing during those years that you lived in the U.A.E?'

'I swear this is utterly new to me. I did not know Dad was involved in anything criminal. I mean, I knew he was a difficult person to live with and my mum had a tough time with him, but this is in a whole different league.'

An uncomfortable silence followed before Zanco decided to take up the mantle once again. 'Richard

Fleming was not the only man who was preparing to give evidence against these gangs. There were two other individuals about to provide crucial testimony for us. Both of them also ended up dead after an unexplained accident.'

'Did these cases take place in the UK? I certainly don't recall hearing anything about it in the press,' Michael asked.

'One of the incidents happened on the coastal road between Dubai and Oman a couple of years ago. The other involved a Chinook crash en route to an oil rig in middle of the Arabian Gulf in 2009,' Frost stated.

'So, the Flemings and their pilot are the only deaths to have taken place on British soil, as it were. I find it hard to believe these criminals could have pulled off something as incredibly bold as this. There was no suggestion of foul play in the accident report,' Michael pressed.

'No, you're quite right Mr Nichols. For a long while we did not make the connection ourselves. But Mr Frost and his team have been painstakingly gathering evidence for us and recently they had something of a breakthrough in all three of the cases.'

The faintest flicker of a smile passed across the American's face. 'A few days ago we were fortunate enough to arrest two members of a criminal gang we have been chasing down for over a decade. These men are extremely well connected. We rarely get an opportunity to interrogate people from within the organisation itself. So we needed to make the most of it.' He sat forward in his plastic seat for emphasis. 'We offered the men we apprehended total immunity plus new identities - this was despite the seriousness of their past crimes. In return, they provided us with valuable information about all three of our unsolved cases. These individuals gave us details about how their gang used a complicated network of bribes and coercion in order to achieve their ultimate goals. In the case of Richard Fleming and the other three men, the incentive the criminals offered had been money. But this was not the only method employed by these operatives. They also regularly utilised the threat of violence in order to get what they wanted.' Frost relaxed back into his chair again, in what amounted to a dramatic pause.

Michael, who's mind had been ticking away during this monologue, suddenly declared, 'are you suggesting, Agent Frost, that someone could have been threatened to cause these accidents? That would mean there didn't have to be any kind of technical failure at all. It would be a case of sabotage, I suppose.'

Adam Frost beamed brightly, as if he were a teacher, gratified by the quick response of his cleverest pupil. 'That is exactly what we started to believe. You see, we had been totally perplexed by the fact these accidents were all so different. The circumstances, locations and vehicles involved were too varied for us to come up with any kind of pattern. Not as it is with a terrorist attack, where there are certain similarities and parallels in the way in which each one is carried out. These events just seemed so random. Then, when we spoke to our two henchmen in custody, the pieces just began to fall into place. The connection was not, after all, in the mechanics of the three accidents, but in the nature of the human beings caught up in them.'

Michael glanced across at Cameron, who appeared completely puzzled by what he was hearing.

'We switched the direction of our

investigation. We started to dig around into the lives of some of the individuals involved; their family situations, friends, social interactions and so forth. It was through this line of enquiry that we finally began to make real progress. What we discovered was that the chauffeur who was driving his boss to a business meeting in Oman had a wife and a three month old baby boy. Alec Armstrong, the man in charge of the Chinook which was taking a group of oil workers out to a rig back in 2009, had three young children at home in Birmingham. Then there was Tom Watson - a pilot with an unblemished safety record and fifteen years of experience. He had two lovely kids back in Troon and what appeared to be a happy, settled life. When we began to interview the unfortunate families, each one of their wives told us how their husbands had become depressed and withdrawn in the weeks and days leading up to their deaths. None of the ladies wanted to volunteer this information during the original investigations as they were worried their spouses' deteriorating mental health might cause them to be blamed for the crashes. This time around, it was simply a matter of asking the right questions.'

'Once we had finally made this connection, we went back to the accident reports themselves. For the first time, all the facts appeared to fit,' Zanco chipped in. 'It was most clear to us in the case of your flight, Cameron. At first, we were totally perplexed by the fact the helicopter just seemed to have pitched into the water at the last moment, for no good reason we could identify. But now we understood it. Tom Watson ditched the chopper deliberately. The storm provided him with the perfect opportunity, as the crash could then be blamed on bad weather. Tom was probably hoping this would avoid his family having to know it was him who was culpable.'

'But what could have made him do such a thing, with the whole of Cameron's family on board?' Michael was visibly dismayed.

'It was either the Fleming family or his own, Mr Nichols. It must have been a terrible choice,' Frost answered this time. 'The guys we arrested said it was common practice for their employers. They would make it crystal clear these poor men's wives and kids would be at risk if they didn't do exactly what they told them. To begin with, we had thought there must have been an altercation on board the aircraft mid-flight - between Richard and Watson. Then, when your account didn't support this scenario, Cameron, we had convinced ourselves you must have been lying to us, to protect your father perhaps. But now it looks like you're in the clear, kid. What you reported to have seen, actually fits with what we now think happened on that night. The fact Tom Watson ignored your father's suggestion that he take the chopper over to Kintyre to do an emergency landing corresponds with our belief he truly wanted the craft to crash.'

Frost's endorsement of Cameron's version of events was entirely lost on the young man. He seemed to have disengaged from the discussions going on around him. He abruptly placed his head in his hands and started to gently sob. This uncomfortable situation persisted for some minutes until Michael was finally given permission to lead the distraught boy away from the oppressive interview room and out into the fresher air of the busy street.

32

Michael decided to take Cameron Fleming back to Garansay with him that very afternoon. Having lost his beloved wife, Miriam, over ten years ago, he felt he had some insight into the most effective ways to deal with one's grief. On this occasion, Michael decided it would be prudent for them to keep busy, by concentrating on their future plans for the new sailing school.

With the investigation into the events of the crash gradually reaching its conclusion, Michael sincerely hoped this would provide his young friend with closure. Detective Zanco made it clear to them both, as they left the Police Headquarters yesterday, that no legal blame was being levelled at the men who had been forced, through intimidation and fear, into causing the tragic accidents. They had already paid the price with their own lives. He stressed that the real perpetrators were the faceless organisations who made money out of the misery of others. Zanco pledged they would continue to work hard to bring these wicked people to justice.

Michael noted with relief that Cameron was in better spirits this morning, although still somewhat quiet and reflective. They ate a hearty breakfast before setting out to walk the two or so miles along the Kilduggan shore to the old jetty. Michael had arranged for them to meet with Colin Walmsley there, as he wanted Cameron to have the benefit of his neighbour's valuable business advice.

There was a chilly breeze rushing in off the Sound but the sun remained high in the sky and provided them with both warmth and good cheer. Michael had always believed that being by the sea could provide comfort in even the most trying of times. Perhaps this was because he grew up next to the water and it was like a familiar friend to him. Or it could purely have been as Cameron eloquently put it, when Zanco told him about the discovery of his father's body, that the ocean seemed so vast it made their own lives much less significant by comparison.

The brisk trek took the two men across terrain consisting of both sand and granite. In one place they had to take a brief detour inland in order to ascend a small grassy headland before they could make their way back to the beach once again. But eventually, they reached the pretty little pebbled cove. As soon as they had scrambled down from the rocky promontory which supported the crumbling landing stage, Michael spotted Colin waiting for them. He was standing by his 4x4, up on the main road. Colin made his way down to greet them. They spent the next half an hour surveying the site.

'The first thing you need to consider is the ease of access,' Colin said decisively. 'If you're going to have building work done here, you need to be able to get lorries in and out. The road is reasonably wide and there's a parking bay nearby so you should be okay from that point of view.'

'Do you think we will get permission from the

council?' Michael enquired.

'As long as the owners of the boathouse don't object you won't have a problem. This area has had a similar use in the past. That will always go in your favour. The main thing you want to think about is whether the business is going to be viable. Can you attract the tourists in Kilross to come all the way over here to the west coast when they can hire boats a stone's throw from their hotel?'

'But my school will provide a different kind of service,' Cameron spoke up. 'I will actually be teaching the skills of sailing. I'm going to pitch to both beginners and those who are more experienced on the water. Ultimately, it would be great if I could attract outward bound types, who will come to Garansay specifically to learn to sail. Then I wouldn't just be reliant on the day-trippers who travel to the more accessible, eastern side of the island.'

'It's an original idea,' Colin said, sounding more interested. 'But what would work best of all, in my opinion, is if you offered the whole package. You could provide bed and breakfast plus a week's worth of tuition, people will pay high prices for that kind of holiday. It's very popular on the continent.'

'I hadn't budgeted for building accommodation in addition to the business premises,' Cameron added, sounding disappointed. 'I don't think my trustees could stretch to that. There isn't the quantity of funds in my bequest that we first thought there would be.'

'Well, if it was me setting up this operation, I'd use Lower Kilduggan for the overnight stays. It used to be a boarding house in Isabel's time.

You've certainly got the space up there. Then get yourselves a really high-end operation up and running, with gourmet meals in the evening and all that stuff. You could charge a fortune.'

'I really don't believe Imogen and Allan would be very happy with the idea,' Michael quickly added.

'You never know what people are going to think until you try them out, Mike. Imogen's a good friend and we've been through a lot together but I still wouldn't like to predict what she'd say to anything. She's definitely got her own mind that lady,' the farmer replied with great feeling.

No more was said about Colin's recommendation. Cameron clambered off to investigate the tiny natural harbour created by an unusual outcrop of rocks to the northern side of the beach. When he was safely out of earshot, Michael explained to his neighbour the outcome of the police inquiry into the helicopter crash.

Colin whistled through his teeth. 'Those poor guys. Imagine being put in a position like that? It doesn't bear thinking about. It's a sobering thought that even out here on Garansay we can be affected by a crime that was committed thousands of miles away. I often like to think we exist in our own little bubble on this remote island, but I suppose it's just not true.'

'If we rely on business and tourism to make a living then we're going to have to accept we are very much a part of the big bad world outside,' Michael replied. 'Speaking of which, I hope this recent unpleasantness over the land bid hasn't put you off expanding your operations, Colin.'

'I'm afraid it did at first. But there's a dairy

farm on the 'South-End' that's just come up for sale. I'm thinking of putting in an offer. The climate's so much milder down there which would mean I could diversify a bit. I won't be considering buying any property on the mainland in the immediate future, though.'

'Well, don't let it put you off forever. You never quite know what's around the corner. Life's too short to be reticent,' Michael said, eschewing his usually cautious attitude.

Cameron and Michael then parted company with Colin, thanking him profusely for his advice. Their ramble back to the farm, across the jagged contours of the rugged coastline was performed for the most part in a companionable silence. The older man was mulling over some of the interesting suggestions his neighbour had made. They certainly provided him with food for thought.

Michael had known for a little while that he was reaching a stage where he must consider just how involved he was going to get with this young man, Cameron Fleming. Currently, they were enjoying each other's company and providing one another with some comfort and solace. Michael was self-aware enough to know that the boy was filling a gap in his life that had been created ever since his wife had died. This young boy was also at a stage when he, too, was in need of love and protection. He had his grandmother, of course, but Cameron had barely known her while he was growing up. She was too old to be able to provide him with the parental guidance he so obviously needed.

If Michael were to get involved in Cameron's business so wholeheartedly that he was prepared to bring Kilduggan Farm into the venture, he would effectively be making a long-term commitment to the lad. Cameron would become a regular part of their family. It could possibly mean opening the farm up to visitors again, just like his mother had done when he was a boy. Michael wasn't sure what he felt about that. He had always been more involved in the farming side of the operation and had never shown the slightest interest in the guesthouse, which was entirely Isabel's domain. Despite what Colin had said earlier, Michael could not envisage his sister going for the idea at all. Allan would probably eagerly embrace the whole project, especially if there was a chance of making some money out of it.

Michael glanced across at his young companion, striding in step beside him and gazing out to sea with a contented expression on his face. The easy camaraderie that exists between them when they spent time together was very refreshing to Michael. On that breezy shore, about half a mile from the pathway leading up to Lower Kilduggan Farm, he suddenly wondered if a more permanent type of arrangement for the two of them wouldn't be such a bad thing after all.

33

Cameron had just heard back from the trustees in charge of his parents' inheritance. They were rather impressed by the business plan presented to them and agreed to release a fixed sum to their young client. This would allow him to make a start on the building work necessary for his exciting project.

The youngster had only just received the news as he bounded athletically into the kitchen of Lower Kilduggan Farm to tell Michael about this piece of good fortune. Cameron would have to supply the bank with a detailed account of his expenditure at every stage, but at least it meant they could begin the task of searching for a suitable contractor to take on the job. It was still only September, but it was important they began the ground works now, before the weather deteriorated as the season wore on. The western edge of the island was particularly susceptible to the terrible winter storms that battered the Scottish coast during the darker months.

Michael decided to delay making any hard and fast decisions about involving Lower Kilduggan in Cameron's plans. He had not yet spoken to Imogen and when he did he would like to be mending bridges with her rather than introducing an issue which could drive them further apart. Michael was also unsure if he wanted to take on the running of a boarding house at his time of life. He remembered how hard his mother worked at the height of the summer and wasn't getting any younger. Besides, he had been quite enjoying the days he spent working on his designs from the farm on Garansay. He then had the added bonus of being able to escape back to the city whenever the fancy took him. In addition to this, he'd found Julia to be a proficient and creative assistant who provided him with extremely useful advice on his building projects.

There was another reason for his reticence. Cameron had asked him some questions last night after dinner which made him query whether it was really wise for the boy to spend all of his days so close to the watery resting place of his unfortunate parents and sister. Perhaps Imogen was correct after all and the fact Cameron wanted to spend so much time there was actually unhealthy and even a little morbid. Hugh seemed to think it wouldn't do him any harm, but after yesterday evening, Michael wasn't quite so sure.

When they had retired to the sitting room, as the light was disappearing beyond the rolling hills of Kintyre in the far distance, Cameron had gone to stand at the tall bay window. He remained quietly impassive for some time but then he had turned back towards his host and said, in a quite matter-of-fact way, 'if a ship or a boat were to break up in a bad storm, out there in the Sound, is it possible that the wreckage might never be found?'

Michael had considered the question for a while and answered, 'well, it would all depend on the severity of the storm, I suppose. You would have to take into account the direction of the tides, prevailing winds, currents and all that kind of thing. If it were a small enough vessel, then probably it would never be recovered. I mean, you might get some fragments of wood and debris getting washed up in various places, but it wouldn't amount to a conspicuous quantity, why do you ask?'

'I was just thinking, that's all. Do you remember how I told you we used to visit the lighthouse on the Mull of Kintyre, when I was younger and my Grandad would take us? The museum there held lots of memorabilia about shipwrecks over the centuries. The cliffs at the headland are pretty treacherous and when the mist is down, hanging low over the water, sailors can't spot the rocks until it is too late. I just recalled reading that many of the boats were simply dashed to bits and then washed out to sea. Do you think some of the pieces might have ended up on the coast of America - or Canada even?'

Not wishing to pursue this line of conversation any further Michael didn't respond but instead changed the subject. Cameron hadn't raised the maudlin topic again. Today, however, Michael was thinking about the boy's strange enquiry once more. He was beginning to feel it might not be so beneficial to Cameron's recovery to be encouraging him to devote his career to travelling the seas that so cruelly robbed him of his family. Michael found himself wanting to hear his little sister's advice on this. Imogen had two young lads of her own and perhaps he should have heeded her wise words sooner.

Before he got in touch with the Crofts,

Michael was determined to spend the day temporarily diverting Cameron from his plans for the boat yard. They had spent so much time recently poring over the detailed diagrams they needed to submit to the council, he believed it would do them both the power of good to apply themselves to a task which was quite different. Michael intended to take a tour around the island's finest hotels. He would check out the wedding packages they had on offer and report the details back to Sarah and Ross.

Cameron was still in high spirits after getting the go ahead from the bank, so he was surprisingly enthusiastic when his host proposed the itinerary for the day. The two men set off in Michael's sports car. The weather was so mild they were able to lower the roof and gain the best possible views from the winding coastal roads which circumnavigated the island. Their first stop was at Port na Mara, where the village's main hotel was situated halfway up the hillside and boasted impressive views over the old Norman Castle on the narrow spit of land at the centre of the bay.

Despite the striking panorama visible from the vast windows of the hotel's dining room, Michael felt, on the whole, the venue would be too small. Its position far up the glen meant the gardens were on a steep slope. He sensed Sarah would not be happy to host her drinks reception there. Beginning to understand the difficulties his daughter had experienced finding the right location, he and Cameron reluctantly decided to move on.

As they wound their way past the Garansay

Whisky Distillery, Michael recalled how a colleague of his hosted a large function there a few years back. He made a sharp turn to the right and pulled up outside the visitor's centre entrance. Grabbing themselves a coffee and a pastry in the galleried café, Michael spoke with the manager about the events packages they offered. By the time he and Cameron returned to the car, the older man was quietly confident this might be just the right place for his daughter's special day. However, he knew that Sarah would need persuading away from the vision she had in her mind of a traditional, hotel based wedding. Despite its truly unique and stunning position, the Distillery might just prove to be too quirky a setting for her.

Taking the mountainous road which cut through the middle of the island and connected the west to the east, Michael weaved his high performance car through hairpin bends and amidst gushing burns and dark, brooding peaks. Some visitors to Garansay found the north of the island a little bleak, but Michael had always felt its rugged and remote beauty provided the most compelling landscape of all and was well worth the strenuous drive.

The route then dropped into a steep descent, where rough heather and gorse gave way to deep green forests of scented pine trees. Streams began to widen out, slowing their flow as they gradually found themselves reunited with the sparkling, clear waters of the sea. The eastern coast, of course had its own attractions. Not least the pretty little fishing village of Gilstone. This tiny natural harbour faced the gentle contours of the Ayrshire hills which lay a short distance away across the Firth of Clyde. It had long attracted the various communities of artists and writers who were drawn to its unspoilt charms.

The Gilstone Hotel was positioned right in the heart of the village. It had a lounge bar popular amongst both locals and tourists alike. Although serving a famously decent pub lunch, Michael did not think this squarely set stone building would suit his daughter's grand plans at all. So the men continued their drive along the meandering and sunny lanes which ran directly parallel to the shoreline. This stretch of the coast was where you were most likely to spot a seal, warming itself on a rock in the sun or poking a whiskered nose out of the rolling surf. In the height of the tourist season you needed to keep a look out for cars stopping unexpectedly along the twisting road ahead. You might also encounter folk suddenly leaping out of their vehicles with binoculars in hand, eager to observe the incredible wildlife on show. People new to Garansay could discover that this strange phenomenon took them by surprise. Some even found it frustrating. But to Michael it was all part of the appeal of the Scottish islands and allowed visitors to feel they'd left the hurly-burly of everyday life far behind.

Realising they would soon be arriving in the island's main port town of Kilross, Michael slowed his speed a little and called across to his companion. 'Cameron, I'm going to need to go and check out the 'Glenrannoch' for Sarah.' He paused, shifting his line of vision back to the road. 'I will absolutely understand if you don't want to go back in there again. It is grossly

259

insensitive of me even to mention the place, I know. If you want to head off and get yourself a coffee in the town - or a beer if you'd prefer, then I'm perfectly happy to do it on my own.'

'It'll be fine, Michael, really. But thank you for being so considerate of my feelings. If I'm going to be living on Garansay permanently then I've just got to get used to everything about the island and that includes the Glenrannoch Hotel.'

Michael gripped the steering wheel and kept his eyes fixed dead ahead. He couldn't tell if the young man next to him was being brave or was simply in denial. Michael knew only too well how painful it was for him to go home to his house in Bearsden after Miriam had passed away. In fact, he was never comfortable within its walls again. He had to sell up and move away, knowing he would never regain a sense of contentment while he was living there. Sarah had been very upset when she had to leave the place she'd grown up in. But at the time, he genuinely believed he had no choice but to go and had never regretted the decision. It hadn't done his daughter any harm either. He still had his memories of the happy times they spent there together as a family. Nothing could take that away from him. So to Michael, Cameron's behaviour was beginning to seem pretty odd.

Their convertible sports-car fitted in perfectly. Nestling neatly amongst its neighbours the car joined the litany of expensive high performance vehicles which were lined up along the sweeping gravel drive of Garansay's premier hotel. Entering the impressive lobby area of the 'Glenrannoch', resplendent even down to its McDonald Tartan carpet, Michael became immediately concerned that this venue would be way out of his price range. Nevertheless, he had promised his daughter he would look at everything on the island. He and Cameron waited patiently at the reception desk for the events manager to come and speak with them.

The thin and slightly harassed figure of Gordon Ingle finally appeared from a side office. He quickly adopted a beaming smile and made his way over to greet them. When Michael introduced his young companion, Ingle looked both uncomfortable and embarrassed. He offered the boy his heartfelt condolences but while doing so, the man barely knew where to look. He seemed much more comfortable when they got onto the subject of weddings. Whilst the manager guided Michael through a huge lever arch file consisting of price lists and photographs, Cameron drifted off to browse in the hotel's small gift shop which was crammed full of overpriced, Scottish related souvenirs.

After half an hour of the manager's sales pitch, Michael felt he had heard enough. Just as he was about to make his excuses and leave, an attractive Indian couple entered through the lobby's revolving doors. As soon as Ingle caught sight of them, he became extremely animated and excited.

'Ah, Mr Nichols, now here are a couple who can tell you everything you need to know about getting married at the 'Glenrannoch'. They did it themselves and in absolutely grand style just last Christmas. Mr and Mrs Malhotra do please come over here for a minute.'

The smart, business-like couple looked as if the very last thing they would want to do is spend even one second in the company of Gordon Ingle. But they politely walked across to join Michael, who took hold of Krish Malhotra's hand in a firm shake. Ingle continued to gabble on endlessly about the flamboyant nature of the Malhotra nuptuals and how well the hotel had catered for their very specialist needs. Just as the pair appeared on the verge of being rude to the man and withdrawing immediately to their room, Cameron emerged from the gift shop and began to stroll nonchalantly in their direction.

The events manager declared rather loudly, 'silly me! But of course you already know Mr Nichols' companion. He was one of the guests on your 'Big Day'. What a fool I am for not making the connection sooner.'

Krish and Akuti looked towards the young man Ingle was apparently talking about and then they glanced at each other, but to Michael, they merely seemed confused by the whole scenario.

Gordon Ingle mercifully lowered his voice a fraction, realising the situation may need to be approached with greater sensitivity. 'The lad over there, coming out of the shop, he happens to be Cameron Fleming - you know, the boy whose parents and sister were killed in that dreadful accident. After they had left *our* premises, you understand.'

The Indian newlyweds still looked completely bemused. Then two strange things happened at one and the same time.

Krish Malhotra announced quite calmly, 'I'm afraid you've made a mistake, Mr Ingle. The boy you are pointing at is most certainly not Cameron Fleming.'

And in that moment, the handsome young blond man who had been making his way across the thick tartan carpet suddenly looked up. He quickly assessed the expressions on the faces of the group directly in front of him. In a split second, he made a run for it. Gently shoving an overdressed middle aged couple aside, he sprinted nimbly out of the impressive entrance doors, down the steep gravel drive and out of sight.

34

Imogen was directed towards the interview rooms of the Holland Street Police Station by a very helpful female officer. Looking frantically up and down the maze of corridors, she finally spotted her brother. He was sitting stiffly in an austere plastic chair with an unreadable expression on his face.

'Michael!' She called, running over and throwing her arms around his shoulders. 'I'm so sorry.'

The tired and drawn-looking man stood up and returned her embrace, but without any enthusiasm. 'I'm glad you've come, Imogen. You really didn't have to.'

'But I was already here - has D.I. Zanco not explained that to you?'

'I've not seen him yet. I've spoken to various detectives over the phone in the last few hours. This is the first time I've met anyone face to face since the boy disappeared.'

'Have they any idea where he might be?' Imogen asked with genuine concern.

'Not a clue. They've been so busy chastising me for letting him get away, I don't think anyone's even begun the search. Apparently, he could have got on a ferry in the time it took me to call the police. I'm starting to believe they actually suspect me of helping him to escape.'

Just as Imogen was about to explain some of the facts to her older brother, Zanco finally appeared. Rather than leading them to a stuffy and cramped cubicle, they were instead taken into the incident room itself. Open plan and full of busy looking plain-clothed officers, they were directed towards the desk of the detective in charge.

'Please sit down,' Zanco began cautiously. 'This turn of events has taken us somewhat by surprise, I'm afraid. Mrs Croft had come to see me yesterday with the fresh evidence she uncovered as a result of her trip to Dubai. Unfortunately, we didn't find ourselves with enough time to bring the young lad in for questioning before he absconded.'

Michael twisted around to look at his sister, 'does this mean you already knew he was an imposter?'

'Only since yesterday lunchtime. I had been given some papers which belonged to Isla Fleming when she lived in Dubai. They needed to be delivered to her mother, Nancy Cook. Amongst them was a photograph which must have been taken about a year ago. It showed Isla at a barbecue with Lucy and Cameron. It was only when I saw that picture I realised it wasn't him,' she hastily explained.

'Regrettably, not long after Mrs Croft came to us with her remarkable evidence, the young man was 'unmasked', as it were, by the Malhotras and now he is gone. To be frank, this discovery is something of an embarrassment to me and my team. We certainly did have photographs of the family, but unhappily, they were all several years old. The young man who has duped us does appear to bear a striking resemblance to

Cameron Fleming.' Zanco shifted about in his chair.

'But his grandmother recognised him straight away,' Michael inserted.

'I may be able to explain that phenomenon, Mike,' Imogen quickly put in. 'Mrs Cook had barely seen her grandchildren in the last few years. The only photos she had in the house were the ones the police were using which were taken when the children were very young. Since the Flemings moved to Dubai sixteen years ago Nancy had all but lost touch with them. When 'Cameron' arrived at her house, in the weeks after the crash, and you all told her it was her grandson, she had no reason to believe it wasn't. There is another factor in this story that I think is crucial. When I started to dig around into Cameron's past - the real one that is - I discovered he was not a very nice person at all. He was arrogant, violent and regularly bullied his mother. Because the 'new' Cameron Fleming was charming, helpful and kind, the people he met *wanted* to believe it was actually him. They could explain away the changes in his character by suggesting the accident had somehow made him into a better person, when of course there was absolutely no reason why it should. In fact, after everything I had learned about the true Fleming boy I was actually relieved to discover that the young man we spent the summer holidays with wasn't really him.'

'But you always knew he was lying about something,' Michael responded.

'I thought he hadn't told the truth about the crash, sure. I couldn't see how anyone could have survived that helicopter ditching into high seas. It turns out they didn't. All of the Flemings died in the water that night. The boy's account of the events was pure fiction,' Imogen said sadly.

'There were so many details that he appeared to know about the Fleming family, right from the very start of it all. Could the whole pretence have been a set-up, to get hold of the inheritance, I mean?' Michael suddenly asked.

'We did consider that possibility, Mr Nichols. But we are now fairly certain he operated alone. One of my officers had a long conversation with Mr Colin Walmsley, who was present when you were treating the boy back at the lifeboat station, just after he had been pulled out of the sea,' Zanco explained.

'I'm not sure why that would be relevant,' Michael added petulantly.

'Mr Walmsley told us that the two of you discussed the details of the crash in front of the boy, while he was lying on the stretcher,' Zanco went on.

'Yes,' Michael was forced to concede, casting his mind back to that terrible night. 'We did read out the telegram from RAF Kinloss. But the lad was unconscious during that time.'

Zanco ignored this point, asking instead, 'and when the survivor finally did wake up, Mr Nichols, who the first person to suggest he was Cameron Fleming - you or the boy?'

Michael was obviously thinking very hard about this. A cold flood of realisation seemed to pass through his entire being. 'It was me.'

'Then how did he know all those details about the family, Inspector? When he gave his description of what happened in the aircraft, the lad appeared to know about Richard Fleming's fear of flying. He seemed to understand the dynamic which existed between them all,' Imogen persisted.

'We believe the young man in question probably lives an itinerant existence, which is why no one had noticed he was missing from where he should really have been for all these months. I suspect he's done this kind of thing before - assuming new identities and conning decent folk out of their money. A lot of it must have come down to thinking on his feet, mixing experiences from his own life with what he had learnt on the internet. He was most likely amazed he'd got away with it for so long. Did he have access to a computer in those early hours and days after the crash?'

'I gave him my smartphone,' Michael replied, almost inaudibly.

'There we have it,' said Zanco, a little smugly.

'I found it incredibly straightforward to source the newspaper reports about Richard Fleming's criminal record. If this boy did his research well enough, he would have known Fleming had violent tendencies and gone on to form a picture of the man from that. I never dug around to see if there was anything online about the father being involved in a light aircraft crash or a near miss, as I never performed a full search on the guy. But this boy could easily have discovered it during his inquiries. It's rather clever really.' Imogen quickly shot an apologetic glance at her brother, who appeared utterly crestfallen and not at all impressed by how good a con job the whole thing was.

'These confidence trickster types are very good at telling people what they want to hear. They've almost got an instinct for it. This young lad could probably sense when he was supposed to be acting upset or being polite and helpful, it's a sort of sixth sense that they're either born with or they quickly acquire in order to survive.' Zanco sounded like he was now an expert in the field.

'Does that mean absolutely nothing the boy did or said was real,' Michael muttered into his lap.

'I don't think that's true, Mike. Apart from what he told us about the crash, I believe he was pretty much honest. Despite the impressive homework he did on the family and their lifestyle in Dubai, I don't actually believe the lad made much of an attempt to be Cameron Fleming at all. Most of the time he was just being himself.' Imogen laid a hand on her brother's arm.

'Was it all for the money?' Michael asked plaintively.

Imogen answered this one quickly, before Zanco got a chance, 'oh, no, it wasn't about the money at all. That boy just wanted to be accepted. As soon as you suggested he might be Cameron Fleming he instinctively took on the role. At that point, he had no idea there was the possibility of any material gain from the deception whatsoever. What he immediately craved was the sympathy and the love. That boy pretended to be Cameron Fleming because he wanted to please you, Michael. Right from the beginning of this whole sorry episode that is all he has ever desired.'

35

Imogen accompanied her brother back to his flat in the West-End of the city. He was subdued and withdrawn for the entire tube journey. She resolved to leave him to his own thoughts. It was not until she had prepared a light supper and laid some crockery out on the small but functional breakfast bar in the kitchen that Michael was ready to talk about the situation.

'So Zanco has no idea yet who the boy might be or how he ended up in the water that night?'

The Detective had already been through all the details with them earlier in the day. But Imogen believed her older brother had drifted off into his own private reflections by the second half of the interview.

'No. He wanted you to think very carefully about all the conversations you had with him to see if you could come up with any possible clues,' she explained, dishing the pasta straight out of the saucepan onto their plates.

'The aspect of this which upsets me the most is how I don't even know what to call the boy any longer. I spent so much time with him and grew to become really quite fond of him. Now I find there is no way of actually referring to this person. It's somehow as if he now doesn't exist.'

Before sitting down she placed a hand on Michael's shoulder and said with feeling, 'then let's give him a name. We can find out who this boy is, I'm certain of it. There will have been clues in everything he has said and done over the last few months. It will just have to be a case of piecing them all together and seeing what we can come up with.'

'Would you really help me to do that, Imogen?'

'Of course, Mike. I think I probably want to know the answers even more than you do.' She smiled broadly and began to eat, hugely relieved to see Michael's face had brightened up a little and that he too had started to tuck in.

*

When Imogen told Hugh about the latest turn of events, he was shocked and a little disgruntled he hadn't picked up on the boy's subterfuge himself. He viewed the oversight as a stain on his professional reputation. What seemed to hurt her husband the most was that he had accepted the lad's suggestion he'd been abused by Richard Fleming. Hugh did not ever like to feel he had been gullible in any way. Imogen did reassure him that the young imposter could well have been ill-treated by his own father and this was why the story was so convincing. Hugh begrudgingly acknowledged this possibility. He keenly offered to provide his advice whenever they needed it in their search for the boy's true identity. Hugh was in the midst of his busiest term at the University. He and his parents were going to stay put in Essex to look after Bridie and Ian so Imogen could remain in Glasgow for a few more days. Michael had taken some time off work. They would be devoting themselves fully to the investigation.

Imogen decided that the best place to begin the search was to analyse Michael's memories of his time spent with the boy. For the purposes of clarity and to make her big brother feel better, she suggested that we might refer to the lad as 'Artie', which was the name of their beloved and slightly mad-cap border terrier. The dog had played such a key role in their childhood she thought it might be a nice idea. To her great relief, Michael thought so too.

They sat on the large leather sofa in the grand living room of the flat, with its tall ceilings and beautiful sash and case windows. The sun was positioned high above Kelvingrove Park and the lawns below them were scattered with bright orange leaves. Both armed with a pad and pen they were ready to brainstorm ideas. Hugh suggested they should write down anything at all they could remember about their time with Artie. He said that even the most innocent of comments could hold a vital clue to his real identity. But before they even began, Michael suddenly looked concerned.

'If we do manage to find out who and where Artie is, what will he be charged with do you think?'

'Zanco said it could be fraud and deception, maybe? I think it all depends on what charges the Bank wants to bring against him. Apparently, he didn't actually spend very much of the inheritance. Most of it was kept in trust anyway. There was money for a wardrobe full of new clothes, albeit expensive, designer ones. Then there was the rent on the Glasgow flat for a couple of months. It amounts to a few thousand pounds in total. At least he was never able to go ahead with his business project. He might have ended up serving a long stretch after spending all that cash.'

'Let's start there,' Michael interjected. 'Artie was a wonderful sailor and he loved boats. I might even go as far as to say he knew that stretch of water between Garansay and Kintyre very well. Now I think about it, he said something strange to me on the evening before his lies were finally exposed. It unsettled me a little and made me think it wasn't going to be a good idea to go ahead with the sailing school after all.'

Imogen leant in closer, her pen poised over the pad.

'He asked if it were possible for a ship that had been broken to pieces in bad weather to never again be recovered. I thought he was being a bit morbid and dwelling on the deaths of his parents. Now I see it could mean something else.'

'Okay, so Artie may have been on a sailing boat the night of the helicopter crash. There was a dreadful storm and his boat capsized or was dashed on a rocky headland or something like that,' Imogen joined in.

'When we brought him back to the Lifeboat Centre he had a nasty gash across his forehead. He could have been knocked overboard by the mast or the boom. That would explain how he seemed to know all those details about the storm suddenly coming over without warning. He would have experienced exactly the same thing as the chopper, but from the sea rather than the air.'

273

'Right, so he comes around in the water and he's looking for something to cling on to - but, hang on a minute, when he was found, he didn't have a lifejacket on. Wouldn't he have been wearing one if he'd been out on a boat in that weather?'

'It depends, if the storm came on without warning he may not have done. Or if he was below deck for example, actually, that's the most likely scenario. He was in the cabin, making a drink or having a kip. Then the ship started rolling around in the high waves, he came up to see what was going on and bam - he's caught in the centre of it all.' Michael stopped, as a revelation seemed to strike him mid-flow.

'What is it?

'Well, if Artie was able to go below deck and take some time out, making a snack or a drink, then it means there had to be someone else on that boat with him, somebody who was taking the helm and guiding them through the channel. So the question is - who was this person and where are they now?'

'No-one was reported missing at around that time were they?' Imogen certainly didn't remember Zanco mentioning anything about it during the initial enquiry.

'Sadly, dozens of people go missing every day, Imogen. If there wasn't anyone who knew this person had gone out sailing on the Kilbrannan Sound then the police wouldn't necessarily make the connection,' Michael explained.

'What about the boat, then? It would surely be missed if it never returned to its original mooring. The yacht or sailing club would raise the alarm, surely.' Imogen wanted to ensure they had covered all eventualities.

'Unless this person had a private mooring, or they regularly moved from place to place. They could even have been setting out on an extended voyage, one that might be expected to take them several weeks or months even. Then it would be a long time before they were missed.'

'Let's consider Artie again. He was only a young man. I'd say twenty years old at the most. He wouldn't have owned a sailing boat at his age, especially if what Zanco says is true and he was a petty con-artist and thief. So what was his role on that ship?'

'If the wreckage was able to disappear, pretty much without any trace, then the vessel must have been reasonably small, maybe just a two-hander. So there would have been a Skipper, who had rented or owned the boat, and then there was Artie. Perhaps the boy was hired to crew for this man. I think we have to assume he was a man. Or, he may have known him already. Artie could have been related to him.' Michael seemed on a roll now.

Imogen grabbed the pen and paper and began to summarize: 'we are looking for a male, in his thirties or older,' she paused, looking at her brother who nodded his agreement. 'He would have gone missing from somewhere on the western coast of Scotland in the week after Christmas of last year. This man could have told people he was going away for a while. But my suspicion is that he had no immediate family, otherwise we would have heard more about it in the press by now.' Imogen took a breath, feeling suddenly excited, as if they had made a kind of breakthrough.

'Now all we need to do is persuade D.I Zanco to let us take a look at the missing persons' register for last year,' Michael concluded with satisfaction.

'I do believe,' Imogen declared, vigorously tapping the pad with her pen, 'that we now have a very good place to start.'

36

Zanco proved to be surprisingly cooperative when Imogen asked for the missing persons' report. He said the information was within the public domain and they had a right to take a look at it. She still had to get over to the Strathclyde Police Headquarters and survey the list herself, as the Scots-Italian detective wasn't keen on emailing her a copy. Zanco appeared interested by the theory that Artie had been out on a boat the night of the crash. He promised to pursue this line of enquiry further.

Imogen got the distinct impression that the DI wasn't taking the case of Artie's disappearance very seriously. To him, the boy's deception hadn't really amounted to a great deal in the end. The real prize for Zanco and Frost was in discovering the link between the death of the Flemings and their investigation into a wider network of criminal gangs. Imogen could see that to the two policemen Artie's deceit must have appeared pretty small-time by comparison. Her only quibble with this dismissal of the boy's ruse was that both investigating teams had based the foundation of their entire case on what Artie had said happened inside that helicopter.

As she understood it, Frost's theory that the pilot was coerced into crashing the aircraft remained purely conjecture. Zanco admitted last week that they couldn't actually make a water tight case. No physical evidence existed which proved Tom Watson received threatening letters or phone calls before the accident. The team only had the testimony of the men's wives to suggest they'd been put under pressure during the preceding months. However compelling that may have been, it wasn't enough for a court of law.

To Imogen's mind, with Artie's account of what occurred inside the chopper having been totally discredited, they needed to look at re-opening the whole investigation. For the moment, that was not her concern. Michael and Imogen were focussing their attention on trying to identify the man who was on the boat with Artie the night of the terrible storm.

Imogen met her brother in a small and slightly seedy café on Douglas Street. She showed him her photocopy of the missing persons' register. It didn't take them long to eliminate the individuals who did not fit the profile they'd devised.

'It's tragic isn't it? Most of these reports have been filed for boys and girls in their teens and twenties.' Imogen sighed, taking a sip of stewed tea.

'And those are the missing who actually had someone in their lives who noticed they'd gone. Imagine how many others simply go unrecorded,' Michael added.

'Oh don't say that, it's just too depressing.' She continued to run her eyes down the list, underlining any names that could be a possibility for their man. There really weren't that many. Imogen took a copy of both years, imagining that if this person lived on their own, with few family and friends, it might take several months before anyone clocked their absence.

'I've got a couple of names here who could be candidates for our lost Skipper,' she finally announced, handing the sheets to Michael.

He took a few minutes to study their details. Pointing at one of the highlighted entries he stated, 'this chap seems the most likely: Lachlan White, 66 years old, lives at Ard na Machair Farm, Carradale, Kintyre. Reported missing by his daughter-in-law on 22nd February of this year. Unfortunately, that's nearly two months after the day of the storm, but the details are still the closest thing we've got to a match.'

'Carradale is just across the Sound from Lower Kilduggan. You can see the lights of the village from the windows of the guest bedrooms,' Imogen pointed out unnecessarily. 'Doesn't 'Ard' mean 'high-up', or cliffs, or something like that in Gaelic? This farm must be on the hillside then, beyond the town itself. Not exactly prime sailing territory, is it?'

'No, it isn't and this fellow is a little older than I had envisaged too. But it's still worth us looking into, especially as it's the only name we've got to go on so far,' Michael added encouragingly.

Imogen didn't like to mention how their mystery man might never have been reported missing at all. Her brother seemed so positive about this line of enquiry that she said instead, 'Okay, have we got any contact details for the daughter-in-law? We can start by talking to her.'

According to the report filed by the Strathclyde Police, Lachlan White's daughter-in-law lived in Garelochhead. Michael and Imogen decided to take his car to make the journey. It

279

was a picturesque drive past the banks of the lovely Gareloch itself. On the way, they tried to decide what on earth to say to the woman.

They pulled up outside the address by early afternoon. Imagining the lady would very likely be out at this time of the day they remained in their seats for a few moments and took a good look at the exterior of the property. It was a modern semi-detached house. Instead of a front garden there was a newly paved driveway. No car was parked outside but when Imogen spotted a pram crammed into the tiny porch area she decided there might very well be someone at home.

The lady's name was Cathy Henderson. As soon as she answered the door, Imogen caught her breath at the striking familiarity of her features. She wondered if Michael had noticed it too. The woman seemed harassed but ushered them in when they told her they represented a charity that helped to locate missing relatives. There was a baby asleep in a bouncer on the floor. Imogen could see photographs of two more children looking smart and smiling in school uniforms displayed proudly on the window sill.

'Is this about Lachlan?' Cathy asked in a hushed voice. 'Hang on a minute.' she promptly lifted the bouncer into another room and pulled the door shut behind her. 'You've not found him have you?' she enquired, looking a little more relaxed. Cathy Henderson was blond and pretty and could have been any age between thirty and forty.

'I'm afraid not, Mrs Henderson, but we're doing our best. We just wanted to take a few more details from you,' Michael said, seizing the initiative.

Cathy gestured towards the sofa and they all sat down. 'There's really not much more I can tell you. It's a miracle I even noticed he'd gone off somewhere. We didn't see very much of him.'

'Perhaps your husband could provide us with the information we require?' Imogen asked tentatively.

Cathy Henderson looked puzzled for a moment and then broke into a smile. 'Oh, Lachlan's not Kenny's dad. He was the father of my first husband. That's the reason why we don't see him very often. I got married young. Dave died within just a couple of years of us tying the knot. He was a fisherman and his boat was caught in a storm. None of the young men on board came back. Absolutely tragic it was for all of us families. So I've always kept in touch with Lachlan - on and off. But when I met Kenny and had the kids, well, you get pretty busy don't you? I'm afraid we visited him less and less.'

'Perhaps you could simply tell us a little about what Lachlan is like as a person,' Imogen gentle encouraged.

'Erm, well, his wife died a couple of years back and he did struggle to cope on his own for a while. The Farm has fallen into disrepair but he keeps the cottage quite neat and cosy. Lachlan's still pretty hale and hearty so it is possible he's gone away on a trip or something. He wouldn't necessarily tell me about it beforehand. But when I kept ringing and getting no response at the end of last February I sent Kenny down there to check he was okay. He said that all his clothes were in the wardrobe and the food had gone off in the fridge. Ken said it just wasn't really as it

281

should be.'

'Did Lachlan have any hobbies?' When he realised the query sounded a bit odd Michael quickly clarified, 'did he take part in any activities that might have caused him to have an accident somewhere, perhaps?'

Cathy shrugged but then said, 'there's only his old boat.'

Imogen sat forward in her seat. 'Oh yes. Was he interested in sailing?'

'In a manner of speaking. He's got an ancient wooden boat in one of the outhouses at the farm, he worked quite hard doing it up.'

'Did he ever take it out on the Sound?' Michael asked lightly.

'Every so often, yes. But it was a huge effort to launch it. He had to shift it onto the back of a trailer and then get it off again at the other end. It was definitely a two man job. He maybe sailed once a year at the most.'

Suddenly, they heard the muffled cries of the baby, waking from its sleep in the adjacent room. Cathy jumped out of her seat.

Imogen said quickly, 'and was it still in the shed when your husband went to check on Lachlan - the boat, I mean?'

'Oh.' Cathy stopped in her tracks, despite the baby's cries becoming progressively more frantic, 'I don't think Kenny thought to have a look.'

They stood up to leave. When Cathy returned with the now serene child cradled in her arms, Imogen decided to try one more question. 'Mrs Henderson, is there anybody else in your family who spent time with your father-in-law, a cousin perhaps or a nephew. He would be in his late teens or early twenties, athletic looking and with very light blond hair.'

Cathy studied each of them in turn, her attractive face adopting a guarded expression. 'Do you mean Murray?'

'Yes,' said Michael, with as much confidence as he could muster. 'We have received a tip off that your father-in-law was seen recently with this young man.'

'Well he could have been. Murray is my son - from my marriage to Dave. He'll be nineteen next birthday. He left home years ago. It got a bit cramped in here when Ken and I got hitched and started our own family. You can imagine what it was like I'm sure. He doesn't come back and see his mum very often. You know what boys of that age are like. But he was quite close to his grandad when he was little so this tip-off of yours might just be correct.'

There was something defensive and self-justifying about Cathy Henderson's tone when she referred to her first-born child. It made Imogen feel both sad and uncomfortable.

'Thank you very much for your time,' Imogen said with a cold finality.

They squeezed out through the confined space of the cluttered entranceway and despite the unseasonal warmth of the late afternoon, Imogen shuddered.

37

When they had returned to the privacy of the car, Michael rested both hands on the wheel and pronounced, 'do you think we've found him?'

'I very much believe we have. Didn't you see the likeness? I noticed it as soon as we walked through the door.'

'Then we can thankfully lay poor old Artie back to rest. The boy who we knew as Cameron Fleming is really Murray Henderson,' Michael concluded flatly.

'Actually, I have a hunch the boy would not have wanted to take on his step-father's name. I think he's called Murray White. We can give both names to DI Zanco and see what he comes up with.'

Before Michael started up the engine, he shifted around in his seat to look at her directly. 'Imogen, you've got good instincts about these things. I'm finding the more I discover about Murray, the more I feel he needs our help and support rather than our censure.'

Imogen smiled wryly, 'You're a good man Michael Nichols. Sometimes I believe you are a far better person than Allan or me. Yes, I am coming around to that way of thinking myself. I also suspect Zanco is wrong. I don't think Murray is a petty thief and con-artist. I'm willing to bet he's never done anything like this before. He was in a state of shock when he woke up in that hospital bed. He'd just lost his grandfather remember, so the grief he exhibited was absolutely real. You showed him so much kindness in those first few hours that the boy simply wanted to go along with the whole pretence so he could be with you for a little longer. Like so much in life, there was never any great master-plan.'

'I'd like to go and look at the farm - the one in Carradale. I want to check and see if that old boat is still there, because if it is then our theory has been quite wrong from the very start,' Michael suddenly announced.

The drive from Garelochhead to Carradale proved to be extremely scenic. Imogen always found it fascinating to view the hills of Garansay from the other side of the water, especially in Kintyre where the distance across the Kilbrannan Sound was at its narrowest. They had only a very basic address for Lachlan White's property. They did possess their theory that the small-holding would be raised up somehow; positioned on a promontory perhaps. This was based solely on the meaning of its name in Gaelic. Michael drove up and down tiny tracks for what seemed like hours until they found it.

Imogen finally spotted a small sign, almost hidden behind dense brambles which displayed the faint lettering: Ard na Machair Farm. It was getting dark as they parked up and approached the little cream coloured cottage, which lay about four hundred yards ahead.

'Let's check out the sheds,' Imogen suggested.

Michael rushed back to grab a flashlight from the boot.

Cathy Henderson was certainly right when she said the farm had fallen into disrepair. The outhouses were in a pretty ramshackle state and those that were meant to be padlocked could easily be accessed through rotten and flimsy wooden panels. There was very little of interest out there, just rusty broken machinery and an old tractor. It reminded Imogen of how her mum had left Lower Kilduggan by the time she died, except in this place the decay seemed to have set in about twenty years sooner.

There was a barn, however, that appeared in better condition than the others. Similar to Isabel's pottery shed, Lachlan had obviously still been using this one up until the time of his death. There was a workbench with various tools and jars of polish set out on it, ready for use. A Glasgow Rangers mug, now green with mould, sat on a small foldable table which also housed a kettle and a tin full of instant coffee.

'He must have had electricity in here at one stage,' Michael commented, 'although I expect it's disconnected now.'

The centre of the barn was completely empty although a neat pile of timber supports lay in each corner, indicating that a large object was once comfortably accommodated within the space. They quickly exited this damp, cold place where nothing had been touched by human hand for months on end.

Now they had the confirmation they were seeking, Imogen began to make her way purposefully down the unkempt lane to where they'd left the sports car. But Michael was standing dead still and swinging his torch's beam around the front of the farmhouse itself.

'Imogen,' he called. 'I just want to check out

the cottage before we go.'

She said nothing but resignedly trudged back up the slope to join him. The house was in darkness. Peering through a small side window Imogen cast a look at the cottage's well-kept and clean little kitchen. They walked the whole way round the modest property; checking door handles and latches as they went. There was a narrow brick extension at the rear of the house which appeared to have been built to contain a new bathroom. When Michael pulled at the sneck, the window immediately swung out on its hinges. The aperture it created was about four foot square. Imogen's brother turned towards her with an uncharacteristically mischievous look on his face.

'There's no way I can get through that gap,' he stated and if Imogen didn't know any better she would say he was enjoying himself.

'Well, don't look at me.'

'You're tall, yes, but you're also a lot more slender than I am. If I give you a push from out here, you should be able to squeeze yourself through.'

'I do believe there may have been a compliment in there somewhere,' Imogen replied stonily, placing her bag on the ground and quickly removing her coat.

Michael gave his sister a foot up. She slowly pulled herself through the window, using her hands to grip the bottom of the frame. Imogen called back to him, telling her brother to keep hold of her legs so he could lower her gently down. She ended up in an awkward position, crouched over the sink, desperately hoping her weight wasn't about to dislodge it from the wall. But she was in.

Michael passed her the flashlight. Imogen made her way gingerly through the unfamiliar layout of the ground floor. She finally located the back door and a set of keys hanging in the kitchen which could be used to let her partner-in-crime into the house. Unsure of what they might be looking for, the pair kept close together and swept through each of the rooms in turn.

Although smelling badly of damp, Lachlan's cottage had clearly been better looked after than the rest of the farm. There was a cosy sitting room which had what looked like a fairly recently installed wood-burner. There was no sign of any fuel. Bookshelves lined the walls of the dining room. Many of the titles were nautical adventures. Imogen spotted a shelf full of Patrick O'Brian novels and smiled in recognition of the addictive quality of these sea-faring tales.

They padded up the narrow staircase and visually took in the contents of the three low-ceilinged bedrooms. Just as Imogen was about to suggest they call it a day, a faint rustling noise came from the bathroom behind them. Suddenly, the door flew open and a dark figure ran straight at them, attempting to barge Michael out of the way. Her brother acted instinctively and grappled the escapee around the chest and waist, leaving him wriggling futilely in the stronger man's grip.

'Calm down Murray, it's alright,' he said soothingly. 'We don't wish to do you any harm. Imogen and I have come to help.'

38

Once Murray had recognised them, he gave up the struggle. After that, the boy was far more composed. He led his guests into the neat little kitchen and lit a couple of candles, apologising for not having yet gathered any wood for the fire.

When they were seated around the chipped table Murray looked his mentor in the eye and beseeched, 'I'm so sorry I lied to you Michael. There's nothing I can really say to explain what I did. Please believe it wasn't for the money. At first, I pretended to be Cameron because that's who everyone expected me to be. I know this is going to sound weird, but I found it hard to contradict them. Then, as time went on, selfishly, I just didn't want to give it all up.'

'I think I understand, Murray. But you've got yourself into real trouble. I would have helped you in the aftermath of the accident whoever you happened to be. It made no odds to me if you were Cameron Fleming or not.'

The boy hung his head down in shame.

'Murray, can you tell us what happened to your grandad?' Imogen asked gently.

The boy raised his vision. He definitely appeared to be more comfortable with this topic. Imogen even saw a brief smile flicker across his handsome face. 'My grandad got me into sailing in the first place. I spent a lot of time staying here at the farm after my dad died. Gran and Grandad liked to take me out in their boat, although we couldn't do it very often because it was a real palaver to get it down to the shore. When I left home a few years ago I made my money by crewing on yachts and working in the boat yards during the off-seasons. I enjoyed the work and it got me out on the water which I loved. There wasn't much room at Mum and Kenny's place so if I had any time off then I came here. Grandad needed cheering up after Gran died, he didn't like being on his own much. We were working on the old boat together whenever there was a spare moment. Then, last Christmas day, Grandad suggested we take her out for a sail, the weather had been really lovely, you see.'

'So you were out sailing on the Kilbrannan Sound that Saturday between Christmas and New Year, when the Flemings had their accident,' Imogen stated.

'That's right. The conditions had been very good when we set out. For a few hours that afternoon the sailing was glorious. I don't remember Grandad and I having a better time since Gran had passed away. As it started to get dark we decided we might moor up somewhere. The boat had a couple of berths and it was great fun to spend the night on board.' Murray stopped for a second, the memory starting to become less pleasant. 'I was down in the cabin, looking at the maps and deciding where might be nice to tie up for the evening. That was when the weather began to turn. The boat started to roll really violently. I immediately went up top to see what was going on. I thought we might have been caught in the wash of a big ship or something. As soon as I stepped out onto the deck the strength of the gale hit me square in the face. I called out for Grandad but my words were completely swallowed up by the roar of the wind and spray. Then I saw that the boom was untethered and swinging completely free. It must have been whipping back and forth with a terrific momentum because before I had a chance to duck out of the way it struck me hard across the forehead. I don't remember anything else after that until I came to in the water. The waves seemed to be as tall as houses. I couldn't see the boat anywhere. There was a terrible blackness all around me but then I glimpsed the flashing light. I don't know if I managed to swim towards it or if the current simply took me there but as I got closer I found there was debris to hold on to. It felt like a miracle.'

'You'd reached the wreckage of the helicopter crash,' Michael said.

'When I made out the shape of the aircraft, as I drifted closer, it was as if I was imagining it. Like when someone's lost in the desert and they see a watering hole with a palm tree - what's it called again?'

'A mirage,' Imogen supplied.

'It just looked so out of place in the middle of those rough seas and creepy too. But I also thought - if this is real it's my only hope. I knew Grandad was already gone. He would not have wanted me to drown out there like my father had so I kicked and swam like crazy towards the chopper. I managed to pull myself up onto one of the skids, which seemed to have some kind of buoyancy in it.'

'Did you see any of the passengers at the crash site,' Imogen enquired, with an increased urgency to her tone.

Murray looked decidedly sheepish. It took him a few seconds to form his response. 'This is the part I feel most guilty about. I wanted to tell the police but I knew if I did it would be the end of everything.'

Both Michael and Imogen shifted forward with interest, patiently waiting for the young man to continue.

'I saw the pilot.'

'Tom Watson?' Imogen blurted out, 'was he still alive?'

'Yes. It took me a little while to spot him. I was edging myself along the skid to keep my legs out of the water and then I reached the cockpit. He was sort of hanging forward onto his seat-belt. I dragged myself alongside him and being nearer to the guy I could see he was badly injured. He had a head wound which was bleeding. There was also blood on his body suit. But he was still conscious.'

'Did he say anything to you?' Imogen couldn't prevent herself from interrupting.

'He was pretty groggy at first. Then he asked me to release his belts so I did. I tried to support the man and move him into a more comfortable position, but he was very weak. I got so upset last week when Zanco tried to blame the crash on Tom Watson, because I knew it couldn't be true,' Murray added indignantly. 'I was so frustrated not to be able to set that smug copper straight.'

'How do you know it wasn't Tom Watson who ditched the helicopter?' She pressed.

'Because he told me exactly what *did* happen

on board that flight. He was a dying man, Mrs Croft and I believed him.' Murray said this with such conviction that neither of them dared to contradict it. 'The pilot told me that when they set off that evening, Richard Fleming was really jumpy. He was nervous and kept asking Tom questions even before they were in the air. Once they'd passed the eastern coast and were heading through the mountains, Fleming got increasingly agitated. Once the turbulence started, Tom said the guy just lost it. He thought he might be having some kind of panic attack. Fleming undid his seat belt and was trying to get into the cockpit. Cameron got out of his seat and tried to restrain him, but his father was a big bloke. The pilot said he thought Fleming might have struck the boy. According to Tom Watson, who was desperately trying to lead the chopper safely through the storm, it was pandemonium in the back. He thinks the wife and daughter were both attempting to hold the dad down, but they didn't succeed. As the chopper was half-way across the Sound, Richard Fleming pushed his way into the cockpit. Tom said the bloke was almost hysterical, telling him to land immediately and stuff like that. The pilot tried his best to reason with him but this guy was beyond reach. At some point, Fleming made a grab for the controls and he knocked Tom out cold in the process.'

'And that's when the helicopter dropped into the waves below,' Michael inserted.

'Tom remembered nothing else until he woke up in the wreckage. Sadly, he bore the brunt of the impact.' Murray gazed wistfully out of the

293

window at the pitch blackness beyond.

'So none of the Flemings had a seat-belt on when the chopper hit the sea,' Imogen chipped in.

'They wouldn't have stood a chance,' Michael lamented, 'what happened to Tom Watson after that?'

'He was desperate for me to know the reason why the chopper went down. He didn't want to end up getting the blame for the crash - ironic, eh? I tried my best to get as close to the pilot's version of events as I could when I gave my statement without giving myself away. I wanted to keep my story nice and simple. I also thought the real Cameron Fleming would never have admitted that his dad went crazy on board. But I still wanted to say how Tom had tried so desperately to keep them in the air. I felt I owed it to that poor man who had died out there in my arms.' Murray sniffled at the terrible memory. 'I tried to hold onto his body for as long as I could, but it was bitterly cold and I was so tired. Eventually, I must have dropped off for a while because when I woke up he was gone. I shifted myself back down the skids, just to try and keep my blood flowing. I must have passed out again because the next thing I knew there I was, warm and dry, lying on a stretcher in the medical room of the Garansay Lifeboat Station.'

39

Michael did his best to persuade Murray to return with them to Glasgow and give himself up to the authorities. They were determined not to leave him in that cold house for another night. His grandparents were both long gone. There was nothing left for the boy now. The cottage contained only the ghosts of his previous existence, however benevolent those spirits might be.

Murray finally agreed to come back to Michael's flat, though he had not yet consented to go to the police. The lad packed a small bag to bring with him. Imogen was saddened to observe the few paltry odds and ends he owned. In that moment, she feel she could not blame a boy who had been given so little in his short life for wanting to grasp at something more. Imogen experienced a stab of anger towards the woman who found no room in her shiny new life for the son she already had.

Imogen was also keen that Tom Watson's last testimony was properly recorded. It would give his family some solace to know that he did not die out there in the freezing, dark waters alone. Not to mention holding back the momentum of Zanco and Frost's campaign to place the entire blame for the crash on the poor pilot. Imogen knew Murray's word could not be totally trusted, but his report of Tom's account fitted with the picture she had formed of what happened on board that flight.

An image had been shaping itself in her mind ever since they returned from Dubai. It had appeared clear to Imogen, after all the evidence she had gathered, that by the day of the Malhotra's wedding at the Glenrannoch Hotel, Richard Fleming was a man on the edge.

Fleming was about to give evidence against a group of highly dangerous men. He also possessed a volatile and aggressive personality. Added to this, he found himself confined within a tiny aircraft with events seeming to be spiralling out of his control. Imogen's theory had always been that he 'flipped out' in some way inside the helicopter with absolutely tragic consequences. Everyone on board the flight was a victim of Richard Fleming's mistakes. Imogen noted how unjust it was that he would be the only one to end up receiving a proper burial.

After Murray had a decent night's rest and a long, hot bath the boy realised he had no option but to face the music. Michael promised to accompany him to the Holland Street Headquarters and put up any bail money that may have been required in order to keep him out of custody. In the end, this was not necessary as after Murray gave his full and frank statement to DI Zanco the policeman allowed him to go home. Zanco informed Michael a report would be filed with the Fiscal's office. They'd let him know in due course what charges would be brought.

The Detective was far more interested in the new explanation for the Fleming's crash provided by Murray's altered testimony. He and Agent Frost were going to have to rethink their entire investigation. From Imogen's point of view, she was rather relieved to learn that the world of international organised crime had not in the end extended as far as the remote and beautiful Isle of Garansay.

With Murray comfortably installed in one of Michael's guest bedrooms, Imogen was preparing to return home. Her brother had once again put himself forward as the boy's unofficial guardian and as someone who would provide a character reference for him when the case finally came to court. Michael called Cathy Henderson, to let her know, out of courtesy, where her son could be found. He said she expressed her gratitude to him for his hospitality but her tone was curt. Michael got the distinct impression that his kindness towards Murray merely highlighted her own deficiencies. Cathy wanted to end the exchange as quickly as possible so she could return to the new life she had made for herself.

On her last evening in Glasgow, as they sipped red wine and enjoyed a simple meal looking out over Kelvingrove Park, there was something Imogen was dying to say to her two companions, but in the end she did not. Imogen yearned to point out how both of them had dads whom they had never known. She longed to tell Michael how his own father had been lost at sea - just like Murray's father had.

She wanted to inform them of these facts because Imogen believed it was this shared heritage that created the special connection which existed between her older brother and this quiet and reserved young man. She knew in her heart of hearts that Michael did not wish to be told anything about his biological father. Of course, she would respect his decision.

Instead, Imogen raised an elegant, long-stemmed glass and proposed a toast: to the future of their families and to this very welcome new addition to the Nichols clan.

40

It was the Saturday afternoon of that non-descript week which lay aimlessly between Christmas and New Year. The winter had been a bitterly cold one on the Isle of Garansay, but today the almost blindingly bright sun was positioned high in the cloudless sky. The crystal waters of Port na Mara bay were glistening in the light. If it wasn't for the distinct chill present in the air and the stark bareness of the surrounding trees, you could easily mistake it for a perfect summer's day.

Michael Nichols was looking elegant and handsome in a dark morning suit. He effortlessly guided his guests towards the wonderfully distinctive setting provided by the Garansay Whisky Distillery building. His daughter's fiancé Ross stood right beside him, looking equally resplendent in his smart wedding outfit. The young man was clearly nervous but his future father-in-law took charge of the proceedings. Every so often he placed a reassuring arm around the groom's tense shoulders.

Everyone was pleased the rain had held off for the Big Day. The excitement and joy which accompanied this event meant no-one was really feeling the cold. Hugh and Imogen had been staying with their children at the local hotel. The stone villa was situated high up the glen, enjoying absolutely splendid views of the old Norman castle and out across the Kilbrannan Sound to Kintyre in the west. The Crofts thought it was best to leave Lower Kilduggan Farm for Michael and Sarah to use. They wanted the bride to have plenty of space and privacy in which to prepare for her wonderfully special day. She and her father could then have some time alone together.

Ross and his Best Man were also staying at the Port na Mara Hotel as was Imogen's brother Allan and his partner Abigail. There had been a lovely, almost party-like atmosphere at their comfortable and hospitable lodgings for the previous couple of nights. They spent several jolly evenings gathered around the roaring log fires of the hotel bar, with whiskies and coffees, sharing the colourful tales of their Garansay childhoods. Imogen just loved an island wedding. There was something absolutely magical about it.

A significant number of the guests were there representing Miriam's side of the family. Most of them had travelled from the 'Granite City' to attend this special occasion. None of them seemed to begrudge making the long journey down from Aberdeen. Ross's folks had come over from Perthshire and were staying at a lovely guesthouse nearby.

Bridie was desperate to be the one to catch the first glimpse of Sarah as she arrived in the wedding car. Imogen stood with her daughter at the entrance to the Visitors' Centre whilst Hugh took the boys inside to find their seats. Ewan's girlfriend Chloe was invited to the celebrations but was spending Christmas with her parents in Dubai and sadly could not attend. In fact, it would be her last visit to the UAE for some time as Howard and Liz had decided to return home to Manchester. Chloe said her mother never really settled happily out there. It just didn't quite feel like home. Selfishly, Imogen was glad they were coming back to the UK. She had grown to like them both very much.

Bridie excitedly nudged her mother's arm as she spotted the sleek sports car negotiating a bend up at the harbour and slowly winding its way in their direction. Sarah had insisted on making the grand entrance in her father's prized automobile, even though she had to squeeze her huge billowing train into the cramped passenger seat.

As the car pulled up, Bridie let out a hearty cheer. The handsome young driver gave them an enthusiastic wave before opening the door for Sarah with a flourish and taking her elegant arm in his.

'Hi Murray!' Bridie shouted over to the temporary chauffeur. He smiled broadly in her direction. Imogen could tell the boy was absolutely brimming over with pride.

Sarah looked simply stunning. Her thick copper curls contrasted strikingly with the cream colour of her long, silk dress. Bridie sighed with pure adolescent admiration as Michael stepped forward to lead his beloved daughter inside.

Murray White's journey to this point had not been an easy one. Just a few months ago, he faced charges of fraud, deception and of attempting to pervert the course of justice by giving a false statement to the police. The Fiscal's office took into account the boy's eventual full confession and his difficult family background. Michael made a private arrangement with the bank's trustees to pay back all the money Murray had spent.

There was also an unexpected development which went in the boy's favour. With the discovery that Cameron Fleming had, after all, perished alongside his parents and sister, Nancy Cook became the sole beneficiary of what remained of the family's estate. It turned out that Isla's mother had no intention of pressing charges against Murray White. In fact, they remained in close contact with each other. Nancy apparently commented to the trustees, after she was told of her sizeable inheritance, that Murray had been more of a grandson to her in the past year than Cameron Fleming ever had.

So Murray White avoided a custodial sentence. Michael wanted him to learn the error of his ways. He recommended a programme of community service for the boy. As a result, he had been helping out in an old people's home in Greenock for a few hours every week. Murray had shown a worrying propensity towards deception. Imogen's brother was keen to channel the lad's obvious ingenuity and skills in a more positive direction instead.

The service was very touching and the venue had been decorated beautifully. The guests sat down to a formal meal in an elevated dining room which possessed angled windows in the sloping roof. They were ideally designed to give panoramic views far up the mountainside. The sunlight was spilling romantically onto the Croft's table from above. Imogen leant towards Hugh and rested her head on his shoulder.

'How long do you think it will be before it is

Ewan and Chloe tying the knot?' Hugh joked, with his mouth full of prime Scottish venison.

'Don't say that!' Imogen jabbed him gently with her elbow. 'They're only kids!'

Hugh chuckled and then observed, 'I'm surprised to see Julia Laing here. I thought she and Colin had split up ages ago.'

'Oh, didn't you know? She is working for Michael now. Just for a couple of days a week. She helps him with his paperwork,' Imogen explained with a cheeky grin and a twinkle in her eye.

'You can wipe that smirk off your face, Mrs Croft. Julia must be over twenty years younger than Mike,' her husband replied, quite earnestly.

'Come on Hugh, this is my older brother we're talking about. Women find it extremely difficult to resist him. Anyway, that kind of age gap doesn't seem quite so significant when you get to our age.'

'Michael hasn't so much as glanced at another woman since Miriam died. I'd be very surprised if there's anything going on between them.' Hugh took a sip of champagne before qualifying this by adding, 'of course, I've been wrong about so many things recently it might not be wise for you to take my word for it.'

'You certainly had the right instincts about Murray. He's not a bad kid after all and he does need someone to protect him. What I picked up on were the lies; I knew he wasn't being truthful about something but I wasn't sure what it was. He was sending out a great deal of mixed messages. For instance, when I found him apparently in the depths of anguish, staring into the distance by the water's edge at the Kilduggan point, at that moment I truly believed he was grieving for his lost parents and sister.'

'The tears were probably for his grandad instead. Or it could even have been sorrow for the father he never had an opportunity to get to know. He might even have been expressing remorse for the tangled web of lies he had created,' Hugh suggested thoughtfully. 'Human beings can prove to be rather complicated and difficult to read at times, I'm afraid.'

Once the speeches were over, the formalities rapidly gave way to a good old Scottish shindig. A local Ceilidh band struck up some immediately recognisable tunes. Hugh decided to join in with the dancing by spinning Bridie expertly around the floor. Suddenly noticing that she was left sitting by herself, Colin Walmsley strode over and took the chair next to Imogen.

'It's been a very enjoyable 'do',' he commented over the sound of the music. 'Can I get you a drink?'

'I'm fine, thank you Colin. How's the farm?'

'Aye, business is no' bad. I'm still itching to get involved in something new, though. Having my fingers burnt with that property deal has made me a little cautious, however.'

'Don't let it. You just had some bad luck. It could happen to anyone,' Imogen advised.

'What would you say if I told you I was thinking about going into partnership with your brother Michael?'

She stopped watching her husband and daughter for a moment, turning to face the man seated beside her. 'I'd be extremely surprised.'

'I was really quite impressed when he and Murray showed me the plans for the sailing school a few months ago. I loved the location; it's only about a mile away from Loch Crannox. The designs have all been completed. The council were about to grant permission before the whole thing stalled. I was thinking it might be a good project to invest in. I'll need a few skilled sailors to manage the thing for me, so it could create some much needed local jobs. But I'll only go ahead if you think it's a good idea, Imogen. I know how you weren't terribly keen on the boy. It would mean him sticking around the area for the long term. If you would prefer it if Murray were to steer well clear of Garansay and of Lower Kilduggan Farm then just say the word. I'll back right off.' Colin's tone was grave and his brows furrowed, giving his usually handsome face a very solemn expression.

Imogen broke the serious mood by smiling warmly at her friend and neighbour. 'That's a fantastic plan!' She exclaimed.

Before they had time to discuss the details any further, Hugh swept past and took Imogen by the hand. Bridie had run off to join her cousins, so her husband was free to lead her purposefully into the centre of this delightfully sunlit room.

Hugh pulled Imogen close and whispered into her ear, 'you didn't think I was going to leave my wife deep in conversation with another man did you?'

Following their lead, the dancefloor suddenly filled up with couples. The band instinctively slowed down the tempo of its lively tunes. This was how the couple remained for much of the afternoon, wrapped tightly in one another's arms

305

until darkness fell. Surrounded by family and friends they became caught up in the wonderful enchantment of the occasion. It was almost as if they'd been temporarily charmed by the magic of this very special and totally unique place.

*

Hugh and Imogen return in 'Lawful Death' available now.

© Katherine Pathak 2013.

If you enjoyed this novel, please spare a few moments to write a brief review. Reviews really help to introduce new readers to my books. This means I can keep on writing.

Many thanks,

Katherine.

Find out more about my books at:

www.katherinepathak.wordpress.com

For special offers and news of new releases, follow me @KatherinePathak on Twitter.

Steele, C., & Aronson, J. (1998). Stereotype threat and test performance in academically successful African Americans. In C. Jencks & M. Phillips (Eds), *The black–white test score gap* (pp. 401–427). Washington, DC: Brookings Institution Press.

Street, B. (1984). *Literacy in theory and practice*. Cambridge: Cambridge University Press.

Street, B. (1997). The implications of the "New Literacy Studies" for literacy education. *English in Education* 31: 45–59.

Street, B. (2003). What's new in new literacy studies? *Current Issues in Comparative Education* 5: 1–14.

Street, B. (2005). At last: Recent applications of New Literacy Studies in educational contexts. *Research in the Teaching of English* 39: 417–423.

Stucky, S. (1987). *Slave culture: Nationalist theory and the foundations of black America*. Oxford: Oxford University Press.

Taylor, D. (1996). *Toxic literacies: Exposing the injustice of bureaucratic texts*. Portsmouth, NH: Heinemann.

Teale, W. H. (1987), Emergent literacy: Reading and writing development in early childhood. *National Reading Conference Yearbook* 36: 45–74.

Teale, W. H., & Sulzby, E. (1986). *Emergent literacy: Writing and reading*. New York: Praeger.

Tedlock, D. (1983). *The spoken word and the work of interpretation*. Philadelphia: University of Pennsylvania Press.

Tough, P. (2012). *How children succeed: Grit, curiosity, and the hidden power of character*. New York: Mariner Books.

Vygotsky, L. S. (1987). *The Collected Works of L. S. Vygotsky, Vol. 1. Problems of General Psychology. Including the Volume Thinking and Speech*. Edited by R. W. Rieber & A. S. Carton. New York: Plenum.

Wells, G. (1986). *The meaning makers: Children learning language and using language to learn*. Portsmouth, New Hampshire: Heinemann.

Wieder, D. L., & Pratt, S. (1990a). On being a recognizable Indian among Indians. In D. Carbaugh (Ed.), *Cultural communication and intercultural contact* (pp. 45–64). Hillsdale, NJ: Lawrence Erlbaum.

Wieder, D. L., & Pratt, S. (1990b). On the occasioned and situated character of members' questions and answers: Reflections on the question, "Is he or she a real Indian?" In D. Carbaugh (Ed.), *Cultural communication and intercultural contact* (pp. 65–75). Hillsdale, NJ: Lawrence Erlbaum.

INDEX

For my two boys, things are only
recently made flesh, made mortal –
our uprooted palm tree, two goldfish,
the bird a neighbour's cat brought down
last week – and they are almost holy
with this knowledge. 'Let's die now,
then let's go home for tea,' Lee says,
putting into words as best he can
the sea's helpless love affair with the land.

Three Lines for Leland

A housefly settles
on the still end of my pen:
haiku counterweight.

Poetry in hard times

The last few months have been worrying ones throughout the country, and across the world, as a result of what increasingly looks like a combination of greed and financial mismanagement. The coming year, and perhaps 2010, looks like it will bring even more challenging times for all. After the extravagance and waste of the Celtic Tiger years, it seems we are set for a rude awakening. One is reminded of Cavafy's famous poem, 'Waiting for the Barbarians', in which the senators and high officials of imperial Rome run around in confusion at the impending invasion of their city and destruction of their way of life; a poem which ends with a no-show by the threatened horde, and the thought-provoking question:

> Now what is to become of us without barbarians?
> These people were some kind of a solution.

In what form and from what direction our own barbarian horde might approach remains to be seen. But it may well be that the 'barbaric yawp' (to use Whitman's phrase) we need to hear and heed will prove to be the voice of a part of our own selves that we have dangerously managed to ignore in recent times.

As well as necessary public debate and the redirecting of shared resources, hard times, on whatever scale they come, also inevitably demand some aspect of that inner quarrel Yeats had in mind when he wrote: 'We make out of the quarrel with others, rhetoric, but of the quarrel with ourselves, poetry'. If the unexamined life is not worth living, in times of hardship the bringing to light of that interior quarrel is an essential step towards the rebalancing of a society.

Hardship also requires a kind of endurance, the ability to let go without giving up, that winter each year might be said to provide the ideal training for. This is not to say that poets require or deserve hardship. Let it be clear. There is no glamour in poverty for poets or artists, or for anyone else for that matter; poets, like all citizens, should resist any attempt to condemn them to garrets or to remove to the sidelines their contribution to the psychic life of their communities.

Good poets work like gardeners with the language; they meet it as a living thing and feel it change and grow and wither and seem to die but then, miraculously, spring to life again, with the passing of the lines, the stanzas, the days and months and years.

In this sense, and perhaps especially in challenging times, poetry is, whatever its subject matter or style, almost ideally equipped to descend again into 'the foul rag and bone shop of the heart'.

The barbarians are ever with us. We fear them and we need them: we can't make up our minds. But we know they are there and we meet up with them from time to time, often at the darkest time of the year when the Rhine, if not our own hearts, freezes over, and they come charging across the borders, waving their arms in the air, calling out in a language that is both terrible and beautiful, a language that tells us things we do not always wish to hear but need to know.

Hard times require a steady hand and a steady gaze, but they also require the reassertion of the worth of careful attention to the things that really matter, the things we would not survive without when all the distractions we have accumulated have mercifully been carried off.

18502441R00173

Printed in Great Britain
by Amazon